Travis, Elizabeth
Deadlines

DEADLINES

DEADLINES

DEADLINES

Elizabeth Travis

ST. MARTIN'S PRESS

New York

Design by Laura Rohrer

Library of Congress Cataloging in Publication Data

Travis, Elizabeth.
    Deadlines.

    I. Title.
PS3570.R346D43   1987   813'.54   87-13979
ISBN 0-312-01018-4

First Edition
10 9 8 7 6 5 4 3 2 1

*My thanks to Deborah Travis Willis, R.N.,
and John K. Willis, M.D.,
for their valuable assistance.*

DEADLINES

CHAPTER 1

Trudging through the terminal at La Guardia, I sensed the faint disappointment that came to me upon arrival anywhere in the world—Detroit, New Orleans, London, Milan. All airports were similarly anonymous, being designed, apparently, to erase any unrealistic expectations aroused by bright-colored travel brochures. And yet, after generating all that promotional material, one might think the airlines would follow through and give arriving passengers at least the illusion of having journeyed to an interesting place.

This might be a subject worth looking into, I reflected, if my new agency turned out to have some airline accounts. *My new agency.* The thought caused a flutter of apprehension. It would be bad luck to take anything for granted at this point, even mentally. Still I could not help feeling confident after the promising interview I had just concluded in Chicago.

Stepping onto an escalator, I caught sight of my reflection in a polished metal panel. Although blurred, it was the image of a successful young businesswoman: head held high and topped with shining, light brown hair; the straight line of pants just right with the longish, unstructured blazer and slouchy shoulderbag. I smiled deliberately as I glided past the reflection. Nice job on the veneer, very nice indeed.

At the baggage carousel I stood, still musing, watching expensive leather cases being chummily nudged by their lesser, often damaged, counterparts and speculating, as I always did, on which passengers would seize which pieces. People and luggage did not always match.

There, suddenly, was one of mine, tan canvas, dirtier and lumpier than it had appeared in private, bumping along toward me like a homely pet certain of its owner's welcome. I looked about for a porter. The bag was heavy, I remembered, and another, only slightly smaller, would soon appear. I saw two tall black men in uniform leaning on their flat baggage trucks, enjoying an animated conversation. I gestured, holding my hand high, but the two did not look in my direction, so I hurried over to them.

"Can you help me with my bags?" I smiled—too eagerly, it was soon made clear. One of the porters, the taller, ignored me completely. He simply nodded to his friend and departed, pushing his cart before him.

The second surveyed me coolly. "When you ready I be over," he said.

I was in New York. I knew it now. No need to give this terminal a distinctive decor; the personnel set the scene, unmistakably.

I felt my pulse speed up as I recalled the technique necessary to these encounters. I fixed my gaze on his. "I'm not allowed to lift things," I said. I cupped my right elbow in my left hand. No wavering of the glance. "My arm is still healing."

Nothing moved but his lips, which he compressed. He remained slouched comfortably against the handle of his cart, dark eyes boring into mine. "Liar!" quivered silently in the air between us, but I did not move either as I said, "My bags are ready now, on the carousel. Will you help me, please?"

A mixture of firmness and courtesy, that was what Granny had always recommended. No shrillness, however maddened one becomes; and on the other hand, no pleading. Above all, no backing down.

He said nothing, but ever so slowly straightened and began shambling over to the carousel as if on impulse. I drew a deep breath. California courtesy hadn't spoiled me completely, it seemed.

My next test came in the taxi, after we had crossed the Whitestone Bridge with its incredible view of the city's skyline on one hand and the long, eastward-stretching shoreline on the other. Remembering that we would soon come to the turnoff for the Hutchinson River Parkway, I asked the driver to use that route, as my grandmother's chauffeur had always done. The man grumbled; the trip would take longer; the traffic would be worse than on the turnpike; he had other fares to think about. Again I held firm, this time fixing my unflinching gaze on the rearview mirror, but uncertain of victory until we reached the turnoff.

Then I tried to sit back and relax while he picked up speed in order to make up the time I was costing him. Fortunately, the Hutch was not designed for the kind of travel he had in mind, and soon we were going along at a rate that allowed me to enjoy the remembered contours of the land and the richness of the budding foliage that lined the road. After five years it was like plunging into a pale green sea. I could not identify all the trees I saw, but I knew there were maples, oaks, willows. I saw slim white birches and, standing straight and strong behind the others or clumped aloofly to themselves, tall evergreens.

The road ran well inland of the shoreline of Long Island

Sound, but I lowered the car window and sniffed, hoping to catch the tang of salt in the air. Instead, there was the nearly forgotten scent of moist earth and young grass, and a hint of a blossom's fragrance—suggested, perhaps, by the tender hues of the budding tree limbs.

We crossed the state line into Connecticut, and I sat forward, counting the exits we passed until it was time to turn off on the road that ran to the center of Granny's town. After the flatness of Los Angeles it was intensely satisfying to drive on hilly, curving roads across land that had once been farmland and looked it.

The road we had turned onto bordered a country club for a mile or two, and I saw several golfers trudging along the damp fairways, carrying their own clubs, since the boys who caddied in the summer were still in school. We were very near Granny's house now, and I could feel my heart pounding with excitement. I felt just as I had coming home on school vacations. I pictured my grandmother standing in the doorway of the big white house as she had then, her eyes alight with the joy of seeing me. Always as I ran to her from the car I would see her lively glance go over me from head to toe, instantly taking in every detail of hair, complexion, and clothing; but any disapproval went unexpressed, consumed in the happiness of reunion.

Basically Granny and I approved of each other; we were in accord on the issues that mattered and we never forgot it, although there were things about my way of dress, my friends, and my mores that she was desperately anxious to change. I sighed now, remembering how I had tested her tolerance, her love actually, and wishing I'd made certain to show the extent of mine while she was able to understand.

It was too late now; that had been made clear in the telephone conversations with my brother. I tried to prepare myself for what I would find—a sick old woman lying uncomprehending in her bed—but it was impossible. It would not be real until I saw her, and as the taxi turned into her long, gravel drive I was filled with the irrational hope that when we reached the house she would be standing in the doorway to greet me and I would once more know the warmth and reassurance of her welcome.

But the big square house loomed blank and silent as we approached. Except for the freshness of the paint on white clapboard walls and black shutters, and the trimness of the grounds, the house might have been deserted. While I paid the driver and pulled my bags from the car I cast expectant glances at the front door. Surely my uncle would be here, or my brother. But the tall black door with its gleaming brass knocker remained fixed, and I had the irrational impression that some hostile force was shutting me out. I felt tempted to climb back into the taxi, but instead I stood uncertainly in the drive while it pulled away. Then I took a deep breath, mounted the flagstone steps, and lifted the heavy knocker.

Ten minutes later I was standing outside my grandmother's bedroom door once again trying to muster my courage, for the prospect of entering the room and facing the sick woman filled me with terror. My heart seemed to have moved into my throat, where it pounded with increasing fury as I hesitated. Soon it would choke me, that was certain, but as I looked about for some comforting presence I saw only the housekeeper, Mrs. Berger, who had greeted me at the door a few minutes earlier. No help there. Mrs. Berger mustered what was meant to be a reassuring smile, but I saw that her lips were twitching nervously and that she was clasping her fidgety hands together to hide their trembling.

We were a pair of "timorous beasties," no question about it, and suddenly I was nearly overcome with nervous laughter:

How ludicrous it was for two grown women to be quaking with fear at the prospect of facing a helpless, possibly comatose, old lady. Clearly, it was the recollection of Granny's once forceful personality that was undoing us; as soon as I saw her I would be all right, and with a view to getting it over with I seized the handle of the partly open door, pulled it wide, and stepped into the room.

Instantly I forgot Mrs. Berger and forgot my own nerves in the familiar aura of Granny's elegant surroundings. Nothing had changed. After five years it was as if I had left that pale brocade sanctuary only hours before, and I felt my eyes fill with sudden sharp tears of nostalgia.

It could not be called a stately room. As in many formal suburban houses, the master bedroom was not unduly large; but the proportions were graceful, the ceiling high, the windows large and well spaced, and the furnishings and fabrics that Granny or her decorator had selected so long ago completed an effect of sumptuous serenity. Three of the walls were painted in a pale, watery green, brushed by hand with a slightly deeper tone to achieve an almost iridescent texture. The fourth wall was covered by a sheet of mirror framed all around by a border of glass etched with soft pink and green peonies, and below it stretched a many-drawered French dresser painted ivory and antiqued in dull gold. A lace cover stretched across its surface like a rippling sheet of foam, and I found my glance going automatically to the silver-framed photographs that had always stood upon it. There I was as a child of five, a beguiling little face smiling shyly from a gleaming silver oval, and beside me in a rectangular frame better suited to a boy I saw the mischievous countenance of my brother at the age of three. Next, set apart from us by reason of size and the space allotted to it, was the picture of my mother in her wedding dress. Even now I found it difficult to wrench my gaze from what in childhood had seemed the utter personification of beauty, glamour, and, of course, mystery. Even now, I felt that if I looked long enough at that face, probed intently enough into those smiling, long-lashed eyes, I would fathom her secret. I felt the questioning begin again, the inner voice beseeching, pleading for an answer I could accept. Why, Mother? Why did you leave me, the one you loved best in the world? How could you do it and never tell me why?

A new and surprising element had been added to my mother's photograph since I had last studied it. Glancing slightly to the left of the tall silver frame, I caught sight of my own reflection in Granny's mirror, and with a little thrill of happiness saw that whatever the last few years of my life had done to me they had also given me a marked resemblance to my mother. My face, which I had once considered hopelessly narrow and unappealing, had filled out. The line of my jaw curved upward to high, rounded cheekbones just like my mother's; my deep blue eyes matched hers exactly; and I noticed for the first time that her smile was like mine, with a quizzical lift at one corner that suggested a wry sense of humor.

Even my hair was like hers, or like what I could see through the gauzy bridal veil: parted on the side and falling in soft, natural waves that framed her face. I wondered fleetingly what unconscious urge had impelled me to have mine cut that way only the week before. In the white satin dress with its wide scooped neckline and with the same strand of pearls about my neck I would almost be the twin of the bride in the photograph. What had become of that dress, I wondered, and those pearls?

A voice interrupted my reverie and I turned apologetically to the nurse who had addressed me from Granny's bedside.

"I'm sorry. It's been a long time since I've seen that picture of my mother." I moved toward the bed as I spoke. The moment I had been dreading was at hand. "You are Miss Kelly?"

She must have heard the quaver in my voice, for she said soothingly, "Don't worry, Mrs. Templeton; you won't disturb her." She indicated the motionless figure in the bed almost proudly, as though Granny were a doll she had dressed especially for the occasion. She stepped back with what appeared to me in my rattled state an excessive display of tact, and I forced my unwilling feet to make the final steps to the bedside.

Granny had never been a big woman, but I was stunned to see how tiny was the figure that now lay so perfectly still in the center of the bed. The form I discerned beneath the creamy, lace-bound blanket cover seemed about the size of a ten-year-old child, and with that image in mind it was a shock when my eyes traveled to the pillow to see the sharp features of an old woman beneath a fluffy crown of feathery, white curls.

"Granny," I breathed, and I inadvertently reached out to touch her gently on the shoulder. My fear had completely evaporated, to be replaced by an unexpected upwelling of tenderness. Suddenly I was aware of how much I had missed the vital, engaging presence that had been Granny's, and I longed to have her open her eyes and speak to me.

"Granny," I said again, "it's Sally." I looked up at Miss Kelly. "Can't she hear me?"

The woman stepped forward, and I saw on her plain, broad face the superior expression worn by those who are familiar with a situation when they are confronted by the ignorance of a newcomer.

"I think she can hear you, yes. It's just that your words

don't mean anything to her." She bent over my grandmother and said, as clearly and slowly as if she were addressing a small child, "Sally is here, dear. Aren't you going to speak to her?" Then she reached out and actually shook Granny's shoulder, gently but firmly.

I was appalled. "Don't do that!" I said sharply, and to my horror, found myself gripping the nurse's arm to restrain her.

She turned to me slowly as she straightened, and for a moment we studied each other like wary adversaries. Miss Kelly appeared to be a type I knew well from my years in a convent school; prim and spinsterish, her face displaying the same smug righteousness that had so frequently stirred me to rebellion. It was unbearable to have such a person in charge of my grandmother, manhandling her to make her mind.

"Come over here please, Miss Kelly," I said, moving away from the bed to a grouping of small, brocade-covered armchairs placed before the tall french doors. I gestured to one of them as the nurse joined me. "Sit down, please. I would like you to describe my grandmother's condition, if you don't mind. I'm afraid I don't understand why you are treating her like a baby."

She looked shaken, but I saw the determined set of her lips as she stiffly lowered herself to a chair.

"Your grandmother is suffering from senile dementia. You have probably heard the disease referred to as senility or, when it strikes younger people, as Alzheimer's disease." Miss Kelly looked at me questioningly, and I nodded slowly. "It is a deterioration of the brain, due to an impaired blood supply, and it can come on gradually or, as in your grandmother's case, quite suddenly." She bent forward and gazed earnestly into my eyes. "I don't know whether you are aware that I have taken care of Mrs. Ryder on and off for several years. When she had pneumonia, when she broke her hip . . . sometimes just to keep her company when the servants took vacations. I came to know her well, and I can tell you that as recently as six months ago she was as alert and humorous and demanding as ever. If only you had come then . . ."

"I didn't know. No one wrote me about her illnesses, and she never would have mentioned them herself."

Miss Kelly smiled, a fond sad smile that made me suspect I had misjudged her. "Mrs. Ryder had no intention of becoming a tiresome, complaining old bore, like some of her friends. That's exactly what she called them. 'I don't want to see Ethel Crane anymore,' she'd say. 'She's turned into an old bore.' The fact that poor Mrs. Crane was not only blind, but crippled with arthritis, made no difference. To your grandmother she was a bore, and that was unforgivable."

I laughed softly. "She's always had strong opinions, and God help anyone who disagreed with them. I gather you managed to get along with her pretty well."

There was a hint of shyness in Miss Kelly's eyes as she glanced quickly over at me, then concentrated on smoothing the skirt of her crisp uniform over her knees. "We became good friends, yes, and that makes it hard for me now. I miss her, you know." She looked up at me with the regretful smile she had worn before. "It's funny when I think of our first few times together. She was so imperious. I don't need to tell you, I'm sure, how difficult she could be. But when I realized that sometimes she was testing me I learned to stand up for myself, and it made a difference. She respected that. She really had no use for people she could push around. And then when I began to understand her sense of humor . . ." Miss Kelly shook her head slowly from side to side. "We had some good times together, Mrs. Templeton."

"I'm glad she had you with her," I said, "as long as I couldn't be here myself. I hope she didn't feel I neglected her. She wasn't resentful, was she, because I didn't come out?" I gripped the arms of my chair, surprised at the frankness of my question, and at the anxiety I felt as I waited for the answer.

"She understood. She knew you were having problems of your own." I heard an undercurrent of apology in Miss Kelly's tone as she continued. "She talked about you a lot; I couldn't help knowing about your divorce and your attempt to start a new life. Your grandmother was proud of you. She admired your courage when you left your husband. I would rather not tell you what she said about him."

I sighed as I sank back into the stiff little French chair. "I can imagine what she said, but it's wonderful to know that she had faith in me. I wanted to get everything straightened out before I saw her. I wanted to come to her with a new job, a new lease on life, so she'd see that I'd pulled out of the mess I'd made for myself. But now I wish I hadn't waited." I felt my anger rising again as I said, "Why didn't anyone tell me she was slipping into this condition? I would have rushed out immediately if I'd known."

"As I told you, it hit her very suddenly. In the late fall when she started to become forgetful I did mention to your uncle that it might be nice to invite you for a visit before Mrs. Ryder's condition deteriorated. He didn't see any urgency." Miss Kelly sighed. "I've seen it before, of course. Men, especially the sons of women who are failing, hate to face the reality of what's happening."

I smiled. It was only too easy to imagine my charming, adorable Uncle John pushing aside the notion of his mother's illness as he had other distasteful issues throughout his entire pleasure-filled life.

Miss Kelly went on. "Only a few weeks later she was totally withdrawn. I think she realized what was happening and gave in to it at once, instead of putting up a fight." I was shaking my head in protest, and she said, "I know. It sounds like the last thing your grandmother would do. But all she wanted when she saw that her mind was going was to get it over with, to get herself out of it quickly. It's a form of self-protection, really."

"I guess so," I said slowly. The concept was difficult to accept. "It's hard for me to go along with that idea. I hate to think that Granny would let go without seeing me once more. I suppose this is a ridiculous thing to say, but it sort of hurts my feelings."

I could hardly believe I was talking this way to Miss Kelly, a woman I had thought I despised only minutes earlier. She did not seem to find it surprising, however. Her plain, pale face was soft with sympathy.

"Your reaction is not uncommon," she said. "I remember feeling anger mixed with the grief when my mother died. You may have felt the same." There was a question in her eyes; but after a pause she shook her head doubtfully. "You were so young, you probably don't remember."

"I've never forgotten," I murmured. I sat forcing myself to focus on my fingers, which were linked tensely in my lap. It was happening again, just as it always had in Dr. Zeigler's office when we talked about my mother's death. My eyes were blurred with tears, and the thickness in my throat made speech difficult, but I retained enough detachment to marvel at the power of the emotion that still overwhelmed me after nearly thirty years. Miss Kelly must have noticed the huskiness in my voice when I asked for more details about Granny's condition, and she proceeded to supply them, in a dispassionate monotone that exercised a soothing effect on my nerves.

Apparently my grandmother drifted in and out of consciousness, but her periods of awareness were becoming less frequent with each passing day. Only rarely did she seem to know the people who cared for her, and although she had been cooperative so far, she was beginning to resist their efforts to bathe or feed her.

"Then I suppose we'll soon be facing one of those decisions we read about so often in the papers—whether to provide her with life-support systems, intravenous feedings, and so forth? Is that why I was sent for?"

Miss Kelly nodded. "Yes. You see, as medical professionals Dr. McGinnis and I must try to keep our patients alive at all costs. But in the last few years, with new techniques making it easier to sustain life . . ." She shook her head slowly. "It means that someone has to decide whether the quality of the patient's life warrants the time and expertise and, to be honest, the money being spent on it. The relatives are the only ones who can do that."

I glanced again at the quiet figure on the bed, then turned back to Miss Kelly. "I must tell you that I find it a terrifying responsibility," I said. I stopped there; I did not dare go on to say that I found it even more terrifying to think that Granny's fate lay in the hands of my brother as well.

"At least you won't have to decide all on your own." Miss Kelly's voice was once again reassuring. "There will be three of you involved. That's bound to make it easier."

Three of us, of course, counting Uncle John. He was Granny's only surviving offspring, after all. Dear Uncle John—my heart warmed at the thought of his kind, handsome face. He would make all of this bearable. He would provide the wise counsel I needed, and he would be arriving on the three o'clock train from the city.

I consulted my watch and saw that it was twelve-thirty. No wonder I felt weak and incompetent to cope with issues of life and death. My airline breakfast of rubbery and startlingly yellow scrambled eggs had been served at seven. I was famished. Also thirsty. I wondered how Mrs. Berger felt about ladies who drank Bloody Marys at lunch. Not too much seasoning, I heard myself requesting; then Miss Kelly's voice broke into my thoughts, and I started guiltily.

She was looking beyond me, I saw, smiling rather nervously as she spoke to someone who had just entered the room. "And this is Mrs. Templeton, Dr. McGinnis, Mrs. Ryder's granddaughter. She flew all the way from Los Angeles this morning."

Again her simplicity caused me to feel a wave of annoyance. One might think I had been the pilot of the plane. Turning toward the door, I said, "No, I came from Chicago this morning. I spent the night there . . ." I stopped. Granny's doctor could not care about my travel arrangements.

Automatically I rose to my feet; again it was the influence of the convent, where doctors ran a close second to nuns and priests when it came to commanding respect. Then I felt rather foolish, for Dr. McGinnis was young and casually dressed, and he wore a broad, friendly grin as he approached to shake hands.

"Terry McGinnis," he announced as he took my hand. "You're Sally, isn't that right?"

I found myself looking up at him. Close up, he was taller than he had appeared from across the room. He appeared to be about my age, possibly even younger, I thought, observing the fresh, rosy tint of his skin and the boyish manner in which a lock of brown hair fell across his forehead. He wore a beige Shetland pullover over his white shirt and dark knit tie, and his trousers were tan corduroy, slightly rumpled. He smiled happily into my eyes, giving my hand an extra, final squeeze before he relinquished it, as if we were good old pals who understood one another perfectly.

"I hope you know my name because of Granny's mentioning

it," I said. I was smiling back at him; it was quite impossible not to.

His brown eyes softened as he flashed a look in the direction of the bed. "I only knew her for a short time before she fell into this state, but I think she spoke of you every time I came to see her." He was regarding me thoughtfully, as if to see whether I merited as much of Granny's attention as I had been awarded. "She often read me parts of your letters," he went on, "and I've missed them in the last few months. You write very well."

Suddenly I was blushing and I turned away, feeling an uneasy flutter at the notion of this attractive, terribly nice man hearing the thoughts I had always shared so unguardedly with Granny. I wanted to scold her for quoting my letters to a stranger; then I remembered that she had always possessed an exquisite sense of suitability. Granny would have edited my letters as she read from them, keeping the more astringent bits for her private entertainment.

Dr. McGinnis did not seem to notice my distress. Miss Kelly had brought a chart for his perusal, and he scanned it quickly, then went over to the bed and gently drew Granny's thin right arm out from under the covers. I hesitated, uncertain whether to leave the room or remain, and he looked up and smiled at me encouragingly.

"Come over while I take her pulse," he said quietly. "It's good for her to have you near."

Moving to the bedside, I marveled that Granny could lie passive and unresponsive in this man's presence. I had never encountered a doctor who exuded such compassion. After a moment he tucked Granny's arm beneath the blankets again, then reached out to place his warm, tanned hand against her face.

"She is a beautiful woman," he said.

He hadn't said she *was* beautiful, I realized. Terry Mc-Ginnis wasn't looking at Granny as if she were the empty shell of a once lovely creature; he saw loveliness in her as she was now at that moment, and as I stared at her face I saw it too. Though her skin was pale and softly wrinkled, her features were winsomely proportioned. Her nose was narrow and straight, her cheekbones and mouth finely sculpted. Her lips twitched slightly as I watched, as if about to part in a smile. I held my breath, waiting for her eyes to fly open, longing to see them brighten with delight at finding me there. They were the bluest eyes in the world, I remembered that, though I nearly always pictured them crinkling with laughter.

I glanced at Terry McGinnis to see whether he too expected Granny to wake up, but he turned his head so abruptly that I knew he had been watching me.

"My grandmother looks as if she's about to wake up and speak to us. She seems to be sleeping so normally. Isn't there a chance that she'll recover from this in time?" I was peering into the doctor's eyes as I spoke and finding them the warmest, kindest, the most concerned . . . or was it the fatigue I felt engulfing me that made me so impressionable? I actually swayed toward him, and he took my arm to draw me away from the bedside.

I followed him over to one of the tall windows that looked out on the smooth green lawn and the tall trees beyond. The window had been raised a few inches, and the gentle April breeze stirred the filmy embroidered curtain, making it brush against my hand.

Terry McGinnis gazed thoughtfully and unseeingly, it appeared to me, out the window before he turned to speak to me, and when he did the warm, dark eyes were somber.

"You must understand that your grandmother's brain has been permanently damaged because of a lessened blood supply. The most we can hope for is a continuation of her lucid periods. That's why we're being very careful about her drug dosage." He looked across at Miss Kelly and she nodded slowly, her earnest hazel eyes fixed on his face in what I suddenly realized was helpless devotion.

She wrenched them away as she said to me, "Dr. McGinnis has prescribed a very light tranquilizer to be given when Mrs. Ryder becomes agitated, as she sometimes does. That is the only drug she ever takes."

And are you on duty twenty-four hours a day? As quickly as the thought flashed in my mind I quenched it. Perhaps Joe was right, and my nature was becoming impossibly suspicious and negative, otherwise why would I leap to challenge a harmless soul like Miss Kelly? Picturing the angry face of my former husband, I was once again overwhelmed with fatigue. I looked about for something to sit on and Dr. McGinnis glanced at me with concern. He grasped my arm while reaching for a nearby chair with his other hand. I must have turned white; I certainly felt drained all at once.

"You look all in." The doctor studied my face with narrowed eyes, and Miss Kelly hurried over to hand me a glass of water. I smiled at her gratefully as I sipped.

"It's been a long morning, "I said, "and finding Granny in this state has hit me harder than I expected."

"You'd better have something to eat." Dr. McGinnis looked at his watch, then shook his head. "As usual, I'm behind schedule with my calls or I'd stay and have lunch with you. On my way out I'll mention to Mrs. Berger that you need to be fed."

"I'll go down with you," I said, getting to my feet. Again I smiled in the direction of Miss Kelly. "I'll come back this afternoon. Perhaps I can sit with Granny while you take a break."

I was so tired and so caught up with my sudden over-whelming need of sustenance that I did not stop to wonder at Miss Kelly's reaction to my words. It registered on my unconscious mind, however; the frown that creased her fore-head, and the tightening of her lips as she glanced anxiously toward the bed. It was to be many days before I recalled that puzzling response, and when I did I would bitterly regret my inattention.

CHAPTER 2

Lunch wasn't bad: chicken salad and popovers, served on the flowered Spode that was Granny's second-best china. No cocktails were offered, but I did request a glass of sherry, and after a slight hesitation Mrs. Berger asked the maid to bring her one as well. We sat politely facing one another in the high-ceilinged living room like two little girls who had been forced by their mothers to spend the day together.

Mrs. Berger appeared to be in her early fifties. Her light brown hair was liberally streaked with gray and she wore it in what was meant to be a smoothly controlled style suitable to her role, but rebellious tendrils kept escaping as she patted it nervously. She was like a photograph that was slightly out of focus, it occurred to me as we talked. The impression she wished to create was clear in her mind, but the hair was a little mussed, the pale rose lipstick slightly smudged, her deep blue cardigan sweater was missing a button and was a distinctly different tone from the skirt it was meant to match.

Her eyes behind pale plastic-rimmed glasses were a watery gray green, and they blinked earnestly when she spoke. It was difficult to imagine that Mrs. Berger had ever had a life of her own, but there on her left hand was a narrow gold wedding band, and when I asked about children her face brightened. A boy and a girl, the perfect family, we agreed; both grown now and living in Boston, both with excellent jobs; she would show me pictures at dinner time. As she spoke of her children she sat straighter and I heard the confidence that had entered her tone.

She was a widow, I had assumed, but no, there was a husband with Parkinson's disease in a veteran's hospital. It was very sad, but also very difficult to be with him, and the care they gave him there was wonderful. No more than he deserved, of course; he had served in the air force in World War II. That meant more pictures to look at, I was certain. I was beginning to dread the dinner hour, and we hadn't yet had lunch.

I was also beginning to long for some time to myself in which to savor the well-remembered atmosphere of Granny's house, to drift at leisure through the rooms, reacquainting myself with the pictures and furniture that had been a part of my childhood. It seemed peculiar to recognize the chintzes on the chairs and at the windows, the Meissen pieces in the tall fruitwood cabinet, the heavy crystal lamps on the end tables, yet find the familiar setting peopled with completely strange characters. Except for my grandmother, it was as if actors in a play had wandered into the wrong theater; I was beginning to wonder what had become of the ones who belonged here.

I had never seen the timid young maid who served our sherry, but Nancy Harris, whom I had known so well, couldn't be old enough for retirement, nor could her husband, Michael, who had been Granny's chauffeur. Since I had been told to take a taxi from the airport, I assumed that someone had decided that with Granny housebound there was no longer any need for a chauffeur. I wondered whether it was Uncle John who made such decisions. It wouldn't be like him to think of economizing, yet Mrs. Berger hardly seemed the type to be entrusted with full responsibility for running such a household. It was easier to imagine her taking orders than giving them. Perhaps Granny's lawyer was in charge—Gillian Clark, the woman who had signed several letters to me in such a firm, bold hand that her name had become imprinted on my memory.

Lunch was announced and Mrs. Berger and I moved to the dining room. Seated at the long, highly polished table with its exquisite linens, I felt uncomfortably grubby and travel-worn. I had washed my face and brushed my hair, but my black silk blouse was wrinkled, as were the tan gabardine pants I had pulled on so thoughtlessly in my Chicago hotel room. The pants were also too tight, I had discovered after an hour in the air; and I should have worn stockings under my high-heeled sling pumps instead of slipping them onto my bare feet in casual California fashion.

It was a relief to escape to my room when lunch was over and stretch out for a badly needed nap. The early-morning flight, the anxiety about Granny, the tedium of Mrs. Berger's company, had combined with the sedative effect of the sherry to make me groggy with fatigue. Anyway, I want to be fresh when I see Uncle John, I thought as I drifted off. Dear Uncle John; he'll make everything all right again.

I was awakened by a gentle but insistent knocking on my door, and when I fuzzily responded it opened just wide enough for the maid, Jenny, to peer in and say, "Your uncle is on the phone, Mrs. Templeton. He would like to speak to you."

Dimly I remembered unplugging the bedside phone from

its jack so that I could sleep undisturbed. Seeing me fumble for the cord, Jenny hurried into the room and quickly connected the instrument. She handed it to me, and I sat up in bed, brushing my untidy hair back from my face.

"Is that you, Uncle John?" I said into the phone, watching Jenny slip through the door and silently pull it shut.

"Sally, my girl. I'm sorry if I woke you, but at my age I can't afford to be patient."

The sound of the well-loved gravelly voice was so comforting that I lay happily back among the pillows. "I don't recall that patience was ever among the virtues you cultivated, at any age," I replied.

"I believe I'll take that remark as a compliment," my uncle responded. "Now, how quickly can you be ready? I thought I'd pick you up and bring you over to my house for supper."

"Why—that's a wonderful idea!" I had pictured the two of us carrying on whispered conversations in Granny's library, with the restricting presence of Mrs. Berger a constant threat. My heart lifted at the prospect of escaping to the small but enchanting house he occupied in a wooded enclave a mile or two away. In his cozy kitchen we could talk freely and openly while we cooked dinner together. It would be the kind of evening I had been needing for a long time.

"Give me twenty minutes," I said. "I suppose you'll come in to see Granny, won't you?"

There was a silence, and when my uncle spoke again I heard such sorrow in his voice that my throat went tight with pity. "It is very hard for me to see her like that, Sally. You must feel it too. It's like losing her over and over again, not just once."

That was my feeling, exactly, but I hadn't found the words to describe it.

"I understand. I'll be downstairs and ready to go when you get here."

We said good-bye and I scrambled out of bed and hurried to the bathroom to turn on the taps in the white marble tub. I hadn't taken time to unpack, and while the tub filled I pulled my clothes out of my hang-up bag, looking them over critically as I hung them in the closet. I'd brought several pairs of pants including my blue jeans, a denim skirt, and a navy crepe dress that would do in case Granny . . . I did not finish the thought, but rummaged hastily through my supply of silk shirts, searching for the least wrinkled of them. My favorite, a deep amethyst color, looked almost wearable, and I carried it in to the steam-filled bathroom and hung it on the shower rod to freshen.

I had poured a liberal amount of foaming bath oil into the tub, and as I stepped into the froth and felt the bubbles prickle against my skin I thought fleetingly of my cramped little bathroom in Los Angeles and of how my toes curled in disgust when they touched the floor of the shower stall. It seemed that no amount of scrubbing would make it really clean after all the neglectful tenants who had preceded me, any more than my sanding and scraping would ever remove all the layers of thick, bumpy paint that coated the woodwork. It was no wonder a near smirk of satisfaction had appeared on Joe's face the one time he had visited the apartment, causing me to reflect, not for the first time, how wonderfully protective were certain men's egos. Joe did not find it insulting that I would rather live on my own in squalid surroundings than stay with him in comparative luxury. No, I think he saw my poverty as the punishment I deserved for leaving him. That was my guess, at any rate, but I never had been good at following the intricate twists and turns of Joe's reasoning process.

Lying in the warm, fragrant water with foamy bubbles tickling my chin, I thought of the costly struggle it had taken to achieve my present objectivity. I wondered if I could unburden myself to Uncle John about all this in addition to sharing my distress over Granny. It would be wonderful to hear a mature judgment of my situation, but perhaps he would simply find it boring. I certainly didn't want to bore Uncle John, of all people in the world, and with that thought came the realization that I'd been dawdling. He would be pulling into the driveway any moment now.

I stepped out of the tub and wrapped myself in one of the thick French bathtowels that hung on the chrome warming rack. The mirror that filled the wall above the marble basin was apparently heated to keep it from steaming, and I stole a moment to admire my appearance. Wrapped in the fluffy, oversized white towel, with my face rosy and my hair curling a little from the steam, I looked like a figure in a sleek cosmetics ad. The glowing tan of my arms and legs was set off by the snowy background, the marble walls and fixtures smooth and gleaming, the stacks of giant towels like soft, fleecy clouds. I looked rich and pampered, I realized as I dried myself and began to dress. I was exactly the image of what I had scorned for so many years, but now that image seemed merely amusing, hardly worth the pain and deprivation I had endured trying to escape it. I pulled on the amethyst blouse and quickly buttoned it, then rummaged in my makeup kit for eyeshadow and mascara. Escape. My mother wanted to escape, that's why she ran away. Suddenly I knew it as surely as if she had told me herself. But from what? I bent forward, peering closely into the mirror as I brushed mascara against my lashes. Mother must have looked just like this as she dressed for the evening, perhaps peering into this very mirror. I shivered. Being in Granny's house again and seeing with fresh eyes how closely I resembled my mother had set me on a startling train of thought. Perhaps our resemblance went deeper than the physical; perhaps mother had been running as I had from a life she could not tolerate. What hurt so terribly was the knowledge that I was part of that life. It was a wound that would not heal. I picked up my brush and attacked my hair with savage fury, as if to beat the sorry realization from my brain.

Five minutes later I was running down the broad, curving staircase to the front hall. I paused halfway to enjoy the way the late-afternoon sun sparkled on the crystal chandelier that hung there and sent tiny rainbows dancing about the walls.

On either side of the front door were narrow lunettes of beveled glass, and I hurried over to peer out at the circular driveway. It was empty; no one had left a smart foreign car parked there, and as I turned away I smiled at my certainty that Uncle John would pull up in a glamorous convertible of some sort. It would be amusing to tease him some day about the movie star image he had assumed in my mind.

Standing indecisively in the silent, carpeted hall I heard the sound of a door quietly closing on the floor above. It was the door to Granny's room, I deduced, for that was the one nearest the top of the stairs. Suddenly I remembered my offer to sit with her. Uncle John's call had put it clean out of my head; I'd better run back upstairs and explain to Miss Kelly.

I hurried up the steps I had just descended, keeping an ear cocked for the crunch of tires on the gravel outside. The upstairs hall was shadowy, so I reached to pull the switch on the small jade lamp that stood on a cabinet at the top of the stairs. As I did so I heard a gasp. Peering beyond the sudden circle of brightness I was astonished to see the figure of Miss Kelly flattened against the wall beside Granny's door, her eyes wide with the shock of my unexpected appearance.

"Miss Kelly, I was just coming to see you." I was almost babbling in my bewilderment at finding her there, looking so frightened and guilty. Then I saw that her eyes were no longer fixed on me, but on the door to Granny's room, which was slowly swinging open.

"I thought you had gone, Miss Kelly." The woman who

stood in the doorway was tall and sleek and stunning, not at all the type to emerge from a sickroom; she couldn't possibly be a nurse. Her dark eyes with their long, thick lashes were narrowed as she studied Miss Kelly's face, and on her lips was the suggestion of a smile. Then as if she had all the time in the world at her disposal she turned her attention to me. The faint, enigmatic smile remained as she looked me over in leisurely fashion, then graciously offered her hand. "You must be Sally Templeton," she said softly. "I am Gillian Clark, and I'm very glad to see you."

So this was Granny's lawyer. As we shook hands I swiftly took in the well-cut beige gabardine suit, the shining black hair that looked sleek and soft at the same time, the glowing, rose-tinted skin, the radiant self-possession. I understood instantly how my brother might feel unsettled in the presence of this splendid creature. I remembered his exasperated voice on the telephone: "With all the good law firms around here Uncle John has to pick this *woman*." When I failed to echo his disgust he went on, "I don't mean to be insulting, Sally, but I think when you see her you'll agree that she wasn't hired for her brains."

Maybe, maybe not, I thought as we faced each other on the threshold of Granny's bedroom. Gillian Clark was indeed a beautiful woman, as smooth and perfectly groomed as a TV anchorperson. Perhaps she was also as artificial as that ridiculous term implied, but she did not appear to have a shortage of brains. For one thing, I've never thought it stupid to make the most of one's appearance; for another, I saw sharp intelligence in the dark eyes that flashed once more toward Miss Kelly.

"Did you forget something?" Again her voice was soft. Control, that was the word for this woman. "Please come in if you wish, Miss Kelly. There is no need to hang about in the hall."

The dark eyes glinted when she turned back to me, as if inviting me to share her amusement at the cloddish behavior of this simple girl. "And won't you come in too, Mrs. Templeton?"

I stepped into the softly lighted bedroom feeling like a privileged guest, while behind me Nurse Kelly explained that she need not come in, after all, and would be on her way if Miss Clark really didn't mind. There were a few more polite murmurings and then Gillian Clark came in, and with a little smiling shake of her head started to close the door.

"Will it bother Granny if we leave the door open?" I explained that I wanted to hear my uncle's car when he arrived, but I knew I had also spoken out of a need to assert myself in the presence of this extraordinarily assured woman. I had been intimidated by such types before, and I knew the symptoms.

She was not even slightly discomfited, but pushed the door wide as she said, "I don't mean to delay you. We will have another opportunity to talk, I'm sure."

"No, this is fine. I'm very anxious to hear what you think about . . ." but I could not seem to discuss Granny in her presence. I gave a little helpless shrug. "I guess she can't hear us," I whispered, "but it makes me awfully uncomfortable to talk about her when she's lying there."

"I felt that way at first myself." Miss Clark's voice was gentle, her lips twisted ruefully, as she stood with her perfectly made-up face bent toward me attentively. I marveled at the smoothness of her shining black hair. Of course dark hair is heavier . . . my unworthy thought was interrupted by sounds from below. The front door was pulled open from the outside, and as a rush of cool, fragrant air blew in I heard my uncle call, "Sally! Where's my Sally?"

"Uncle John! I didn't hear you. I'll be right down. Sorry,

Miss Clark—Gillian. I'll call you tomorrow." I was like a ten-year-old, practically squealing with excitement, but as I ran from the bedroom into the hall I found I was not the only one who felt a joyful lift at the sound of the voice from below.

Gillian Clark was beside me, her step matching mine until we reached the staircase. There we both stopped for an instant to peer down at the man who looked up at us from beneath the crystal chandelier. Before I started my headlong descent some instinct made me steal a quick glance at Gillian's face and I saw that the softness had left it. Her flushed cheeks glowed through the smooth layer of makeup, her eyes sparkled like fiery black gems, and as she stared wordlessly down at my uncle her full red lips slowly parted to reveal even, white teeth. Though he waited for me with smiling expectancy, I saw his eyes move to her as if drawn by a magnetic force. An instant's shadow flickered on his face, but when I reached the bottom of the stairs and flung myself upon him his smile was firmly in place again, and there was nothing but welcome in the strong arms that hugged me close.

CHAPTER 3

"So then you left him. I guess you had to." Uncle John spoke slowly, thoughtfully, but his words had a galvanizing effect on me.

I jumped up from the comfortable old leather chair I'd been sitting in and I'm sure I was smiling with relief as I said, "You understand! I knew, or rather I prayed, you would!" I crossed the room in order to peer down into his face. "I wonder if you know how much it means to have you see how I felt. I don't think Granny did at all. That was one reason I was so anxious to see her before she . . ." My voice was husky as I continued. "I did so want to explain to her. I wanted her to understand. And then I got here too late after all."

My uncle seized my hand and for a moment we gazed wordlessly into each other's eyes. His, like mine, were blurred with unshed tears, but he quickly cleared his throat and dropped my hand. "As long as you're up," he said, reaching for his coffee cup, and I took it from him and went over to fill it from the pot he had placed amidst the clutter on the top of his desk in the bay window.

"I see you're still counting on me to clean up your desk for you." As I replaced the pot, a precariously balanced stack of papers slid off the edge and slithered to the floor. I shook my head in wonderment. "How do you ever get anything done in this mess?"

He was grinning as he took the cup from me; the wonderfully blue eyes with their unexpected fringe of dark lashes were cloudless again. "Seems to me you've asked that question before." His fond glance followed me as I filled my own cup and settled once more in the shapeless old chair across the hearth from him.

"I remember when your mother brought you over here before you could talk and you would toddle over and look at that desk with the same disgusted expression you had on your face just now. Even then you thought it was a disgrace."

We sipped our coffee in silence. To my surprise I felt sleepy again, but it was a different kind of fatigue now; instead of the exhausting nervous tension I had felt earlier, I was succumbing to the blissful security of being with my uncle again. Here, sitting before the fire in his warm, paneled library, I knew I had really come home.

Granny's house had seemed an anachronism, somehow, because everything in it, every curtain, lampshade, and rug had been cleaned or replaced as they wore out so that there was no sense of the passage of time. The rooms probably looked exactly as they had on the day her decorator placed the last ashtray and pronounced the job completed. So it was doubly shocking to see the tragic change in Granny. There, on a once vibrant and beautiful woman, time had left its disfiguring stamp. I wished the house had been allowed to age with her.

Uncle John's house was another story, as it always had been. The oriental rug at my feet, with its soft pattern of beige and rust, now bore a faint threadbare path leading from the door to the desk. The chintz curtains had been drawn to shut out the blackness and I could see in the inner folds the green leaves and coral flowers which, on the exposed pleats, had faded to a colorless mass. I had always loved to curl myself into the vast brown leather chairs that flanked the hearth; I found them no less comfortable now that some of the seams had split and the arms were worn and roughened in spots.

Here, I realized, was the opposite of what I had found at Granny's. The house had aged, but it appeared that its occupant had not. The man who sat across the hearth from me must have been in his mid-fifties, but he looked at least ten years younger. I saw a few changes, of course, from five years ago. The streaks in his light brown hair were no longer blond but gray, and his face seemed a bit coarser; the crisp outline had softened. It had never been a smooth, bland, model's face anyway, but mobile and expressive, like Granny's, with laugh lines crinkling at the corners of the beautiful deep eyes and finely chiseled mouth.

He had always been a natural athlete, if a lazy one, and it was plain that he had kept himself in shape, or his genes had done it for him. He seemed as lean and lithe as ever, lying back in his chair with his long legs stretched toward the warm flames. The gray flannel slacks he wore might well be turned down by any self-respecting thrift shop and his camel hair sweater appeared to have been darned by a number of different needlewomen over the years; even so, it was about to go through at the elbows.

This was the way Uncle John had always dressed; in fact, I thought I remembered that terrible sweater. It was amusing to think of all the women who had tried to spruce him up. I imagined the gifts of cashmere and tweed that no doubt filled his closets; I could hear the cajolery: "You're such a handsome man, John, it's a crime the way you dress when you could look so wonderful."

Granny had given up years ago, asking only that he pull himself together for holiday dinners and formal occasions, and to please her he always had.

This was his form of rebellion, I suppose, or maybe it was a challenge; take me as I am or not at all. Plenty of women had been happy to comply, finding the invitation in the blue eyes irresistible, feeling in his company a buoyant gladness other men could not provide. Even as a child I had sensed it, the electric prickle when he entered a room. I'd seen the women's eyes follow him, noticed the way they often lost the thread of their conversations while they strained to catch the wry pronouncements issued in that intriguing gravelly voice.

In fact, it occurred to me at some point that having Uncle John around during my growing up had been enormously instructive. No one ever had to explain the term sex appeal for me. It was what my only uncle possessed in almost embarrassing abundance, and what every woman who came within his ken longed to have him discover in herself.

Obviously it wasn't this quality that gave Uncle John such a special place in my regard, though I became more aware of his magnetism as I grew older, and more impressed by the power it gave him to wound or delight those who fell under his spell. I also began to observe that as his niece I had an enviable relationship to this charming man. I had known him to leave a beautiful woman looking through magazines on the terrace while he took me, a grubby little five-year-old, wading in the brook. Later, when Granny put in a swimming pool, it was Uncle John who swam laps with me, often while someone young and lovely looked on, her smile becoming noticeably rigid as the summer afternoon went by.

When I played Priscilla in the Thanksgiving play my uncle sat in the audience and led the applause, and I knew he had turned down a luncheon party in the city in order to be there. That was the year I came down with mumps during the holidays, and although I won't claim that Uncle John stayed home every night to read to me, he passed up a number of New York balls and the Army-Navy football game in order to keep me from becoming utterly despondent.

My mother had died by then; in fact, must have been dead for about four years; so I should have been used to it, if one ever gets used to that particular fact. Even after thirty years of knowing it to be true, I find that the statement rings false to me. Yet I suppose I should have been better prepared than most because of that strange thing she did, the disappearance that was never explained. Though the sharp pain of it passed with time, it remained an unanswered question that rose again and again to torment me. If I could ever learn why she had run away, if I could ever fully understand, perhaps I could bear it that she had died. I had always felt a stubborn certainty that she had wanted me to know and that it was her sudden death that had prevented her explaining it to me.

I think it was that certainty that held me together when I might very well have become traumatized by the blows that came so fast: my father's death in Korea, followed in a few weeks by my mother's unexplained absence, which was in turn followed by her accidental death, the most stunning shock of all.

I was four when Daddy was killed and Mother ran away. My brother, Philip, was two and a half. He didn't seem involved in it at all. I felt it was my burden, possibly my punishment, though I didn't know for what. And when she came home to see us that one last time I felt she belonged to me alone. It didn't matter how often she snatched my brother up and hugged him; he was just a baby, and a boy at that. I was the one Mother had been longing to see; I was the eldest, the first and—I knew it—the best-loved, the daughter, the cherished one. I would grow up and some day she would explain it all to me, even if to no one else.

Later I marveled at the strength of the bond between us. How iron-forged it must have been to give me such conviction, to outweigh the damage she had inflicted and was unwittingly still to inflict.

My uncle put down his empty coffee cup and picked up the long-handled poker to give the fire a nudge. He couldn't quite do the job from his chair, so he pulled himself out of its comfortable depths and went over to the hearth. When I saw him reach into the wood basket for a fresh log, I spoke up.

"Don't put another on for my sake. I've got to get home to bed."

He hesitated, peering over at me with a quizzical, questioning smile. "You're sure? Seems to me we've barely scratched the surface. I still haven't heard what attracted you to Mr. Templeton in the first place. He doesn't sound like your type at all."

I felt the blood rise to my cheeks, and was grateful for the fire's warmth to excuse it. "I'd hate to tell you; it makes me seem like such an ass." Reluctant to leave, but suddenly unwilling to say any more on the subject of my disastrous marriage, I dragged myself to my feet and straightened my twisted skirt.

"Can you call me a taxi? I don't want you to have to go out again."

He was shaking his head as he put an arm about my shoulders to lead me to the hall where I had dropped my jacket. "Doting uncles don't send beloved nieces home in cabs: old Chinese proverb." He glanced at his watch. "Anyway, it's much too early for bed as far as I'm concerned. You'll have to get over these priggish hours if I'm ever going to hear the rest of your life story."

"It's your turn next," I said, climbing into the car he'd left parked in his driveway. My instinct had been half-right; the car was imported, but it was old, heavy, well cared for—not the lowslung Hollywood model I had expected.

We drove the few blocks to Granny's house in companionable silence, both worn out, I think, from the emotion of reunion. There was still much to be said, but we had plenty of time. I had given notice at the Los Angeles advertising agency where I worked as a copywriter, and if my Chicago job interview had gone as well as I thought it had I would soon be starting a new life there. I felt a thrill of anticipation at the prospect, as well as a sense of pride in at last being strong enough to break completely with my mismanaged past.

It was a night of scudding clouds, often parting as we went along to illuminate a remembered landmark. There was the entrance to the country club, then the stone house where Betsy Marsh lived or had lived. I had forgotten it was so near. And just before we turned onto Granny's road I recognized the shadowy trees and rolling lawns of the Ball estate. Many a night I had wandered there with one boy or another, and now as the moon shone briefly on the tall, pointed firs I saw that it looked just as dreamlike as it had to the foolish, romantic girl I had been those long years ago.

I was nearly undone by a wave of nostalgia, and as we pulled into Granny's drive I clutched the sleeve of Uncle John's tweed jacket. "I'm so glad to see you I can hardly stand it," I said. I tried to keep my voice light, but he heard the quaver in it, and he switched off the motor and covered my hand with his.

The light of the fine old coach lamps beside the front door

shone on his strongly modeled face as he gazed at me sitting there half in darkness. He seemed about to speak, but his eyes narrowed as he studied me, and then I saw them fill with a desperate sadness, and instead of answering me he pulled me close, pressing his lean jaw against my cheek with a strange intensity. It was only for the space of a breath that he held me like that, but later I was to discover that of the entire evening we had spent together it was those few seconds that had really mattered.

The next morning I found myself again hesitating outside Granny's door. It was not apprehension that held me back this time, however, but a desire to take just the right stance with Miss Kelly. It had been puzzling to find her in the hall the night before. She had shrunk into the shadows almost as if she had been eavesdropping on some conversation taking place in Granny's bedroom, but when the door was opened by the redoubtable Gillian Clark it was plain that Gillian had been alone in there with Granny. So it couldn't have been a conversation the nurse was attempting to overhear; she must have had some other reason for lingering outside the sickroom. I very much wanted to know what the reason was, so I decided to do my best to win Miss Kelly's confidence. I rapped lightly on the door, then pushed it open and entered the room with what I hoped was an air of disarming friendliness.

"Good morning! How's my grandmother today?" Smiling, I strode over to the bedside where Miss Kelly was apparently feeding Granny her breakfast. She had propped her up on a mountain of fat, white pillows and draped a turkish towel about her shoulders while she carefully spooned some thin cereal into her mouth. I had been dreading any such scene as this, but as I watched, my tendency toward revulsion was replaced by admiration for the gentle, caring way Miss Kelly handled Granny. She had brushed her silvery hair into a fluffy crown; the bedcovers were smooth and fresh; the breakfast tray was covered with a delicately embroidered linen mat, and the cereal bowl was the blue-sprigged china Granny had always used on her tray. If she had suddenly regained her awareness and looked about, she would have seen little to criticize.

Miss Kelly placed the heavy silver spoon on the plate and turned to greet me. All she said was, "Good morning, Mrs. Templeton," but in her large round eyes I thought I saw a flicker of uncertainty, and her lips twitched nervously in the instant before she turned back to her patient.

It wouldn't do to have her proffer some trumped-up explanation for the previous night's scene. If I were to establish a relationship of trust between us I must not put her in a position of having to lie to me, especially as instinct told me she was not one who could lie well. So I said, "I have to tell you I'm impressed with the kind of care you're giving my grandmother. You and Dr. McGinnis. Even in a short time I've seen that she is very lucky to have you with her."

Another spoonful was on its way to Granny's mouth, but I saw Miss Kelly's hand pause at my words, and when the task was completed she turned and said, "Thank you, Mrs. Templeton. You're certainly right about Dr. McGinnis, and we do seem to work well together." She glanced at the figure on the bed. "And then of course Mrs. Ryder is an easy patient."

I chuckled. "You might not be saying that if she had her wits about her, Miss . . . by the way, do you mind telling me your first name? We're being entirely too formal."

"It's Jane," she replied, looking up at me almost shyly, and I suddenly felt remorseful about the high-handed way I had treated her the day before.

"I guess you know my name is Sally," I said.

She looked uncomfortable, and I quickly changed the subject, asking her whether Dr. McGinnis would be there that morning and feeling a surprising stab of disappointment when she said he would not.

"He doesn't come in every day," she said, and I detected a note of wistfulness in her voice. "But he's more than willing to run over whenever I think Mrs. Ryder needs him."

"And Miss Clark. I was surprised to see her in here last night," I said. "She is a lawyer, isn't she?"

Jane Kelly's face darkened, but she merely replied, "Yes, she takes care of Mrs. Ryder's affairs; and sometimes she sits with her between shifts." I looked puzzled, I guess, and she went on, "The night nurse doesn't come until seven. I don't know why they set it up that way; it seems crazy to me." Her cheeks were flushed now and a bright spark glowed in the hazel eyes that had seemed so placid.

"Then you leave at five, is that right?" I regretted the question the minute I had asked it. The last thing in the world I wanted was to become involved in Granny's domestic arrangements.

She nodded, then glanced protectively toward the bed. "They seem to think she can be left alone for a spell now and then, but I don't agree with them. That's why I stay an extra hour, sometimes more, whenever I can. I will say it's nice of Miss Clark to fill in. I wouldn't have thought . . ."

She allowed the sentence to trail off, and I thought I knew why. Gillian Clark, to all appearances, wasn't the sort to inconvenience herself for others. She didn't fit Jane Kelly's image of one who made humanitarian gestures, nor mine either, I realized; yet there it was, an irrefutable fact.

"Appearances can be misleading," I said softly. "Miss Clark has been acting as my grandmother's lawyer for several years. They probably got to be good friends."

Nurse Kelly looked startled. Perhaps it had never occurred to her that Gillian Clark might have become genuinely attached to Granny before her illness, but I had seen my grandmother's charm at work over the years. I knew she had a talent for binding people to her, and I'd seen it affect many who were just as polished and worldly as her lawyer appeared to be. Many of the mighty had fallen under Granny's spell.

I watched while the breakfast tray was removed and Granny rearranged in her bed. Her cheeks had lost some of their pallor, and she looked more like her old self than at any time since I had arrived. She was peering at me in a friendly manner, with a little smile on her lips, and it seemed impossible that she did not recognize me.

"Granny," I said, "it's Sally. You know me, don't you?" I took her hand and shook it playfully. "Come on, Granny, stop pretending."

"Sally," she said, and I caught my breath. "Sally. Of course."

I would have thrown my arms around her, but the flatness of her voice told me that she did not really comprehend. She was merely parroting what I said. Still, it was something; it was the first reaction I'd had from her, and I turned happily to Nurse Kelly, who had come to stand at my elbow.

"I think she knows me, don't you?"

Miss Kelly looked skeptical, but she spoke softly to Granny, and elicited another smiling response.

"It's Sally. I know. Yes, I know." I heard the impatience in Granny's tone. Even in what must be a misty cloud of confusion she would stand for only so much prompting. I found the hint of exasperation the most heartening sign I'd seen that within that shell of a woman there still lived a remnant of the indomitable spirit that had shaped my life.

I had swung around to find Jane Kelly gazing at me with total understanding, and I was aware that a bond was forming between us, a bond fashioned of our mutual affection for my grandmother and the joy we felt at any indication that she might be regaining her awareness.

We waited in silence, hoping for more, but Granny's eyes were closing, and in a moment she had dropped off into one of her innumerable naps.

I turned to Jane Kelly with a sigh of exasperation. "It's maddening to have her fall asleep just when she's starting to make sense," I said.

"She'll wake up pretty soon. Why don't you go out and get some fresh air? It's a beautiful morning."

She'd sensed my restlessness, possibly because my feet were fairly chattering on the floor. In an instant I had reached the door, where I paused long enough to turn and say, "I'll be back in an hour."

I was like a schoolgirl released early from class, but I felt a qualm as I saw Jane Kelly smiling at me serenely. She couldn't skip out of the room when she felt like it, yet she didn't seem to mind. Well, it's her profession, I said to myself as I closed the door behind me; she's a nurse, and a good one, it appears. Lucky for Granny she's got Jane taking care of her and not me.

I grinned at the thought, but as I started down to the front hall I realized that the bond I felt growing between Jane and me was based partly on respect. Though my work as a copywriter was very different from nursing, I knew what it was to possess high professional standards and I recognized the quality when I found it in others. It created a link that was lacking in friendships with women who were not engaged in work they cared about.

It occurred to me then that Jane Kelly possessed still another admirable quality. It must have taken a good deal of raw courage to hover outside Granny's door on the previous evening, knowing that if she were discovered by Gillian Clark she could be fired on the spot. And indeed she had been discovered, but Miss Clark's reaction had been cool and contained. I stopped dead on the stairway to think what that could mean. Where Gillian Clark might have swooped upon the cornered nurse like a tall, exotic bird demolishing its prey, she had instead made light of the incident, treating her with contempt rather than outrage. She must want to keep Jane Kelly on the job, must want it so much that she would allow herself to appear slightly foolish. It didn't seem to fit her character, at least not as I had analyzed it in my usual lightning-swift fashion.

Ruefully, as I resumed my descent, I recalled that most of the disasters in my life could be blamed on my tendency to make snap judgments. I had better exercise caution now that Granny's welfare was at stake.

CHAPTER 4

Just after lunch Uncle John called to say he had invited my brother and his wife to have dinner with us that evening, and at once my edginess returned. Philip and I had never been close. He simply wasn't my type, and neither was his wife, Barbara. They were perfectly nice, of course, thoughtful and well-mannered, conscientious and dependable. The thing was, they appeared to be in a great hurry to get old. In fact, it seemed to me that Philip had always been old; even as a little boy he had possessed a sense of propriety and a cool reasonableness that had often infuriated me.

We had gotten reversed somehow. Instead of being the older sister who is constantly embarrassed and tormented by her mischievous little brother, I was the one who caused trouble. I think perhaps I was probing for a spark of the life I felt bubbling up in myself when I picked on Philip, though perhaps my teasing and provoking was just plain meanness. Of course I paid the price when I carried it too far, being banished to my room, or forbidden some treat I'd been looking forward to; but I was rarely spanked—that wasn't Granny's style.

I remember the way Philip would watch while sentence was pronounced: the expression of faint shock that started me planning deeds of revenge even more terrible than the one for which I was about to pay the penalty. There was something so pious in his small, pale face as he listened to Granny's grimly controlled words, such solemnity in his round, blue eyes as they looked from her face to mine, that I sometimes thought with envy of my friends whose little brothers were normal and naughty.

Nothing happened to close the space between us as we grew older. Philip became taller and stronger than I and learned to ignore me when I suggested embarking on some escapade that was bound to end in trouble. He applied himself to sports and studies, and by the time he reached his teens he was set, motivated, undeflectable, while I was floundering, experimenting, reaching out greedily to sample all the wonders of life. I'm sure it embarrassed him when my friends and I came home in our ragged cotton clothes and strings of beads. When we smoked pot he left the room, and we barely noticed, for none of us had anything to say to him anyway.

Predictably, he graduated from Princeton with honors and immediately took a job with a Wall Street investment firm. He married the attractive, well-bred Barbara and they bought a house in Larchmont. We communicated by telephone now and then, mainly on the subject of Granny's Christmas or birthday presents, and three years earlier he had taken me to dinner in Beverly Hills when he was making a business trip to the coast. It had been like dinner with one's lawyer or broker, certainly not one's younger brother. I had felt sad when the evening ended, but it was a sadness with a rough edge of anger. His disapproval seemed palpable, like a solid object placed between us on the table, and I was at a point with my marriage and my job where I needed encouragement and support. I probably needed a shoulder to cry on, in fact, and I suppose that was the reason I had greeted him too effusively, actually feeling a mist of tears in my eyes as I hugged him. I also felt the stiffness of his body and sensed the warning conveyed by the touch of his cool, dry lips on my cheek.

He seemed to have filed me somewhere, like a report to which he must occasionally refer, and since I was uncertain as to just where I was filed or when I was allowed to pop out, the prospect of seeing him again was not particularly joyous. However, Uncle John had arranged it, and of course it was necessary for us to talk about Granny's care. We might soon have to agree on the crucial question of life-support systems; for Granny's protection I must establish a harmonious relationship with my brother.

As Philip hurried across the room to embrace me I was amazed at how much he appeared to have aged in the three years since I had last seen him. His face was thin and drawn, his eyes deeply shadowed, and he seemed to have lost some of his fine brown hair. Good lord, you don't go bald at his age, I thought; then felt freshly dismayed by the tension in his thin frame as he gave me a fleeting, almost reluctant, hug. His lips briefly touched my cheek; then he dropped his arms and stood surveying me with a smile that seemed distinctly forced.

"Why Phil, you're Wall Street from head to toe." It seemed wise to confine my comments to his manner of dressing; and he did indeed appear the prototype of the successful, young stockbroker. His charcoal gray suit was cut of flannel so fine that it bore a subtle sheen; a narrow gold watch chain curved importantly across his neat vest; the navy and red regimental striped tie contrasted silkily with his crisp white shirt.

I could not refrain from glancing quickly over his shoulder to where Uncle John was looking on, his blue eyes shining with suppressed merriment, his rumpled tweeds disposed on his lean body with casual grace.

Beside him stood Barbara, my sister-in-law, and I saw her eyes sweep over me appraisingly as she hastened to add her welcome to my brother's. Bobbing like prizefighters, Barbara and I bestowed identical, mothlike salutations on each other's cheeks, then stood back admiringly, our eyes equally glazed and beaming.

"You look marvelous."

"I love your hair."

"You're thinner! What have you done?"

It might have gone on for hours, for Phil just stood watching with that odd, nervous smile coming and going. But Uncle John was handing drinks to Barbara and me, then asking my brother what he would have. Another amused flash appeared in the blue eyes when Phil said stiffly, "Just club soda for me, please."

At that Barbara raised her glass to her lips and took a flickering, hummingbird sip, her hazel eyes wide with apprehension as she gazed over the rim. "Oh John, you've given me —what? Gin, I think." Smiling gently, she held out the glass and my uncle took it from her. "Just club soda for me too, if you don't mind. Only I'd like a twist of lemon in mine."

She glanced about at us with a mischievous twinkle, and to my annoyance I heard myself chuckling appreciatively. Why did such people inevitably reduce everyone else to their own level of inanity, I wondered, as I had many times before. Why instead weren't they ridiculed, thrown out, ostracized, banished from society?

I was gripping my glass as if preparing to hurl it at her. Easy now, I told myself; she's not a criminal, just an idiot. But it was certainly going to be a long evening.

Of course the truth was that no evening spent in the company of my uncle ever seemed long to me, and this one flew as they all did, in spite of my brother's strange reserve and the superficial chatter of my sister-in-law. I was curious about Philip, anxious to know why he was so thin and tense; so at the table I asked a few questions about his work, about Chip, their two-year-old, and the progress of the house they were restoring in Larchmont. But every query was fielded by Barbara; according to her everything was super.

I thought I saw a look of gratitude on my brother's face after she had repeatedly supplied answers to my questions, but of course Philip had always been quiet and somewhat shy. Even so, he possessed a subtle sense of humor, which had given me the reassuring feeling that in his own way he enjoyed life as much as anyone.

I saw no glimpses of that quiet enjoyment that night, however. Though Uncle John and I were several times reduced to helpless laughter over some anecdote of the past, Phil did not seem to share our amusement. Indeed he displayed no animation all evening except, strangely enough, when the conversation turned to Granny. He kept returning to the subject of her illness, the prognosis, her chances of recovery, until finally I turned to him and said, "It is awful, Phil, but I think it's worse for us than it is for her." I looked over at Uncle John and saw him nod slowly in agreement. "She doesn't seem to feel any discomfort and she is getting wonderful care."

"But she could lie there like that for years!" Abruptly, Philip picked up his untouched glass of wine and drank half of it at one gulp. "Ted Stevens was telling me about his mother, who had a stroke fifteen years ago. She's still alive, but the cupboard is nearly bare. Her entire estate has been spent on her care. It's a disaster for Ted and Laura."

There was a silence, and I saw the watchfulness that had appeared in Barbara's eyes. For once she had failed to rush in before Philip could speak, and she turned her attention to the ice cream melting on her dessert plate as if to detach herself from the discussion.

I felt an angry flush rise to my cheeks, but I tried to keep my voice light as I said, "Well, it seems to me Ted Stevens should be thankful that his mother is able to pay for her own care instead of needing help from him. Is there some better use for money than keeping your mother alive?"

"I'm thinking of the quality of her life, Sally. Lying in bed year after year, not recognizing any of us . . ." Phil shook his head, distressed, apparently, by the thought of all those misspent funds.

"Well, civilization hasn't gotten to the point where we put sick old people away, like dogs or horses. Perhaps you think it would be better if it had?"

Philip looked shocked. "Good Lord, no, Sally; whatever gave you that idea? I'm just suggesting that there ought to be some way to care for them that would make sense financially."

I glanced at my uncle, suddenly aware that, given the circumstances, our conversation was in the worst possible taste. He met my eyes and smiled reassuringly, but I had a sharp sense of the pain our words must be causing him.

Springing to my feet, I picked up my dessert plate and reached for Phil's. "Come on, Barbara, we can't leave Uncle John with the dishes after the splendid feed he's given us."

Barbara jumped up at once, as eager as I to put an end to the discussion, it seemed, and we busied ourselves loading the dishwasher while Uncle John carried the coffee pot to the library.

There we settled with our cups while my uncle placed a Mozart piano sonata on the tape deck, then sank into his shapeless old chair at the hearth.

He lifted his coffee cup in a toast. "Here's to more evenings like tonight, with all of us under the same roof at last."

We all raised our cups, but I observed that Philip and Barbara and I kept our eyes fixed on Uncle John, carefully avoiding one another's.

Phil put down his cup and said, "I suppose you've closed on the Palm Beach house by now?"

Uncle John nodded. "Yes, Gillian went down last week. That's one job finished at least." My bewilderment must have shown on my face, for he turned to me. "It seemed foolish to maintain a house in Florida that none of us wanted to use, so we sold it to the people who have been renting it. For a very nice price, I might add."

I felt an odd little pang at having no voice in the decision. On the other hand, there was no reason why I should have been consulted about Granny's business affairs.

"Granny never was the Palm Beach type anyway," I said. I looked questioningly at Uncle John. "I never understood why she kept a house there at all; she was so reluctant to spend any time in it."

"You wouldn't remember, but Father hated cold weather more and more as he got older and began to suffer from arthritis. Then when he died I think Mother kept the house out of habit or respect for his memory—or with an idea that the rest of us might use it. But we never did."

"Any luck with the apartment?" Phil asked, and again I felt a stab of something like jealousy. I didn't like having Granny's framework stripped away, as it were, and I didn't like being ignored while the men of the family made all the decisions— counseled, no doubt, by Miss Gillian Clark.

"But Granny loves that apartment," I exclaimed. I looked from Philip to my uncle and saw the same tolerant look on both faces. Of course they were familiar with the situation and I was new to it, but still . . . "It would cost a fortune to get another apartment in Manhattan. Shouldn't you wait and see what happens?"

"It's extremely unlikely that Granny will ever be strong enough to spend any time in the city again, or alert enough to enjoy it, if she did." Phil spoke slowly, patiently. "Maintaining that apartment is expensive. It would be irresponsible to keep it, under the circumstances."

"But Granny always enjoyed being there so much, with that wonderful view of Central Park. It might be stimulating for her to spend a few days there now and then. It wouldn't hurt to find out at least." I knew I should drop the subject, but I suddenly felt like Granny's advocate. Someone ought to think about ways to rekindle her interest in life, but it was her financial situation that seemed to be getting all the attention.

I saw a flicker of annoyance on Philip's face, but he continued to speak calmly even as he said, "You just got here, Sally. you haven't been involved, haven't carried the responsibility for all this." He glanced understandingly toward my uncle, then back at me. "You've got to leave the decisions up to Uncle John; he's best qualified to make them, after all."

I couldn't account for the sudden tears in my eyes, unless it was that old sense of frustration that had often struck me speechless, as a child, just when I needed to be most persuasive. I cleared my throat, turning my head away so the others would not see my emotion, and then I felt a strong, warm hand on the back of my neck, and my face was pulled over to rest on a familiar, moth-eaten sweater.

"I value Sally's opinion more than I can say." My uncle's voice was huskier than usual, as if he too were struggling to control his feelings. He tilted my head so that he could look into my face. "I didn't realize how much I've been missing my mother's voice in all this. When you spoke up just now I could very well imagine her saying the same words."

I knew my eyes were red and my hair tousled, but it didn't matter. As I gazed into my uncle's eyes I saw the love and understanding I had always found there—and never anywhere else since that long ago, golden time that lived for me more in feeling than in memory.

He started to speak, but the shrill ring of the telephone

broke in and, giving my shoulder an apologetic squeeze, he went over to the desk to answer it.

I smoothed back my hair and bent forward to speak earnestly to my brother. "I don't know why I got so upset. Except that it all sounds so final when you and Uncle John talk about disposing of Granny's property. She's not dead, after all. Let's not give up on her so easily."

Philip's face was expressionless, his eyes cold and unreadable. He sat stiffly in his chair, making no move to acknowledge my appeal, but I could hear sympathetic murmurings from Barbara, on my right. I turned to her, and as I did, I caught sight of Uncle John at the desk behind her. He was hanging up the phone, and it struck me that his face had become as carefully blank as my brother's.

His features relaxed, however, as he returned to our little group by the fire. Philip had risen and was consulting his watch, and Barbara rose alertly to join him. Again we darted at one another in a display of sisterly affection. "Let's have lunch *soon*," she said. I replied that I could hardly wait to see Chip, and saw her glance at Phil as if to call his attention to my normal instincts. "We'll make it dinner," she said. "You need to escape from that gloomy house in the evening."

I was somewhat surprised to see Uncle John coming toward me with my coat in his hands; I had a lot to say to him on the subject of my brother, but apparently it would have to wait. We stood in the open doorway while Philip and Barbara climbed into their car, and when they had driven off Uncle John led me across the gravel to the compact car I had rented to use during my stay.

"I would insist on having a nightcap so we could talk," he said, "but you look done in." His eyes were tender as he brushed a stray lock of hair back from my forehead, then bent to kiss me lightly on the cheek. "I'll be over in the morning.

I want to see Dr. McGinnis when he comes. Then I'll take you to the club for lunch."

My uncle's driveway curved away from the house to the right, to circle a grove of slender white birches, then turned left again before it reached the road. The engine of my little car was cold and as I rounded the stand of tall, pale trees it coughed weakly and died. I sat there in the dark, fumbling to find the ignition key, and managed instead to turn off the headlights. The situation was hopeless until my eyes adjusted to the blackness, for I had neglected to study the owner's manual and had only the vaguest notion of which buttons and knobs controlled the various functions.

I sat there, cursing all auto manufacturers for not standardizing the controls, while I activated the windshield wipers, the distress signals, and the cigarette lighter before locating the ignition key. Finally I got the motor started and was groping for the headlight switch when I heard the sound of a car approaching, then saw a bright band of light sweep the roadway ahead.

My fingers found the headlight switch and pulled it on, and in the same instant I heard the squeal of brakes quickly applied and saw the moving finger of light come to a stop, pointing in my direction.

I pulled to the right to make room, then eased carefully past the car that had entered my uncle's driveway. It was a smart foreign convertible, low and black, and it paused there trembling with the expensive, guttural throb of its engine.

A white face peered searchingly from the wheel, and although the eyes were narrowed against the glare of my headlights I recognized their dark, impatient flash, as well as the full red lips that were parted in annoyance. It was Gillian Clark who had arrived so unexpectedly, and there could be no question that she was headed for my uncle's house at the end of the long, curving drive.

CHAPTER 5

It was a night of brief periods of sleep so bustling with dreams that when I started awake I was uncertain whether I had slept at all. Repeatedly, I saw my uncle's face, wearing the closed, private look I had noticed when he replaced the telephone on the desk; and each time the picture floated into my awareness I felt a stab of sorrow. At the same time I heard the voice of my husband, accusing me in his cool, reasonable way of a variety of shortcomings. We seemed to move slowly through the rooms of our small Los Angeles house while he spoke of chairs and curtains and dinners and I surreptitiously tried one door after another, searching for one that would open.

I had dreamed it before, the part about Joe and the house, and my therapist, Dr. Zeigler, had found the symbolism almost laughably obvious. I wasn't so sure he had it right, however. Though I had benefited enormously from my sessions with him, I couldn't help wondering whether he had caught the real significance of that particular dream. If it illustrated my desire to escape in order to fulfill myself as an individual, why had I never dreamed it during the years of my marriage when I actually felt so trapped? It wasn't until after the divorce, when I had gotten a job and was learning that I possessed some marketable skills, that I began to have that recurring dream. Yet it seemed unnecessary to dream of freedom when I had finally achieved it. Or had I?

To me the inopportune timing of the dream suggested conflicts still to be resolved, but Dr. Zeigler was so pleased with my progress that I kept postponing further discussion of it. Then I began to feel so strong and confident, and my life became so busy, that I no longer wanted to spend two hours a week probing my psyche. I felt it was time to graduate, as it were, and Dr. Zeigler seemed to agree. He had helped a timid, immature, deeply depressed young housewife discover that she was capable of functioning on her own in the world. I was a success and so was he; now we must allow others to benefit from his talents.

But the dream persisted, occurring so infrequently that I gave it little importance, except to wonder at the variations that turned up. Always there was Joe and the house, its rooms much larger and more numerous than in reality; but often a third person joined us in our progress, either visually or as a presence felt. Once it was my boss, the gifted young copy chief who had taught me so much. Now and then it was the misty image of my mother. This was the first time the dream had featured my uncle. I tried to reason out the connection, but in my sleepy state it was impossible to think straight. It would have to wait for morning; but at last I fell into a sound sleep and when I awakened the familiar scenario had slipped from my consciousness.

I felt oddly unsettled that morning. I asked for bacon and eggs for breakfast, sensing a need for extra energy after my unsatisfactory night's sleep; and I drank three cups of Jenny's strong black coffee. Still I could not concentrate on *The New*

York Times, and finally left it half read on the dining room table with the idea of getting through the rest at lunch.

No, I remembered, Uncle John was taking me out to lunch. After he consulted Dr. McGinnis. I wondered how my uncle had known the doctor would be there this morning; I wasn't aware that he appeared on any predictable basis. Then I thought of Gillian Clark, seeing her white, impatient face as it had appeared the night before at the wheel of her car. I recalled the shock of surprise I had felt, realizing now the surprise had been accompanied by a sense of inevitability. In some deep, inner place I had been expecting something like that from the moment I saw Uncle John put down his telephone. I regretted now that I had not brought up the subject of Gillian Clark on the night we had dined alone. I could have questioned him then with a freedom I could not summon now that I knew they shared a relationship he had concealed from me.

Realistically, of course, there was no reason why he should confide the details of his private life to me, just because of my schoolgirlish urge to share my own personal history with him. After all, he had gone his own way and kept his own counsel for a long time, and privacy had become a habit of mind. Still, I felt a twinge of jealousy, there was no denying it, at the thought that Gillian Clark might enjoy a closeness to my uncle that I could never know.

Yet there was more to my reaction than mere jealousy; there was something here I did not understand, and the notion made me so uncomfortable that suddenly I could not tolerate the whine of the vacuum cleaner Jenny was pushing about the hall. I pulled on the cardigan I had brought downstairs with me and slipped out through the french doors that opened onto the terrace. There I paused for a moment to enjoy the spectacular view.

Granny's house was set on the top of a hill in the midst of

what had once been fields and pastures belonging to a prosperous farmer. The land rose so gradually from the road below that it was with a sense of disbelief that one looked beyond the sloping lawn and the treetops that bordered it to discern in the distance the glimmering waters of Long Island Sound. It lifted my spirits to see that patch of water, which on this bright spring morning shone with an inviting glow.

I set out across the lawn, savoring the aroma that rose from the tender, young grass. It was still wet enough to mark my sneakers, but after all my time spent on Los Angeles sidewalks damp sneakers seemed deliciously bucolic. I headed for the stream that began near the boxwood hedge that surrounded the rose garden. I wondered if it was still being stocked, remembering the lively, little brown trout I used to catch for Granny's breakfast. "I want them no longer than that," she would say, indicating a size well below the legal limit; and it was always with a sense of glorious wickedness that I obliged her.

I found the stream swollen from the spring rains, the stretch of flattened grass along the bank indicating that recently it had been even higher. Not so good, I reflected; the fish, if there are any, will be hovering near the bottom. Still I studied the water closely as I picked my way along, searching so avidly for a dark, swirling form that when I rounded a sharp bend and came upon a man standing there I gasped in astonishment.

"Oh! I'm sorry! I mean, I didn't see you."

He was smiling at my confusion, while at the same time giving his attention to the fly line he had cast upstream. "Sorry if I startled you," he said, slowly stripping in the line until he held most of it looped in one hand.

"How's the fishing?" I inquired. "The water's awfully high."

He was apparently ready to quit, for he caught the end of the line as it came near and pulled a pair of small scissors from his pocket with which to cut off the fly. With a motion of his head he indicated the wicker creel that lay on the ground beside a small tackle box.

"Have a look," he said. "I got a few, but they're small."

"They're the best, I think." I bent over the creel to inspect his catch of five small, speckled trout. "I'll have to bring a rod down here this afternoon and get some for myself."

"Oh, you like to fish?" He turned to me, looking faintly amused, and seeing his features squarely for the first time, I felt a shock of recognition.

"Tommy! Tommy Harris!" The name had come to me with no effort, for his face still had the boyish appeal I remembered. The dark blue eyes were thickly lashed, the nose straight and blunt above a mouth that seemed eager to laugh. But the little boy I had known was now a head taller than I, and he peered down into my face without, it appeared, any recollection of ever having seen me before.

I seized his hand and tugged it playfully. "Come on, Tommy, it's Sally. Good Lord, have I aged that much?"

He grinned, white teeth flashing in his ruddy face. "My gosh! Sally . . . I didn't know you were here. I guess that's why I didn't recognize you."

There was an instant's awkwardness as I let go of his hand, and I regretted my mention of aging, for it seemed a reminder of the distance between us. Tommy was about five years younger than I, the son of Granny's former maid and her chauffeur, Nancy and Michael Harris. He had often been brought to the house when he was a toddler, partly for the convenience of his mother, who still worked for Granny then on a part-time basis, and partly because I so much enjoyed playing with him.

At three, Tommy was a plump, lovable little creature who followed me about, prattling happily, and entering enthusiastically into any entertainment I concocted for him. Years later I realized that both Granny and Nancy must have seen that the almost maternal role I adopted with Tommy was a way of assuaging the pain I felt over the loss of my mother. Philip and I were too close in age; he wanted no "mothering" from me, even in play, nor did I feel like giving it to him. He was too cool and reserved, even as a small child, to enjoy the cuddling and scolding and other nurturing sorts of activity that good-natured Tommy accepted so willingly.

As we grew older Tommy became less amenable and I less demonstrative. Still, perhaps because he was an only child and I a lonely one our relationship remained special, with me teaching him to ride his first bike, running for the Band-Aids when he fell off and skinned his knee; helping him with his homework; defending him when he got into trouble. He, in turn, invited me along when he went fishing and sometimes came over to watch television, especially during the period when we owned a color set and Nancy and Michael did not.

He was only eight when I went off to boarding school, and from then on the gap between us widened until all I knew of Tommy was what I heard from Nancy or Michael. Until recently that had been a good deal, for their son had proved to be a gifted scholar, a fine athlete, and a natural leader. He had gone through college on a scholarship, then had worked in hospital administration long enough to realize it was no substitute for the medical vocation that had always appealed to him but which he could not afford. I had been delighted to hear, a few years earlier, that he had taken additional science courses while he worked and saved, and at last had entered medical school.

We talked about that as we walked along together, following the stream in its twisting descent to where it passed beneath the road that led to Granny's. I congratulated him on his perseverance and on the wisdom of his course.

"You're probably much more sure of yourself than if you had gone into medical school straight from college," I said. "But it's a long haul, isn't it?"

"It sure looks like one at the moment." He stopped and began stripping line off his reel almost viciously. "I'm taking a year off to make some money."

"Then when you finish school you have what, a year of internship? Or is it two?"

"One, then two or three of residency." Tommy was scowling as he cast his line out onto the water. "At least I'll get paid for that."

"Well, won't your father help out?" Tommy was shaking his head angrily, so I went on, "Or how about a government loan? You probably have a wonderful record."

"My father won't have it. He doesn't want me taking on a debt that he might have to pay back some day if everything went wrong." Tommy gazed over my head toward the woods, where the newly budding leaves trembled in a green haze. "He's old-fashioned when it comes to money—especially the amount it takes to get a medical education these days. So I'm working in the hospital lab during the day and driving people to the airport at night."

It was all I could do to keep from crying out at the terrible waste of it. Tommy's handsome young face sagged with unhappiness as he contemplated the years ahead. They would be difficult enough without the financial burden his father was forcing upon him.

"What will you specialize in when you get to that point?" I asked, and Tommy turned to me with his face full of light once more.

"Pediatrics," he said. "I really like kids, Sally, and when I see them in the wards . . . I don't know. I just want to do something to make a difference. I've got some ideas about certain diseases, but of course I'll need to put in years of research, and that's another reason Dad is worried about any loans. He doesn't see me as a big money-maker, at least not for a long time."

"But what you'll be doing is so much more important than making money! Oh Tommy, I wish I were rich. I'd give it to you myself, no strings attached!"

Something odd happened to his face when I said that. The eagerness vanished as if at the flick of a switch, his eyes turned bleak again, and his lips tightened as they had before. He looked uneasy all at once, and when he started to speak he quickly bit off the words and glanced at his watch instead.

"I've got to go," he muttered, and indeed it was obvious that he could hardly wait to be on his way. "Good to see you, Sally."

I stood beside the little wooden bridge that crossed the stream near where it joined the road, ready to wave when Tommy turned to look back. But he did not look back. He paced down the road with long, impatient strides, as if to escape my presence as speedily as possible. When he had disappeared around a bend in the road I turned to start back to Granny's house.

I felt forlorn as I trudged along. When I thought of what a sunny little boy Tommy had been and of the ambition he had now to bring sunlight to sick, helpless children, I felt a stab of anger toward Michael Harris. How could he refuse to help a son so gifted and idealistic?

Looking about, I saw that hundreds of crocus shoots were pushing their firm green tips through the grass, and I began to pick my way carefully among them. Piercing sturdily up-ward, the fat, pale green stalks looked tough and healthy, but they would break easily under a careless, trampling foot. Their crisp, young fibers would not spring back, as perhaps they might when old and seasoned. And neither would Tommy Harris's spirit, I reflected. He had worked hard; he had been strong and determined; but how long could he keep to his goal in the face of his father's opposition? Perhaps I should talk to Michael Harris—and try to persuade him. Then, as I emerged onto the neatly clipped lawn surrounding Granny's house it occurred to me that Michael, with his traditional Irish background, would have little respect for any opinions of mine. It would be far better for a man to reason with him on the subject of Tommy's education. I picked up my pace, eager to see whether Uncle John had arrived at the house. He would speak to Michael, I felt sure of it, and it was with a surge of optimism that I ran up the terrace steps and wiped my sneakers on the mat before pulling open the wide french doors.

CHAPTER 6

Mrs. Berger greeted me with the news that my uncle had called to say his plans had changed, and if I were free that night he would like to take me to dinner instead of lunch.

And what about his meeting with Granny's doctor, I wondered? Dr. McGinnis was upstairs, Mrs. Berger told me, so I hurried up to Granny's room, pulling off my sweater on the way. Her door was ajar, and I paused in the hallway to listen to what sounded like an animated conversation being carried on inside. I heard Terry McGinnis say, "You're so peppy this morning we're going to take you for a little walk."

Then there was my grandmother's voice, frail and thin, but with a vibrant undertone that had not been there when she had spoken to me the day before. "You have to disturb me when I get comfortable, don't you?"

She sounded so normal, speaking with the mixture of humor and asperity that had always distinguished her manner, that I half expected to find her sitting at her desk before a litter of correspondence and newspapers.

Instead, I entered the room to find Jane Kelly holding

Granny upright with one arm while she helped her into a warm woolen bathrobe. Terry McGinnis was placing a low footstool beside the bed, and he grinned over at me as he straightened to his feet, then turned to my grandmother and said, "Here's a visitor you'll be glad to see."

He stepped aside to give Granny an unobstructed view, and she peered at me intently, frowning with narrowed eyes, her mouth twitching as if undecided whether to smile or speak.

I didn't wait for the outcome, though I did approach her quietly, sensing that any effusiveness might startle her back into her protective shell. She seemed so tiny, sitting there on the edge of the bed, that I knelt so as not to loom above her; then reached to take her hands in mine. It was a shock when she drew herself up with a suggestion of hauteur, and folded her hands together in her lap. She did not seem angry, but slightly affronted, as though I had no right to presume to such familiarity.

I said, "I don't think you know me, Granny, but I'm Sally, remember? I haven't seen you for several years, so it's no wonder you've forgotten." I spoke lightly, trying not to lapse into the false sprightliness I thought of as "nurse talk."

"What makes you think I've forgotten?" There it was again. Elizabeth Staunton Ryder was not one to accept gracefully any suggestion of mental incompetence, except in others, of course. "I remember you, my dear," she said composedly, and I marveled at the quality of character that gave this small shrunken person with her unruly white hair and pale, dangling shins unquestioned authority over the rest of us.

Jane Kelly's expression was one of awe, or as close to it as could be managed while wrapping the person who inspired it in a bathrobe. No doubt Jane had forgotten, over the last months, how impressive Granny could be, and this was like watching a queen rise to reign again. Terry McGinnis had

moved back from the bedside, but I could imagine the be-
nevolence on his face as he watched the old woman grope in
her memory while pretending she had no need to do any such
thing. I was grateful to him for keeping silent.

Jane gently helped Granny to her feet, having already placed
a pair of soft slippers on them. She tied the sash of the pale
blue robe around Granny's waist and, holding her elbow firmly,
took a few tentative steps in the direction of the french doors.
My grandmother moved forward eagerly, an expectant smile
hovering on her lips, and after a few steps began making
strenuous efforts to break free of her nurse's grip.

"Now, Mrs. Ryder, let me steady you." Jane spoke softly,
but I heard the iron in her tone; there was no question about
Granny "letting" her help. Or so I thought until I saw the old
woman stop dead and turn to look up at Jane with a determined glint in her bright blue eyes.

"Just let me go along on my own," she said. It was not a
request but an order. Her faint smile remained as she went
on to say, "I will not move another inch until you let go."

Jane's lips were compressed as she cast a defeated glance
toward Terry McGinnis, who stood on the far side of the bed,
his face turning red in an effort to contain his amusement.
He threw up his hands in a gesture of helplessness, then came
toward my grandmother to be near if she should start to fall.
He made no move to touch her, but fell into step beside her,
as if they were strolling down the street together.

I was amazed at her strength after so much time in bed.
She walked without faltering, pausing only once to grip the
back of a chair for a moment, then relinquishing it to resume
her progress toward the doors that opened onto her balcony.

When she reached them I was amazed to have her turn
and say, looking directly into my eyes, "Open the door, Sally,
and let's see what kind of day it is."

There had been no emotion, no word of welcome, no instant when I saw the realization strike her, but it seemed that suddenly she knew who I was—or was it more pretending? I could not tell and I dared not challenge her. As I hurried over to do her bidding I asked myself fleetingly why it mattered, and I did not know the answer. I only knew that I felt a desperate need to have her truly recognize me.

Terry McGinnis released the brass catches on the glass-paned doors, and together we pulled them open. Immediately the soft breeze stirred Granny's thin white curls and lifted the flap of her bathrobe. She pulled the robe against her body, then slowly stepped out onto the narrow balcony, seized the iron railing and stood surveying her wide, green lawn with its clumps of budding trees and shrubs. She lifted her head and sniffed the aroma of rain-washed grass. Her lips parted in a faint smile, and as she raised her face to the sun I saw that her eyes were half-closed, like those of a contented cat. After a moment she turned as if to share her delight, and as her glance went from Terry's face to mine her smile widened and a soft chuckle escaped her.

"What a glorious day!" she exclaimed. She reached for my hand, and I stepped to her side and put my arm lightly about her shoulders. I could feel the frail bones close beneath the woolen fabric, and as she swayed against me, like a child leaning confidently toward her mother's skirts, I was swept with a feeling of protectiveness. I looked up to find Terry's eyes upon me, and in their depths I saw my own feelings reflected, the wonder and gratitude expressed more clearly than in words.

But Granny was tired. I felt her small frame sag against me for a moment, then she straightened and walked over to Jane Kelly, who had come to stand in the doorway. "Enough," Granny breathed, and as Jane took her arm she smiled up at her gratefully. "Time for a nap," she murmured. "A little rest and then we'll do this again."

When they had gone inside I quickly closed the balcony doors, then swung around to face Terry. "It's wonderful," I said, "but I don't get it. What made her wake up like this, and why didn't it happen sooner?"

He smiled down at me in silence for a moment and when he spoke it was as if he had to pull himself from some private contemplation. "This sudden alertness; yes, I can see why you find it surprising, but this is what I've been hoping would happen, once we could stop giving her any tranquilizing drugs."

"Tranquilizing? I should think you would give stimulants to people in her condition."

He shook his head. "It's a delicate balance that has to be maintained. In moments of awareness a person can feel immense anger because of what is happening to his mind. Your grandmother had a spell of that just before you arrived, and it was necessary to calm her down, just temporarily, while somewhere, perhaps in her unconscious, she adjusted to her altered state."

"Was she really unmanageable? Throwing things and yelling at Miss Kelly?" I could not help grinning at the thought of it. "I can see where Granny could be a handful if she wanted to."

"Sure. A victim of senile dementia can be like a two-year-old who has no effective tools for getting what he wants. The anger can be worse, really, because someone like your grandmother is aware of having once possessed better means of communication and a two-year-old isn't. So the frustration is maddening." Terry looked out across the wide green lawn and his eyes narrowed as he sought the glimmer of water in the distance. He ran his hand through his hair in a gesture I was beginning to recognize, then he said softly, "Sometimes I think it's panic they feel—understandably—when a window in the mind opens to offer a glimpse of reality. It's necessary to help them then, not only to keep them from striking out and perhaps getting hurt, but also to keep them from slipping into a terrible state of hopelessness."

"Oh, yes, I can see that. It must be ghastly to know you're . . . losing your mind. I hate to think of Granny suffering that way. Maybe it's better to be totally unaware." I was peering at Terry through a mist of tears. "It's no wonder they get furious," I said. "The situation is unacceptable!"

I dashed the tears from my eyes, amazed at my emotional reaction; but Terry did not seem to find it surprising.

"If it makes you mad I guess you can understand how a victim must feel. Your word 'unacceptable' is good, but it's like a lot of other things in life. Sometimes the unacceptable has to be accepted, and since we're programmed to fight, the process can tear us apart." He glanced at his watch and his forehead creased. "I've got to go, but first I want to check on your grandmother's medication. I don't think she's had anything for a couple of days." He quietly opened the door to the bedroom and followed me in.

It was silent in the room. Looking over at the bed, I saw that Granny was sleeping while Jane Kelly sat knitting in a chair nearby. She rose as we approached and placed her needles and bundle of yarn on the table beside her, then picked up a folder that lay there and brought it over to the doctor. There was a questioning little smile on her face as she said softly, "You'll want to see this, won't you, Dr. McGinnis?"

Terry nodded his thanks as he took the file that constituted Granny's chart and flipped over the last few pages. "Mrs. Ryder has had no Haldol for three days, I see." His voice held a question, and after a moment's hesitation Jane Kelly replied.

"That's right, doctor, according to the chart." Her face

was troubled as she continued. "I am afraid Miss Nelson occasionally neglects to enter a dosage, but I can't be certain of that."

Terry's reaction was instantaneous. His heavy brows shot upward in an almost comic expression of alarm, and he said, "What do you mean? I thought we had made it clear to her that every single dose must be recorded."

"I have spoken to her, quite sternly; and she swears she has never given any medication without entering it on the chart." Jane's eyes were anxious as she saw the color rising in the doctor's face. "I don't want to make trouble, Dr. McGinnis, and maybe I'm imagining it; but sometimes when I come in in the morning Mrs. Ryder seems to have regressed. Now and then she seems to have sunk back, as if she had been heavily sedated."

Terry McGinnis drew a deep breath. Again he ran a hand through his hair, while he gripped the chart and scanned the most recent entries. He looked up to find Miss Kelly's eyes fixed on him expectantly, and he forced a smile to his face. "If only you could stay on the job twenty-four hours a day," he said.

His tone was light, but I felt certain he regretted his words when I saw the solemn look that appeared on the nurse's face. "I could certainly work a double shift, Doctor McGinnis. I'm strong, and Mrs. Ryder is an easy patient—most of the time."

But even as she spoke he was shaking his head. "It's not necessary; in fact, it would be unethical to let you wear yourself out like that. No," he went on, "it's up to me to speak to Miss Nelson, or replace her if she won't cooperate."

"Can I help?" I said. "I could very well sit with Granny for a few hours at night. I realize I wouldn't be permitted to give her any medicine, but I could call you if something went wrong. I gather Gillian Clark sometimes does that." There was a silence while both doctor and nurse stared at me speculatively. It went on for so long that I began to feel uncomfortable, and I heard the waspish note in my own voice as I said, "Well, what do you think? I'm not totally incompetent, you know."

A spark of amusement flashed in Terry's eyes, and he said, "Give it a few more days, Sally; then we'll see. Meanwhile, I think you should be near your grandmother as much as you can." He peered down at me intently for a moment, then his face softened and he said gently, "She's reached a point where being with you, someone she both loves and enjoys, can give her the incentive to keep trying. She may have lost much of her memory, but she still has a life to be lived. Now that she's more aware, we have to sell her on that idea, between us." He glanced from me to Miss Kelly, and I saw that she was listening raptly to his words.

He faced me once more and said, "Do you see what I mean?"

I nodded, speechless. As it had the first time I met him, the intense conviction of this young doctor swept over me. His compassion was like an aura that enveloped me when I drew near him, making me feel soft and gentle and close to some simple but vital truth. I had to restrain myself from reaching up to brush the unruly hair back from his face. My fingers fairly itched to do so, and I stepped away from him and clasped my hands behind me.

"I've got to tell you what I told Jane," I said. "I think we're extremely lucky to have you taking care of Granny. Because you really do care, I can tell."

Apparently my remark made him uncomfortable, for the pink color rose in his cheeks, and he said hastily, "For anyone who knew your grandmother it would be impossible not to care." He nodded at Jane, then at me, and hurried from the room. In a moment I heard the sound of his car starting up in the driveway, and I picked up my sweater from the chair where I had tossed it, told Jane I'd be back that afternoon, and started downstairs in search of lunch.

When I returned at around three that afternoon I was disappointed to hear that I had missed out on Granny's second period of wakefulness. Jane reported that she had taken another walk to the balcony, and had been as cheerful and lucid as when I'd seen her that morning.

"All that time in bed has sapped her energy," Jane pointed out. "But if she has more days like today she'll soon get her strength back."

Jane was smiling, but she looked tired, and it took me only a minute to persuade her to leave me with Granny while she went out for a short walk.

"Take a nap in my room if you want to," I said as I settled into a chair near the bedside. "I intend to be here when she wakes up again, so there's no reason for you to rush back."

When Jane had left the silence fell about me like an invisible veil settling softly to the floor. Curled into the comfortable brocade-covered chair, I gazed dreamily around the room, seeing shadowy fragments of dimly remembered scenes, fancying I heard the faint cadences of Granny's voice mingling with my own and Uncle John's. All those long ago sights and sounds existed still no doubt, in some dimension where I could not quite reach them. At least I liked to think they did, and that one day I might find the key to that strange time warp and with it the answers to the questions that nagged at me.

I heard a soft intake of breath, and peered over at the bed to see if Granny was stirring, but she appeared to be sleeping peacefully. I realized then that this was the first time since my arrival that we had been left alone, and I suddenly felt very close to her. Perhaps she seemed more herself when she was asleep than when she was awake and unresponsive to me. Whatever the reason, I began talking to her as I had so often in the past. Without my willing it, the words came tumbling out, and it did not seem at all odd to sit pouring out my thoughts to a sleeping woman; it felt, instead, like a most marvelous and healing release.

"I've got to talk to you about Joe, Granny," I began. "I know you wondered why I married him. There was no hiding what you thought that one time you met him. You were so relieved to have me settle down, after the freewheeling life I'd been leading, that you were obviously doing your best to like him. But I saw the way you looked at dinner when he talked about his job and how although it would mean years of travel for him, and long separations, the rewards at the end would be worth it. I saw you glance at me and I remember sitting straighter in my chair and looking back at you with what I hoped was confidence. Defiance is what it really was, though I didn't realize that until much later. I was ready to get married, that's the truth of it, and it almost didn't matter to whom. As long as he was sexy and able to support me, that is. I was sick of being a semi-hippie. That world never suited me; you knew that long before I did. I needed a solid base to my life. I think most people do, but my need might have been greater because of Mother. In fact, Dr. Zeigler made me see that it was not just sex and love I sought by marrying Joe, but a parent to give me something I did not know I needed. It wasn't security. You had provided that. What I missed by not knowing my parents was a sense of continuity, a connection that reached back to the past and forward to the future, through my unborn children. It must be some basic instinct that keeps the animal species going.

"But, oddly enough, I didn't get pregnant, although I had assumed it would be a sure thing once I stopped taking the pill. And without children I didn't quite know what I was supposed to do, living in a small house in Brentwood. I had wanted to be a painter, remember? I entered every sidewalk art show in Oakland County when I was at Berkeley, and I guess I never realized how terrible my stuff was because it was surrounded by so much that was just as bad. I didn't feel like painting in Brentwood, though, and now I like to think it was because my taste had improved, and I knew I was hopeless.

"In any case, painting didn't seem to fit into a neat stucco house filled with mahogany furniture and flowered chintz curtains. I put furious energy into making that little house a copy of what I saw in the women's magazines. I learned to make slipcovers and draperies. I bought odd pieces of furniture in thrift shops and refinished them. I worked hard at cooking, even though Joe was away almost all week, every week; and when I finally met some people I began giving small dinner parties—again with the help of the women's magazines. Oh, Granny, you would have died over the food I turned out! There was one casserole involving tuna fish and stuffed grapes, if you can imagine such a thing."

I stopped. Granny seemed to be waking up. She turned restlessly and muttered something, but I could not make out the words. She probably wants me to shut up, I thought, shamefaced at the way I had been babbling. I waited anxiously, bending over her to catch any whispered phrase, but she stayed silent, and soon I realized that she had fallen asleep again.

Gazing at her placid face, I suddenly felt a surge of anger. It must have been the memory of my unhappy marriage that triggered it, but there was no way I could blame any of that on Granny. I sprang to my feet impatiently, bewildered by the sudden rush of emotion. I strode to the dresser, picked up Granny's silver-backed hairbrush and began pulling it through my hair. In the wide mirror I saw that my eyes shone with repressed rage and that my lips were set in a tight, straight line. Then my glance moved to the right, to the picture of the lovely young bride in its silver frame, and my hairbrushing came to a sudden stop.

There was the reason for my anger; I must face it. Much as I loved my grandmother, my anxiety about her had another cause, one I had kept hidden from myself until that moment. When she died, or lapsed into mindless senility, any hope of learning the truth about my mother would come to an end. It was that hope that had sped me to Granny's bedside, not concern for her; I must look at the fact squarely, however distasteful I found it.

I replaced the brush and walked slowly back to look down at her. Why should I think that this frail old woman, who loved me devotedly, would keep from me the answer I so urgently needed to find? And why had I always felt so certain she knew the answer? Looking back, it seemed that my life had been a long period of waiting, that I had always carried within me the secret expectancy that one day Granny would quietly tell me the reason my mother ran away. Yet now she lay in her bed sleeping her remaining days away, and it made me feel like shaking her. But steadying myself on the bedpost, I told myself to be patient and stop blaming the poor old lady for something she couldn't help. Meanwhile, I thought, I'll get to work on Uncle John, though he's always said he doesn't know any more than I do.

I heard footsteps approaching in the hall, then a firm knock on the bedroom door, and I hurried over to pull it open. There, instead of Jane Kelly, I was confronted by the arresting presence of Gillian Clark. She was smiling broadly, her wide, dark eyes aglow with friendliness, and as she briefly squeezed my shoulder with one hand I felt the strength of her beautifully manicured fingers.

"I heard the good news," she said breathlessly, then strode past me to the bedside. "Oh, she does look better; there's no question about it!" She turned to me, beaming. "Jane asked me to take over for a while so you could get away. She wanted to run home for a minute."

"Oh I can stay. I'm in no hurry at all." But as I spoke she was settling herself into the chair beside the bed, and the expression on her face was one of bright determination. I saw that if Gillian Clark had decided to be helpful it would be futile to argue with her.

"You're very thoughtful," I said, mustering a smile to show that I wasn't put out by her mastery of the situation; but I moved toward the door with an uncomfortable feeling of inadequacy. It appeared that in the hands of Gillian Clark I was as mindless as Granny, lying over there on the bed.

Indeed, I reflected as I made my way to my room, everyone in the entire household seemed to lie under the spell of this beautiful, self-assured young lawyer. Perhaps that was why they were there. I stopped abruptly outside my door, re-membering the strong-minded housekeeper who had pre-ceded timorous Mrs. Berger. Mrs. Olsen was her name, and her way of speaking her mind had caused many a run-in with Granny. It had also kept the tradesmen from taking as large a slice of the household funds as they would have liked.

In my room I picked up the novel I was reading, but a sound from below impelled me to my window, which over-looked the service area outside the kitchen door. I saw that Jenny had stepped outside to the trash can and locked herself out. She was hammering on the door to attract the cook's attention, just as she had that morning when she had done the very same thing. Not overly endowed with intelligence was Jenny, especially in comparison with Nancy Harris, Tommy's mother. I wondered whether Nancy and Michael had retired of their own volition or whether they had been asked to leave. I would clear up that point with Uncle John that evening. Suddenly I was impatient for our dinner together. We had more to discuss than I had anticipated, and it startled me to realize that many of the questions that troubled me revolved around the shapely figure of Gillian Clark.

CHAPTER 7

As it turned out, my dinner with Uncle John was unsatis-factory on every count. I had looked forward to an evening like our first together, when we sat alone in his warm study and talked of matters close to our hearts, but when he tele-phoned at six it was to tell me that we would be going to the club and that he had asked Gillian Clark to join us.

"I think it's important for you to get acquainted," he said. "Gillian drew up Mother's will, and she has been handling just about all her affairs. She can answer any questions you might have on your mind."

"Yes, I'll bet she can." The disappointment I felt gave a sour edge to my tone that I instantly regretted. "I mean, I've met her, you know, and she certainly seems capable. But I wanted to discuss a couple of things with you—especially after seeing Philip and Barbara. What's going on with them, anyway?"

My uncle laughed softly, and I knew he was recalling those two stiff figures politely grimacing their way through the evening. "They've always been like that, Sally; you've just forgotten."

"Oh, it isn't just their personalities; I know I can't do anything about that. But I didn't like the way Phil talked about Granny. You wouldn't let him persuade you to put her in a nursing home, would you?"

"No, no, I've never considered such a thing and as long as we can afford to keep up the house I never will."

"What do you mean? There's no shortage of money, is there? Everything looks the same as always around here."

There was a pause and when my uncle replied I felt a coolness I had never encountered before. "It's complicated, Sally, and I don't really want to get into it right now; but things aren't quite as serene as they may look to you."

"I'd love to have you explain it to me when you have a chance." Some instinct made me speak gently as I continued. "I don't mean to be nosy, Uncle John; but I can't help being concerned about Granny's . . . situation. And by the way, I hope you'll pay her a visit this evening. She's much livelier today. She actually recognized me, or I think she did."

"Oh? That's good news. I'll come a little early then, around seven. And by the way, Sal, you know how they are at the club." He sounded tentative all at once and I smiled to myself. I knew what was coming.

"I haven't been near that club in so long. It will be nice to see it again." To me I sounded so phony and sugary that I half expected Uncle John to put me firmly in my place, but he didn't.

"If you brought a dress it might be a good idea to wear it," he said. "They rather frown on ladies wearing pants to dinner."

"No problem." But all at once the evening ahead loomed dismally, and for the first time since my arrival I felt a sharp longing for my own surroundings, my own friends, my own style.

It seemed terribly sad that it was my beloved uncle who had made me feel homesick, but it was time I faced it. He wasn't the same; I wasn't the same; our close, loving relationship had subtly changed. Time and distance had come between us, and that was inevitable; but there was another factor in the equation, one not so unavoidable. At least in the beginning, I told myself, Uncle John must have surveyed Gillian Clark with detachment, as he did all attractive women. I was beginning to have an uneasy suspicion, however, that he no longer controlled the situation. It looked very much as though he had allowed the reins to slip from his hands to hers, and that she held them so lightly, tugged on them so imperceptibly, that my uncle was unaware of the change in drivers.

Pulling on the one dress I had brought, I told myself I should be grateful that I was wearing it to dinner, instead of to the solemn obsequies I'd had in mind when I packed it. It occurred to me then that I should ask Terry McGinnis about Granny's general health, although it seemed likely that he would have told me if she had any serious problems other than her mental deterioration.

I heard the crunch of Uncle John's car in the driveway, and quickly slipped into my shoes and took a last, critical look in the mirror. The dress did nothing for me, that was certain. Perhaps because of being mashed into a suitcase for three days, it hung on my slight frame in dark, depressing folds, and I tried vainly to remember what I had liked about it when I bought it. If it hadn't been for my faintly insecure feeling about my standing with Uncle John I would have torn off the dress and thrown it into the back of the closet. Instead, I pulled the belt as tight as I could in hopes of improving the silhouette, picked up my handbag, and hurried out of the room.

I was surprised at the excited anticipation I felt as I headed down the hall in the direction of Granny's door. Then I realized that I had not seen Uncle John and his mother together since my arrival. It would be wonderful to see his face light up with happiness at her improvement. Surely he would want to be with her often now, and his engaging presence would be the best possible tonic for her.

I tapped lightly on the partly open door, not wishing to interrupt what might be an emotional scene of reunion. I heard the rustle of starched cotton, and the door was pulled open by a tall, pale woman who said, "Good evening," and neither smiled nor stood aside to let me enter.

This must be Miss Nelson, the undependable record-keeper, I decided, but standing there like an implacable guardian she gave no impression of flightiness; quite the contrary, in fact.

"I'm Sally Templeton," I said, tilting my head to smile up into the nurse's face. "I'm Mrs. Ryder's granddaughter."

This news seemed to leave her unmoved. Her light gray eyes flickered over me appraisingly before she replied, "How do you do?" then moved ever so slightly to the left, as if admitting me against her better judgment.

My uncle looked over at me from where he stood beside the bed, and one look at his face told me that his visit had been a bitter disappointment. His fine blue eyes were shadowed as he gestured hopelessly toward my grandmother's still figure.

"I guess there's been a change since you saw her," he whispered as I came to join him, and all my uncertainty melted away in a rush of pity for him.

I seized his arm and squeezed it wordlessly as I looked down at Granny, who appeared to be in a deeper sleep than when I had left her that afternoon.

I spoke to her; I went so far as to shake her shoulder gently, but there was no flicker of response, not even the restless half-awareness she had displayed at other times.

"I don't understand," I murmured. "She was wonderful this morning. She went out on the balcony, enjoyed the pretty day . . ."

In my uncle's face there was such sorrow, so much baffled love, that I felt miserably guilty about arousing his expectations. "Let's go," I said softly. "Maybe if you come back in the morning . . ." I was practically tugging him away, but I paused near the door to question Miss Nelson.

Maintaining her cool detachment, the nurse reported that Mrs. Ryder had been asleep when she arrived on duty and that Miss Clark had indicated that she had been sleeping all afternoon, or certainly ever since she had arrived.

I saw a softening in Miss Nelson's stern features as she went on to say that Miss Clark had been let down at finding no improvement in her client's condition.

"It's wonderful, the time she spends with Mrs. Ryder. She's absolutely devoted to her." She was looking at me in a way that seemed to imply that I had a good deal to learn on the subject of devotion, and I felt a surge of anger mixed with astonishment.

It seemed that Gillian Clark had the formidable Miss Nelson, as well as the weaker members of the household, under her thumb. The question that naturally followed concerned the strength of her hold on Uncle John. As we said goodnight and left the room I began to see the evening ahead in a new light. If I kept my wits about me I might find it extremely informative.

Uncle John dropped me at the porticoed entrance of the country club, then drove off to park the car. I entered the reception area and, looking around curiously, saw that the place was very much as I remembered it. The walls were covered with a scenic wallpaper depicting the rolling fairways and imposing stone clubhouse of the St. Andrews golf course in

Scotland, and the green carpet on the floor suggested a continuation of its grassy turf.

The same wallpaper had covered the walls twenty years ago; the club's decorator must have laid in many extra rolls to allow for replacement. Automatically, my eyes picked out the scattered figures of old-time golfers wearing tartan trews and tam-o'-shanters. When I was a child I had thought they were leprechauns, and I remembered how Granny would send Philip and me out to see how many we could count when we became fidgety during the slow Sunday dinner.

It seemed strange to return to the scene of so many of those endless dinners and, later, the dances and parties of my early teenage years. It had been rather fun to dress up and go to the parties, always filled with a tremulous expectancy regarding one boy or another. But as we grew older and the hard-driving message of the sixties reached us, the country club became a place we were dragged to under protest. To be seen there with family members, and wearing an expression of tightly controlled boredom, was just barely acceptable in our group. To appear in the club dining room or snack bar without an adult one was obviously humoring was unthinkable, and the few young people who went there and actually seemed to enjoy it were considered by the rest of us to be hopelessly effete.

For that reason I did not anticipate meeting any of my old friends at the club, although by now we were mature enough to use the place if we wished to without fear of being branded reactionary. It still seemed to me the domain of older people, however, and I felt vaguely uncomfortable as I dawdled there in my unbecoming crepe dress.

It was a relief when Uncle John came striding through the wide doorway and led me into the walnut-paneled cocktail lounge across the foyer from the dining room. As we entered a waiter came to greet us and show us to the table near the back of the room where Gillian Clark sat waiting. To reach it we passed among several seated groups of men and women, and though my uncle paused frequently for a brief word or handshake, he did not take the time to introduce me, but continued purposefully on to join his dinner guest. Poised and smiling, she watched us approach, and when we reached the table she said in her low, vibrant voice, "It's lovely to see you two crossing a room together; you are so alike."

Her dark, velvety eyes glowed at me with affection even as my uncle bent to kiss her cheek. He held a chair for me and I sat down saying, "I've been waiting years for someone to notice the resemblance!" It took an effort to keep my voice light in the face of such bald-faced politicking, for the only physical trait my uncle and I shared was our leanness, our light bone structure, with possibly some likeness of gait as we walked together. Yet Gillian Clark had paid the compliment that once I would have found irresistible. She had figured me out with amazing intuition; but it was the old, adoring me she had pinpointed, not the newly alert, faintly suspicious person I had become in recent days.

She had changed from the sweater and tweed skirt she had been wearing that afternoon to a simple, honey-colored cashmere dress, totally unadorned. Its fine, soft texture suggested an elegance that extended to the body beneath; as if such well-made bones and disciplined curves required the richest of coverings. Her smooth hair was lifted back from her face that night and pinned on one side with a narrow, gold-edged comb. When she turned her head the thin line of gold gave a glimmering accent to her shining, dark eyes, then sparked again in her white teeth and smiling red lips.

She was drinking white wine with club soda, and with a view to sharing her plane of mental alertness, I decided to have the same. Uncle John ordered the drinks, requesting Scotch for himself, as usual; then he turned to Gillian. "Thank you once more for looking after Mother this afternoon." He smiled into her eyes, but it was a slow, sad smile, and he bent forward at the same time to rest his arms on the table with an air of weary defeat.

Gillian's smoothly arching dark brows knotted in compassion. She touched my uncle's hand lightly with one perfect fingertip in a gesture that suggested understanding so complete that it required no greater expression. I found myself staring at her hands as she sat back and lifted her glass to her lips. Her long fingers were white and slim and tipped with shining ovals of rosy polish. They curled about her glass with languid grace, then came to rest on the tabletop near, but not touching, my uncle's.

She did not speak until the waiter had brought our drinks and placed them before us. Then she said softly, the vibrancy of her voice reduced to a silky undertone, "You were disappointed, weren't you, when you saw your mother?"

Uncle John sighed, then straightened and reached for his glass. "Every time she has a good spell I seem to miss out on it."

"And I have the same luck." Gillian smiled over at me, her expression as rueful as my uncle's. "That is one reason I like to sit with your grandmother—when I'm allowed to."

Her mouth twisted wryly and she darted a quick, mischievous glance at my uncle.

I saw the humorous glint as he returned her look, then Gillian went on to say, "Miss Kelly is an excellent nurse, but she's like an excitable watchdog about your grandmother. She doesn't seem to realize that the rest of us want a part in caring for her—because we love her too."

With the last words her voice dropped almost to a whisper,

and she sat studying her hands as if embarrassed by her own emotion.

I glanced at my uncle to catch his reaction to this playacting, and felt my heart sink when instead of meeting my eyes with a flicker of our usual understanding, he kept his attention fixed on the gracefully brooding Gillian.

I said, "It's understandable that you would feel that way, that anyone would, after working so closely with Granny. There's no one like her, is there, really?" To me my voice rang false and tinny as I attempted to make the point that it was Granny's charm that was the marvel, rather than Gillian's capacity for devotion.

But I could see that it didn't matter how I sounded or what I said, for Gillian had rallied, lifting her glowing dark eyes to engage my uncle's in wordless communication. Suddenly aware of the silence that had fallen, they turned and both began to speak at once. Gillian immediately deferred to Uncle John, and he acknowledged the courtesy with a little smile.

"I'm sure you can see, Sally, in your usual perceptive way, that Gillian and Mother have a relationship that goes far beyond the normal one between lawyer and client. That was part of my reason for asking you to come east now instead of . . . later." He paused, and sat turning his glass in his hands as if thinking out what he wanted to say. Gillian, meanwhile, gazed about the room with a tranquil smile on her lips, waving once to a friend seated at a nearby table.

Uncle John looked at me squarely and there was a boyish appeal in his expression as he said, "I've never had much of a head for business, you know. Mother always handled her own affairs after my father died. She enjoyed it, I think, although she always said it would be unfair to burden me with her financial matters when I had my own career to think about. My career . . ." He smiled and shook his head slowly. "I guess

Mother expected me to make a dent in the business world, even though I had no need to earn a living. But I wasn't interested in any sort of commerce, and since my ego didn't prod me, I could only be thankful that my grandfather had made it possible for me to do what I liked full-time, instead of cramming it into weekends and vacations."

I grinned over at him. "That's why you were such a satisfactory uncle. No one else had time to take me to the movies or listen to my problems."

"Not to mention your friends' problems. Some of those tangled romances made my own love life look pretty dim."

He did not look at Gillian as he said this, but she glanced up quickly and we smiled at each other, as any two women would smile at the notion of Uncle John's love life ever being "dim."

"Well, so I gather you helped Granny more and more as she began to lose her grip. Is that right?"

Gillian nodded. "Yes, it was mainly a matter of taxes at first, helping her keep records and all. Then she asked me to work with her broker on such things as capital gains—when to buy and sell and how long to hold certain stocks—and I found it very interesting."

"It was interesting to see what happened to the figures when you got into it." Uncle John signaled to the waiter for another round of drinks, then turned to me. "Gillian just about doubled the income Mother was getting from her capital. It was amazing. Old Mr. Parsons's nose was out of joint until the day he died."

"Is that something lawyers normally get involved with? I always thought they drew up wills and settled estates and handled lawsuits. It sounds as though you have some special qualifications."

"I did take some accounting courses, because of course

there's a good deal of money management involved in any trusteeship. And I turned out to have a head for figures—to my surprise." She spoke thoughtfully, displaying none of the false modesty so many bright women feel called upon to assume, and I liked her for that.

Uncle John seemed eager to bring me up to date on all of Granny's affairs that evening, and this helped erase the uncomfortable feelings I'd had in the presence of Philip and Barbara. He told me more than I could absorb in a short time, equipped as I was with a meagre understanding of the world of finance; but by the time dessert was set before us I had received the impression that it was thanks to Gillian's canny manipulations that both Granny and my uncle were able to live much as they always had.

Uncle John talked knowledgeably about such things as tax shelters, deferred income, living trusts, capital appreciation, and although I saw Gillian look up sharply once or twice, as though about to contradict him, she kept remarkably silent, considering that she was the recognized expert on such matters.

In a way I admired her restraint, for I felt certain Uncle John was getting at least part of it wrong; but her reluctance to correct him implied the deviousness I'd suspected in her from the start. This was disappointing because I wanted to like her. I also wanted to relax. I had resolved to stay alert, wary, observant, like the experienced hero of a spy novel; but the role was new to me, and exhausting. Those master spies, always portrayed as world-weary, were just plain tired, I decided. I wished Gillian Clark would evaporate and leave me alone to talk to Uncle John about really interesting matters.

But it clearly wasn't the night to probe for any facts he might have concealed regarding my mother's disappearance. Nor did I feel inclined to discuss my brother. Some primitive family protectiveness made me reluctant to serve Philip up for Gillian's appraisal, though of course Uncle John and I could speak as we liked in private.

I did manage to ask about Tommy Harris's parents, though, and deduced immediately that the subject made my uncle uncomfortable.

"Oh, gosh, I hate to get into that." He picked up a spoon and stirred his coffee, although he had added no sugar or cream. "Michael and Nancy kind of let us down, Sally. When Mother began to get forgetful—just when we needed them most, that is—they started pressing for more pay, more time off, and so forth. I'd have to say they started taking advantage."

"That amazes me," I said, "after all those years when they were so wonderful. Why, I thought of them as family, and I think Tommy felt the same way about us."

"That made it all the more difficult for your uncle." Again Gillian's dark eyes glowed with sympathy as she directed her attention to Uncle John's troubled face. He did not meet her gaze, and this avoidance seemed as significant as any meaningful glance might have been.

Gillian bent forward earnestly, moving her coffee cup aside as she said, "It is often disillusioning to learn what servants really think of people in your grandmother's position. It's usually not until they are badly needed that the truth comes out. When they decide they are indispensable they take liberties; and, of course, that can't be tolerated."

"I suppose that accounts for Tommy's manner the other day. He seemed quite anxious to get away . . ." I stopped, for my words had affected my dinner companions quite strangely. My uncle had stiffened in his chair and was almost glaring at me, while Gillian held her coffee cup arrested halfway to her lips for a moment, then replaced it on the table without taking a sip.

"Where did you see Tommy Harris?" Uncle John sank back, but his face remained grim, his eyes unnaturally bright.

"I guess I forgot to tell you; I ran into him down at the stream. He didn't recognize me at first, it's been so long since we've seen each other." Faced with my uncle's inexplicable tension, I was prattling on like a hostess with a difficult guest.

"I thought Tommy was away in medical school." Gillian's face was smooth and untroubled; she seemed to be taking only a polite interest.

"He has dropped out of school," I said. "His father refuses to pay any more tuition. I think it's a shame."

I knew I was up to something, with that deliberate exaggeration, but I wasn't sure what, except an attempt to elicit a stronger reaction than the truth might have caused.

Indeed, at my words Uncle John threw his napkin onto the table and abruptly pushed his chair back. "Are you finished, Sally? Gillian? We'd better be on our way."

He was in such a hurry to be gone that I almost had to run to stay with him on the way out of the dining room. "I've been meaning to talk to you about Tommy," I said breathlessly as we strode across the foyer in the direction of the front door. "Can't you do something to help him?"

"Help him!" My uncle stopped so suddenly that I stumbled into him. I clutched his arm with an apologetic laugh, but he stood looking down at me, glaring, actually, just as he had at the table, and I sensed that he was struggling for control. Then he raised his eyes, the angry glare was transferred to someone behind me, and I realized that Gillian had caught up with us.

"Sally wants me to help Tommy Harris!" Uncle John spoke the words in a low tone, his voice vibrating with fury. He pulled away from me, then swung around and strode out the door in search of his car.

CHAPTER 8

Waking in the mornings in my old room in Granny's house, I often lay still in the maple bed enjoying the warm, safe feeling induced by my surroundings. As a child I had accepted that protectedness unquestioningly, barely aware of it until I went away to the battered, anonymous rooms and dusty corridors of boarding school. I reveled again now, as I had since my very first school vacations, in the various sounds of the house about me, the steam rising in the radiators, the subdued voices of Jenny and Mrs. Berger and, when I slept past eight, the ringing of a distant telephone.

It was pleasant, on these bright spring mornings, to prop a second pillow beneath my head and lie watching the filmy embroidered curtain rise and fall on the current of air wafting through my partly opened window. On the ceiling a gossamer shadow danced beside a quivering bar of sunlight whose source I could not discover. Though I pretended I must not get up until I found it, I was usually distracted by the scent of coffee or, on some mornings, of bacon cooking, and that was the end of my daydreaming.

On the morning after my dinner at the club, however, it was not the aroma of breakfast that broke my reverie, but the recollection of my uncle's angry face at the mention of Tommy Harris. I could remember only two or three times in my whole life when I had seen Uncle John so disturbed. His persona, after all, was of a smoothly cultivated, slightly sardonic man of the world. That the thought of my seeing Tommy Harris could discompose him as it had was indeed cause for puzzlement, and I lay in bed that morning examining the question from every angle I could think of.

Perhaps it was my effrontery in suggesting that he help Tommy; perhaps he had already lent the boy some money. But no, I remembered that Uncle John was instantly displeased when I merely said I had seen Tommy. Could he have been so upset by the Harrises as to want them forever banished from our property? That sort of hardness was not like Uncle John, especially since he knew how Tommy loved to fish in our stream and, in fact, had himself taught him to fly cast.

Gillian had given me no clue. After Uncle John had flung out the door of the club, leaving us alone together, I had turned to her in astonishment. "What in the world . . . ?" But I got no further before we were joined by two women whose husbands had also gone for their cars, and while Gillian seemed unruffled as she introduced me, I fancied I saw my own bewilderment reflected on her face.

In the car Uncle John seemed totally himself again, though the easy flow of comment maintained all the way to Granny's might have been designed to prevent any questioning. And I observed with some sadness that once again he was maneuvering it so we were not left alone at the end of the evening. Apparently he hadn't enjoyed that first night as much as I had, though at the time I had thought we shared an enviable rapport. He had seemed entranced with the long, sad tale of my married life, in fact had appeared to find it more amusing than depressing, and his enjoyment had left me with a restless urge to tell him the rest of the story. I smiled at the realization that Joe Templeton, who had once caused me such pain, now could serve as mere conversational fodder.

But however entertained Uncle John might be, I had no desire to include Gillian Clark in my reminiscences. For if I had learned anything over dinner it was the extent of her power, and I found it daunting. I wanted to like this woman; she was beautiful, charming, intelligent, totally in control of her life. But although she exuded warmth and friendliness in my direction, I sensed in her a toughness and a beautifully played artifice that put me on guard. I could not go on about my amusing mistakes in her clear-eyed, evaluating presence. She would join in my uncle's laughter, but where he would be touched as well as entertained by a young girl's foolishness, she would see my misadventures as stupid, crazy, easily avoided.

She would not be honest—or foolish—enough to say so, of course, any more than she had corrected my uncle when he discussed her financial maneuvers. Again the word control came to mind; it was not passivity that distinguished Gillian Clark, nor serenity, but the sense of a strong will keeping original ideas and strong feelings from bursting forth. She was a formidable woman; I had never come up against anyone quite like her.

It was amazing that my brother had allowed the situation to develop as it had. Unlike me, he had been on the spot; it would be natural for him to take both a professional and personal interest in Granny's finances. After all, half of her estate, our mother's share, would be divided between Philip and me—or so I assumed.

So I assumed. The thought was electrifying. I hastily climbed out of bed and went over to the desk beneath the window to find some paper and a pencil. While I had listened to Uncle John the previous evening, some questions had occurred to me and it seemed wise to write them out before I forgot them. At the top of the list would be the matter of Philip's and my inheritance. I sat down in my spindly, old desk chair and wrote: Philip's and Sally's share? I underlined the words, then sat back astonished at myself. My heart was beating fast, my thoughts were racing; I was angry, infuriated suddenly, by the thought of my darling Uncle John—darling, weak Uncle John—surrendering so much authority, not only over Granny's income and his own inheritance, but over the funds that would have been my mother's.

It was just ridiculous, I told myself, to feel so agitated when, if my uncle had it right, Gillian Clark had actually increased the value of Granny's holdings. Well, we'll see, I thought; we'll just look into it all and find out. I would call Philip at his office that morning; that would be much more businesslike than wangling a dinner invitation from Barbara. I would find out what he thought of it all, and we could decide together whether anything should be done to protect our interests.

I rose from the desk and stared thoughtfully at the list I had prepared. Anyone coming upon it would think I was obsessed with Granny's money. I must put it out of sight.

I pulled open the center desk drawer, idly noticing as I did so that this was not the desk at which I had done my homework all those long years ago, but a more elegant, French "lady's" desk. No doubt the old maple one I had used had been banished to a servant's room or thrown away. Too bad, I thought; it might have been entertaining to go over the graffiti I had scrawled on it during my preadolescent years.

I was surprised to find that the drawer contained an untidy jumble of writing paper and envelopes, the first disorderly sight that had met my eyes in this well-organized household. I began automatically arranging the stationery in stacks of notepaper, letter-size sheets, and envelopes, and saw that each sheet of paper was engraved with a monogram. The initials stood out from the yellowing white paper in swirls of thick blue ink, and I felt no surprise, only a quiet certainty, when I saw that they were C.R.L., with the R centered and larger than the other two letters. Catherine Lewis Ryder.

This had been my mother's stationery. Hers might have been the last hands to touch it before mine; certainly anyone who discovered it in the drawer would have arranged it in neat piles or, more logically, thrown it all away. For I assumed that the desk had been carried down from the attic when it was decided that my old school desk was beyond repair. En route the writing paper must have shifted about in the drawer, which apparently no one had bothered to open.

I had the oddly satisfying sense of performing a useful task for my mother as I piled the paper and envelopes neatly in the drawer. I smiled, thinking of Uncle John's desk, and how it had always amused him to watch me put it in order. It was an unusual specialty, desk-straightening, but it had come in handy, for now I could tuck my list of financial queries beneath Mother's writing paper and feel certain it would not be discovered.

In a minute or two I had finished, and the drawer looked like a stationer's display case. Except at the back, where I noticed that a scrap of paper had gotten stuck. It was only a small triangle, and I bent and tried to blow it away, but it would not budge. Frowning, I pulled the drawer all the way out of the desk and balanced it awkwardly on my lap. In the better light I could see that the tiny bit of paper was not a scrap, but the protruding corner of a larger piece. I carefully took out the stationery I had tidied and placed it on the desktop. Then I pulled at the corner of paper and found the lining of the drawer lifting with it. It was a false bottom, a layer of thin polished wood fitted in to cover the rougher material of which the framework and been constructed.

I removed the thin wood lining from the drawer, and as I lifted it the bit of paper at the back came loose and fluttered to the floor. I quickly seized it, bending clumsily over the drawer I held, but before applying myself to the writing I saw on the paper I made sure there were no other surprises concealed between the drawer bottom and the lining.

There was only that one slip of white paper, about two by three inches in size, one evenly perforated edge indicating that it had been torn from a notepad. A name and address were written on it in black ink: Martin Josefson, 2572 Boston Blvd., Detroit, Michigan.

I read it over, spelling out the words as if they were written in a foreign language. I studied the paper closely; I turned it over to examine the back. I placed it in the drawer with the corner sticking up as it had before. Then I lifted the false bottom and slid the little note completely under until it was concealed. I replaced the writing paper in the neat piles I had arranged and slipped my list of questions underneath. I pushed the drawer shut and sat back in my chair, gazing uncomprehendingly out the half-open window.

Here it was at last—a clue to the mystery of my mother's disappearance, the first clue ever. Or was it? Some monitor in my head asked the question: How can you be sure?

Because this name and address were obviously hidden here by my mother. I paused in my self-interrogation to picture my mother's discovery of the drawer's false bottom, her instant recognition of it as a perfect hiding place. If she had possessed my romantic nature, and somehow I thought she had, she would have stored it in her memory in case of future need.

I imagined her smiling as she rose from the desk, enjoying her new secret.

And was she wearing a smile on her face when she carefully placed that slip of paper beneath the false bottom of the drawer? My mental picture did not show me the answer to that question.

I hurried through breakfast that morning, even though the news of Granny's liveliness the day before had inspired the cook to make blueberry muffins. They were deliciously moist and they broke apart to reveal plump, juicy berries that never could have come in a packaged mix. I hoped no word of Granny's disappointing evening had reached the kitchen.

I carried my coffee cup to the library so that I could telephone my uncle before he left his house, but as I started to pick up the instrument it rang, startling me so that I nearly dropped it.

I answered to hear a young woman's voice asking to speak to Sally Ryder. It was my old friend, Betsy Marsh, whose mother had heard that I was in town. Betsy suggested lunch; she had a day off because her office was being painted. We arranged to meet at a restaurant called The Nook, and I then cut the conversation short, too intent upon catching Uncle John to wonder what kind of an office Betsy normally occupied.

I dialed my uncle's number only to find that the line was busy, and since it remained busy for three more attempts, I decided to simply drive over and see him.

I ran upstairs first to get a sweater and check on Granny. Her bedroom door was closed when I came along the hall, so I knocked lightly, and in a moment Jane Kelly opened the door and said, "Good morning."

She stepped back as she spoke, and I looked hopefully over

at Granny's bed. All was as still as it had been the night before, and I turned to Jane in consternation. "Hasn't she been awake at all?"

Jane shook her head. "I'm going to call Dr. McGinnis this morning. This doesn't seem possible after the way she was yesterday."

"He wouldn't have ordered any medication given, would he? She wasn't upset or anything, at least when I saw her."

"He certainly wouldn't have." Jane was frowning, her eyes fixed thoughtfully on the still figure in the bed. "Mrs. Ryder was doing beautifully yesterday, making wonderful progress. I can't help wondering . . ."

"I don't blame you." I said. "But, Jane, I met Miss Nelson last night and she doesn't seem at all the type to give medication without recording it. Of course you're in a better position to judge, but she struck me as thoroughly professional."

"I know what you mean. She's so efficient it's almost funny—except I can tell you it's no laughing matter when I suggest that she hasn't recorded a dosage. She has threatened to quit if I bring it up again. Which puts me on the spot, doesn't it?"

I said slowly, "Jane, I'd like to sit with my grandmother this evening between shifts. Would you have any objection to that?"

There was a moment's silence. Jane's expression did not change. I had the strong sense that she was deliberately concealing her reaction to my suggestion. "I think that would be very nice," she said in what seemed a carefully neutral tone. "I suggest that you come a little early, around a quarter to five, if you can."

She was looking at me searchingly now, her earnest, hazel eyes enlivened by an urgency I had not seen before.

I nodded, returning her gaze unsmilingly. "I'll be here,

don't worry." I turned and hurried out of the room and down the stairs, pulling on my sweater as I went.

If Gillian Clark should come to spend an hour or two at the bedside of her beloved employer that evening she would find me there before her, and this time I would not be so easy to uproot.

CHAPTER 9

"Martin Josefson. No, the name doesn't mean anything to me." Uncle John leaned back in his chair and a feather of steam rose from the coffee cup in his hand to partly obscure his features. "Detroit? I never heard Kitty mention Detroit. What makes you think this name you found has anything to do with her?"

"Because of the way it was hidden in her desk." I saw a faint skeptical smile hover on his lips and I bent forward earnestly. "Well, there it was, in the same drawer with her stationery. The writing paper is marked; there's no question that it was hers, and I don't think there's any question about the name and address either. It was never found and cleared out with the rest of her things because a drawer full of expensive monogrammed stationery is something people are inclined to leave alone—even after the owner of it has died."

Uncle John smiled. "You're right. I still have boxes of my father's in the attic. But Kitty wouldn't have thought of that. She wasn't expecting to die, after all."

"No, of course not; but she must have had some very good

reason for hiding that name and address so carefully." I got to my feet and carried my coffee cup to the sink. I rinsed it out, then reached for a dish towel and slowly dried it. I put the cup away in the cupboard and turned to face my uncle, who remained seated at the kitchen table with his long legs stretched out halfway to the sink.

"I'm dead serious about this," I said, and saw the slightly quizzical expression fade from his face. "It bothers me terribly not to know why Mother ran away when she did. You may think I'm being melodramatic, but it's always haunted me. I don't think I can even begin to live my life properly until I find out."

My voice was shaking so that I had to stop, and once again I was reminded of those tearful sessions in Dr. Zeigler's office. But unlike Dr. Zeigler, who watched with clinical detachment while I helped myself from the ever-ready box of tissues, my uncle sprang to his feet and with one stride came to envelop me in his arms.

"Ah, Sally, I had no idea it mattered so much to you." He held me, gently stroking my hair and murmuring meaningless, comforting words in my ear, until I began to feel warm and cherished in the old familiar way.

I pulled away, reluctant as I was to leave that sheltering embrace. "I'm an awful bore, I guess." I smiled up at him and he slowly shook his head. He started to speak, but I broke in.

"May I explain something, please? Ever since I got here and saw Granny's condition I've been almost in a panic about finding out about my mother. I feel that this is my last chance, and that somehow I've got to get you or Granny, or both of you, to tell me what happened. I've always thought Granny knew and was waiting for some suitable time to tell me."

I paused, but Uncle John did not respond to the question

I had implied. Though the deep blue eyes were fixed on me attentively, I could not guess his thoughts.

"The other thing I've always thought is that you—or Granny—might know something that would help me figure it out, some little remark or incident that might not have seemed significant at the time. Do you know what I mean?"

He nodded. He seemed about to say something, then he sighed and came to put an arm about my shoulders. "Let's go outside and talk. It's too nice to stay in here."

He pushed open the kitchen door and we stepped down onto a narrow flagstone path that curved around the back of the house to the driveway. Beyond it was a stretch of lawn, the grass growing in uneven tufts as it always did in early spring. My uncle frowned as he picked up a fallen branch and tossed it into the rhododendron bushes at the side.

"I've got to get busy on this place," he muttered, and indeed the untidiness of the yard seemed offensive on a day of such sparkling sunshine and soft, caressing air.

I drew a deep breath as we wandered aimlessly onto the damp lawn. "It smells of spring; it's delicious. It doesn't smell like this in Los Angeles."

"The only aroma I've ever noticed out there, other than exhaust fumes, is ultraviolet, like the smell of Mother's sunlamp. I figure the chamber of commerce sprays it around."

I laughed. "Well, I'm through with all that, I guess. I wonder what Chicago smells like in the spring."

Uncle John had stopped beside a tumbled stone wall that divided his lawn from his neighbor's. He stooped to pick up another branch and began pulling the twigs from it. "How much do you remember about your mother?" he asked without looking up. "You were only about five when she died."

"I was five when she died, four when she went away. And of course I don't have any clear picture of her in my mind.

But the photographs I've seen fit my image of her. She was very pretty, wasn't she? It's not just that she was my mother?"

"She was very pretty, oh yes." Uncle John spoke so softly I could barely make out the words. He held the branch absently in his hand while he gazed into the distance, crinkling his eyes against the brightness of the sun. "I'd say your mother, Kitty Lewis, was about the loveliest girl I ever knew. I don't mean the most beautiful, you understand; I mean she had a special kind of energy and interest in other people that seemed—to light her up. She had a radiance. I've heard other people say it too." He stopped and I saw a boyish eagerness in his face, as if remembering my mother as a girl had made him young again.

I was holding my breath. He had never talked this way before. No one ever had. I suppose they thought I remembered her the way they did, but how could I? What is a mother to a small child but a bundle of agreeable scents and sounds and feelings, all of them vitally important to the child's well-being? What I remembered were impressions—a musical laugh with an undertone of kindness; the special, safe warmth when she hugged me; a lock of silky hair brushing my cheek when she kissed me goodnight; the incredible softness of her velvet evening wrap. And sometimes in a crowd I would catch a whiff of an elusive fragrance and turn my head to follow it.

"Do you know what perfume she used?" I almost whispered the words in my anxiety to sustain the mood.

"Mimosa." There was a pause, then Uncle John laughed, so abruptly that I jumped. "From the time he was sixteen, Bill never let us forget that. For every birthday, Christmas, and Valentine's Day he somehow had to save up enough to buy Kitty's bottle of Mimosa. I don't think he ever missed."

I smiled, but I could feel my lips trembling: I felt dazed. Here were two people I had never known, my own mother and father when they were much younger than I was now. This was the sort of recollection I might have heard over the dinner table if they had lived.

My uncle was peering at me thoughtfully. "Apparently it's very important to you to find out all you can about your mother. What about Bill? Aren't you just as curious about your father?"

The question startled me. In my mind's eye I saw the photograph of my father that stood on Granny's crowded dresser top in the largest silver frame of all. He wore the uniform of a lieutenant in the air force, the cap emphasizing the level gaze of his clear blue eyes. As a child I had observed the resemblance between the two brothers; their features were quite alike, but where Uncle John's face seemed to glow with life and mischief, my father's looked solid and responsible. Several times I had stifled the disloyal thought that in a way things had worked out for the best, for I could not imagine getting along as happily with that rather stiff young soldier as I did with my lighthearted uncle.

Even now I could not say that, however, and after a moment's reflection I realized it wasn't the answer to my uncle's question anyway.

"I think the main reason is that my father was killed; he didn't run away and leave me. He didn't have a choice, unless you count enlisting in the air force, and I don't." I paused, searching for the right words. "My mother was killed too, and she couldn't help that. It wasn't her fault that a retired mail clerk had a heart attack on the Hutchinson River Parkway just when she turned onto it. Horrible as it is, a child can accept the fact of a parent's death; he knows that people don't want to die and if they're killed it's against their will. But running away is different. Your mother running away from you is not to be borne. It's unacceptable!"

I stopped, as surprised by the force of my emotion as I had been the day before in Granny's bedroom. It was in her room, too, that I had used that same word, and now I heard again the voice of Terry McGinnis saying that sometimes the un-acceptable has to be accepted. Well, maybe, but not without putting up a fight; not without exhausting every possibil-ity. . . .

"Hey, what's going on?" Uncle John grasped my chin and turned my head to face him. "You're mad at your mother, is that it? After all these years?" His arm was around my shoul-ders, and he pulled me close. "Don't be angry at Kitty," he murmured. "She loved you; I know she did. She wouldn't have left you without a good reason. Give her a break."

I stiffened. "You do know something! I've always thought you must. Tell me, please, Uncle John. Don't hold out any longer. I can take it, whatever it is!"

But my uncle was slowly shaking his head. He did not look at me, but off into the unfathomable distance as he said, "I can't tell you what you want to know. I don't think there's anyone alive who can."

I swallowed. I sank against the stone wall. The sun had heated the rounded old stones, and I could feel their warmth through my flannel pants.

"What about Martin Josefson?"

Uncle John looked around at me blankly.

"The name I found in Mother's desk." Uncle John was shaking his head again and I said impatiently, "Don't you think you're giving up too easily?"

Now I had done it. I saw at once that he was angry, and cursed my inability to hide my feelings.

"It's not up to me to give up or to persevere; this is your project, not mine." The words were clipped and the blue eyes that could be so compelling bore into mine now with a frosty glimmer. "I'll be glad to search my memory all you want; I'll tell you all I can about your parents, but I can't tell you what I don't know. And I'll not encourage you on a fool's errand."

Until his final words I had thought only to soothe him into amiability again; I so desperately needed his affection, even if I could not have his help. But he had stung me, and I pushed myself to my feet and brushed off the twigs and broken leaves that clung to my pants.

"All right, I'll figure it out on my own. I'll hire a detective if I have to. And when I get the answer, you needn't expect me to share it with you!"

I stumped off across the uneven lawn, too upset to watch out for the spongy spots that soaked my shoes, and when I reached the driveway I climbed into my little red car and drove away without glancing back to see whether my uncle had followed.

It was a little too early to go to The Nook to keep my lunch date with Betsy Marsh, yet there wasn't quite enough time to go home and change my muddy shoes. I drove slowly to the village. Perhaps Dominic's shoe repair shop was still in operation. It was quite near the restaurant, as I recalled, and I might be able to get my shoes cleaned and polished before meeting Betsy.

Driving slowly along Main Street in search of Dominic's I was aware of two emotions; anger at Uncle John, and amazement at myself for feeling that anger. We had had an occasional falling out over the years, usually when, as was the case today, he had stubbornly refused to exert himself in support of some project that was passionately dear to me.

In the past when I had goaded my uncle into his special kind of icy rage I had been quick to regret it. The idea that he might stay angry with me was insupportable, and turned me into an anxious, fawning supplicant. Not this time, though. I felt positively exhilarated, and I wondered if I might at last be free of the need for approval that had dogged me all my life.

Ahead on my right I saw Dominic's, and I slowed the car and began looking for a parking place. Just beyond the shop a sign pointed to a municipal parking lot on the next street, so I turned right at the corner, pulled into a space in the lot, and climbed out of my car. As I was about to turn left in the direction of Main Street, the building at the end of the street caught my attention. It was a pale sandstone block, two stories high, and the sign on the roof bore the simple outline of a dark blue bell on a yellow background. The telephone company, yes. What about it?

I would find a Detroit telephone book there, and Martin Josefson's name in it. I could call him up.

I turned and started toward the sandstone building with no further thought for the mud-covered shoes that squelched unattractively with every step. I did glance at my watch, however, and saw that I had a scant ten minutes before my one o'clock date with Betsy. I could look up the number in that time, certainly, and make the call later when I got home.

But of course it wasn't that simple. I was shown to a room containing rows of shelves lined with out-of-town directories arranged in alphabetical order. It was no problem finding Detroit, but I had my first hint of trouble to come when I saw that the city's listings were spread over several directories. I picked the one titled Central Detroit and quickly turned to the J pages. There I found Josephsons, many of them, including a few Martins, but only one Josefson and that an Irving.

I felt discouraged as I surveyed the remaining Detroit area directories. I had no idea which area might contain Boston

Boulevard, so I selected one of the phonebooks and turned
to the yellow pages, hoping the zip code map might tell me
what I needed to know. What I found was a chart of north-
western Detroit and its suburbs divided into postal zones,
with only the major arteries indicated by name.

I looked at my watch. I had to leave immediately, and even
so I would be late if The Nook happened not to be exactly
where I thought it was. I felt intensely frustrated as I replaced
the directory, and my face must have reflected it, for on my
way back through the reception office I was stopped by a
pleasant-faced girl at the desk, inquiring whether I had found
what I was looking for. I explained that I had not and why,
and she offered to locate the number for me.

"We have maps of all the major cities, of course, and I can
easily find the address." Her voice was as soothing as the one
that comes on the line to say that you have misdialed, and
her smile was so wise and gentle that I felt ashamed of showing
my impatience.

I thanked her and quickly scrawled the name and address
on the pad she offered me. Then I explained that I'd be back
after lunch and hurried out to the street, wondering where
the telephone company recruited their sweet-voiced, understanding employees. Their personalities were so uniform it
sometimes seemed they were members of a religious order.

I picked up my pace, suddenly eager to see my old friend
Betsy, and hoping the years had not changed her too much.
My concept of a sisterhood of the telephone was exactly the
sort of thing she used to love. I remembered how we would
sprawl lazily in the sun, embroidering some conceit that amused
us while our friends tore about on the tennis court. Since
those days there had been many tennis players in my life, but
a great shortage of Betsys.

The Nook was aggressively simple: a white clapboard house

set back from the street, with a swing on the porch and clay pots of geraniums everywhere. Inside were bare wood floors, a good deal of old brick, a dozen round tables covered with blue and white checked tablecloths, and more geraniums. The room I looked into was nearly full, and I peered uncertainly around at all the women's faces. I hadn't seen Betsy for a long time.

A hand went up from a table beside the window, and I started forward somewhat hesitantly. The girl who sat there in the sunlight looked too tall and slim and composed. Her hair was blond and straight, cut in a severe blunt style, while I remembered Betsy with a mop of long, brown hair she kept pushing from her face in a habitual nervous gesture. But I saw that the shining hair framed wide, brown eyes, a narrow, turned up nose, and a generous, smiling mouth. It was Betsy, all right.

As I drew near her smile broadened until the whole of her expressive face was alight with pleasure. She reached for my hands, and I seized hers and beamed down at her speechlessly. I think we were overwhelmed by the rush of affection we felt, because outwardly we were so altered. At least I gathered from Betsy's bemused, searching gaze that I wasn't exactly as she had pictured me, either.

"Well, five years have to make a difference," I said. I pulled out a chair and sat down, then I leaned forward to grin across at my old friend. "I swear, Betsy, you've gone chic on me."

"It's all on the surface. Underneath I'm the same unspoiled, untrammeled, untutored . . ."

"Unmarried?"

The brown eyes sparkled. "At the moment."

"Betsy! Tell me . . ." But a waitress had appeared to take our drink order and recite the restaurant's special dishes of the day. The list was numbingly familiar: ginger sorrel soup, radicchio salad, mesquite-grilled fish, fruit sorbet.

When the waitress left us I was pleased to hear Betsy ask mildly, "What ever became of *sherbet*, do you suppose?"

"Too hard to pronounce."

She flicked me a glance that told me she understood perfectly what I meant, and I knew that in one important way she hadn't changed. I hoped her future husband, if she really meant that she had one, appreciated the economy of communicating with Betsy. It saved so much energy, not having to spell everything out.

"I gather you've had a rough time. I'm sorry." The brown eyes were fixed on me soberly now. "You look all right, though. I hope you are."

"Yes, I'm all right. But it's a big thing to go through—divorce. I don't see how people do it more than once."

"That's why some of us are proceeding with caution; too much of it, I sometimes think." Her mouth twisted in a wry little smile for a moment, then it straightened and she gazed at me thoughtfully. "You'll do it again, though, won't you? You're not bitter?"

"No, bitter isn't the word. It's more that I'm still . . . reverberating, you might say; and I can't think about another relationship until the shock waves have dissipated. I need to be still for a while. I need to settle some things." I looked across at her in astonishment. "It's amazing. I didn't know I felt that way until I heard myself saying it to you."

"We never did waste much time." We were silent while the waitress placed our drinks before us. When she had gone Betsy lifted her glass. "Good to see you, Sally. I've missed you."

Her tone was light, but she didn't smile and neither did I as I raised my glass in response.

"What's your job," I asked, "in the office that's closed today?"

She bent forward eagerly. "I'm in public relations, working

for a fantastic woman named Prue Evans. Have you heard of her?"

I nodded vaguely. "The name means something, but I can't exactly remember—"

"Well, we have a fascinating mixture of clients: actors, fashion designers, cosmetic tycoons; people who need to build their personal images. Prue is very selective. She handles only the ones who have potential. They have to have nerve, and stamina too, to take on one of Prue's promotional campaigns."

"You mean you get them invited to the parties and openings that are covered by the press? Things like that?"

"Oh, sure, that's part of it. Plus guest appearances on TV, interviews in popular magazines, and of course an invitation to the White House is always helpful."

I laughed. "It sounds like fun. It also sounds like a job that could take over your life. You must have crazy hours."

"My hours are unpredictable. If we're working with a movie studio to promote the sensational upcoming star of their next blockbuster, for example, I might spend a whole week with the dear girl." Betsy hitched her chair closer and leaned her elbows on the table. "Say it's Darlene Swivet, who spent her formative years stalking the runways at Caesar's Palace in three ounces of sequins and a pair of net stockings. Suddenly she's picked by the head of the studio to play an ethereal poet living in Paris in a possibly, but not definitely, lesbian relationship with Clara Schultz, the founder of women's suffrage. Darlene is going to be on serious talk shows, right? She's got to have the clothes, the haircut, the flattering spectacles— plus a smattering of indoctrination. I mean, she's not supposed to look blank if the interviewer mentions the ERA."

I wiped tears of laughter from my eyes. "But, Betsy, what does she *say*? You can't do a complete Pygmalion job in a week."

"Well, that is where Prue's genius comes in. She supervises Darlene's appearances very carefully, and she knows which interviewers want a real discussion and which are dying to air their own opinions, with maybe a few Hemingway reminiscences thrown in. And if there's any slipup, if our host unexpectedly fixes Darlene with a piercing look and asks about her goals, for instance, we've coached her to talk about 'fulfillment.' It's surefire, as maybe you've found out. There is nothing like the mention of fulfillment to get a man talking —about something else."

"Oh, Betsy, that job was made for you. Does Prue Evans realize how lucky she is? You'll make her fortune for her."

"Well, maybe." Betsy sat back as the waitress appeared with our salmon. "White wine?" she asked, and I nodded.

"How does all this fit in with your other plans?" I said, picking up my fork. "I did hear you hint something about marriage, didn't I?"

"Ah, yes." Betsy took a bite of her salad and gazed over at me speculatively as she chewed. Finally she put down her fork and said, "Tell me, Sally, what do you think of your grandmother's doctor?"

"Who? Terry McGinnis? Why, he's wonderful. At least he seems to be." I stopped, perplexed by the nonsequitur.

"Well?" A gleeful light had appeared in Betsy's brown eyes and her lips were parted expectantly.

"Oh lord, Betsy, you're going to marry *him*? Terry McGinnis? I can't believe it." Indeed the news hit me like a dash of cold water, sobering and oddly unwelcome.

"He's the lucky man. Or so he tells me. What I'm wondering is how I can ever live up to him." She suddenly looked very young and vulnerable and I reached across to quickly squeeze her hand.

"He is . . . very special. Or anyway I've gotten that impression in the two times I've seen him. I've never known a doctor quite like him." I hardly knew what I was saying, I was having such difficulty adjusting to the idea of Betsy marrying Terry McGinnis.

"I know you're wondering how we got together, and I can only remind you that I've always been one to spot quality—in anything: clothes, jewelry, or people. Look how I've hung on to you, for instance." She grinned, all flashing white teeth and sparkling brown eyes, but I knew she meant what she said very seriously. "When I met Terry he knocked me out. He was almost godlike compared to the types I knew in New York. You know, the yuppies who have to make a million by thirty."

I smiled. "I've met a few of those in L.A. They scare me."

"Well, then you know how different Terry is. And Sally, when I say he's godlike, don't get the wrong impression." Her mobile face was suddenly reflective. "Terry is admirable, certainly, but it's his humanity that really gets me. He's more in touch, more accessible, than any man I've ever known."

"Oh yes, I've seen that. You are so lucky, Betsy. And Terry's lucky too."

Betsy looked at me almost shyly. "He was just as thrown as I was. I guess because I'm a little different from the girls he was used to."

I laughed. "Different indeed! You must have been like a comet blazing in from another world. Now I know why he looks kind of dazed sometimes."

When the waitress took our plates away, we fell silent while we waited for our coffee. Betsy, I could tell, was pondering how much more to say on the subject of her marriage plans.

"Are you engaged, officially?" I glanced at her left hand and saw no diamond there. "That's sort of unnecessary now, I guess."

"We haven't announced it, though Mother's pushing for it,

of course. And we're not living together—exactly." Again the wide grin lit her face. "But we go away for weekends when we can, and when we're off in Vermont or somewhere alone together it's pure magic. Then when we come home . . ."

Our coffee had arrived, and as Betsy lifted her cup to her lips I saw that her face had turned somber. When she spoke again she sounded almost wistful.

"Life must have been a lot simpler in the old days, when a woman just settled down to have babies and bake cakes. Have you ever thought that?"

I nodded. "That's about what I had in mind when I married Joe. I was such a simpleton. I thought marriage was a full-time occupation."

"Well, how would you know? You were so young you'd never had a job; and your grandmother kept busy enough. So did my mother, for that matter. It's different for me." She paused for another sip of coffee. "I told you I love my job. Oh, I know I'm not doing anything to improve the world, but I enjoy my crazy work. It makes me use all my ingenuity; it makes me stretch. I love it when I come up with an idea Prue hasn't thought of. I love the excitement, the electricity of working in New York. I love making money. And guess what Terry wants to do?"

I shook my head.

"He wants to move to a small town in Vermont—he's got it picked out—and start a family practice."

"Oh, yes! That would be perfect for him. That's what is needed, now that medicine is so specialized; someone like Terry, who's concerned, who cares . . ."

Betsy was gazing at me, her eyes cool and level. "Sounds great, doesn't it? Brilliant young doctor foresakes chance at fame and fortune to snowshoe around the mountains delivering babies and diagnosing measles. And brilliant

M.D.'s wife, what does she do? Follow him around carrying splints and bandages like some medical caddy? Bake pies and churn butter? Take up weaving? There's a lot of weaving in Vermont."

The words came so fast it was clear that she had gone over and over it. Her voice had become a hard, dry rasp.

I cleared my throat. "And what do you want Terry to do?"

Betsy sighed. "Oh, ideally I'd like to see him set up in New York. He could have a fabulous practice in no time at all. Or, instead of going commercial he could do research at Columbia or NYU. It's all there, Sally. Many of the top medical men in the country are in New York. He could make a real contribution to science." She was leaning forward eagerly now, the brown eyes shining once more. "He wouldn't have to make a lot of money. I could keep working—even with children."

"But he doesn't want that?" It was out of courtesy that I phrased it as a question; I knew the answer.

"He wants no part of it. He's only staying in the suburbs so that we can be together. All he thinks about is the wonderful simplicity of life in Newcastle, Vermont; getting down to basics, truly relating to his patients." Her voice was soft now; she was nearly whispering as she said, "And the trouble is that I love him, so I guess I'll have to give in. I'm stuck, Sally."

We looked across at each other with total understanding and my voice sounded as regretful as hers when I replied, "Yes, it certainly looks like you're stuck."

CHAPTER 10

Back at the phone company, again in a rush because it was after four o'clock, I was dismayed to be told that no Martin Josefson was listed in any Detroit area directory.

"Are you certain of the spelling?" the soft-voiced lady asked me. "There are three Martin Josephsons, spelled with p-h. I can't find a single one spelled with an f."

"It's the spelling I was given." I sagged a little, leaning against the edge of the desk. For some reason I hadn't anticipated any difficulty, but now I realized how foolish it had been to expect to find the listing. It must have been at least thirty years ago that my mother concealed that note in the desk drawer, possibly even earlier. I needed old Detroit phone books; I tried to figure how old.

"Is there any way I could see listings from years back? I think it's 1952 that I want."

"We have them on microfilm," she replied, "but not stored here, unfortunately. I can have the name looked up in New York, but it will take a few days."

"I would appreciate that," I said, "and if it isn't too much trouble ask them to look up 1951 as well."

I was pretty sure that it was in that year that my father had left for Korea and Mother had taken Philip and me to Granny's for what she probably expected to be a few months' stay.

Uncle John could be helpful when it came to pinning down such dates, but for a while at least I would manage without him. As I pulled out of the parking lot I thought about his behavior that morning. He had been extremely quick to take offense, it seemed to me, now that I could view the scene with some detachment. Yet only a moment earlier he had spoken of my mother with such fondness that I had felt close to him in the old, wonderful way of my childhood days. He had seemed to linger over his memory of her as if it were a cherished treasure.

Then why was he so unwilling to help me track down this Martin Josefson? Because he didn't have my burning need to learn more about my mother, of course. He'd obviously found her enchanting and had no doubt been deeply saddened by her tragic death; but he'd accepted it, and for him her story was finished.

I parked my car in Granny's driveway and glanced at my watch before I climbed out. It was four-thirty; I was in plenty of time to plant myself firmly at Granny's bedside. And later, when Miss Nelson arrived, I just might take a fly rod down to the stream. I had no plans that night; seven o'clock would be just right to catch the trout in their evening rise.

I stopped with my hand on the polished brass knob of the front door. In my preoccupation with Martin Josefson I had completely forgotten to press Uncle John for an explanation of his angry reaction to my mention of Tommy Harris. I had not only neglected to ask him, I had gotten him so irritated that now it would take much tactful fence-mending before I dared bring up what was apparently a very sensitive subject.

I sighed as I pushed the door open and entered the hall. I had never expected to see the day when I would have to think and plot how best to handle my beloved Uncle John.

The minute I saw Jane Kelly I knew that Granny must have improved. Jane's face, which when I first met her had seemed stolid and suspicious, was alive with a happy expectancy she had obviously been bursting to share.

When I entered the room after knocking lightly on the door, she hurried over to me with her hand outstretched. She drew me to the bed impatiently, and stood beaming down at my grandmother.

"Mrs. Ryder is much better this afternoon," she said, and indeed I could see that the figure propped on a fat, white mound of pillows was once again Granny and not the lifeless doll I had seen that morning.

Her eyes were bright and blue as she peered up at me, and although an uncertain smile hovered on her lips, her expression seemed genuinely welcoming. She lifted one hand in a weak but graceful gesture, and the lacy sleeve of her bedjacket fell back from her thin, blue-veined wrist.

"My dear," she whispered. "How good it is to see you."

She hadn't called me by name, but never mind. Gratefully, I sank into the chair beside the bed and took her frail hand in mine. At my touch, her hand stiffened, so I quickly let it go. I could imagine how harsh and intrusive it must seem when outsiders came blundering into what must be a misty, echoing world. I spoke to her gently, keeping my voice soft and low.

"Granny, it's lovely to find you feeling better."

"Well, of course I am seldom ill." She was politely correcting me; it seemed a wonderful sign.

"That's true," I said slowly. "But do you remember when

you broke your ankle? For weeks you had us all scurrying around from morning till night."

A sharp glint of amusement appeared in the blue eyes. "I made them pay too, didn't I? Cartier's—for having such a slippery walk."

I heard a quick intake of breath from Jane Kelly, standing behind me, but I didn't dare turn to her and break the spell.

"You wouldn't break your ankle in the A and P, would you, Granny?" I chuckled softly, delighted to have sparked a recollection in her mind.

"What on earth would I be doing in the A and P?" She was smiling broadly now, her eyes crinkling mischievously, just the way Uncle John's did.

I felt certain she knew me, she looked so jolly and confiding; still I was reluctant to press the point. Finding her alert was enough for the moment, and if she continued to improve I might soon be able to ask her some questions. Patience was what was needed, along with a gentle, coaxing manner.

She spoke again, and I had to bend close to hear, for her voice was suddenly as frail and distant as the light breeze that played among the young leaves of the willows. "Ask Nancy to turn off the lamp, will you, dear? I'm going to sleep now."

Her eyes closed before the sentence was finished; the light left her face, and there was no motion except for the barely perceptible rise and fall of the embroidered blanket cover.

I got to my feet and went over to where Jane was putting on her coat. "Isn't it amazing—the change in her?" She was grinning as happily as if she herself had wrought the miracle, and if skill and devotion counted for anything, perhaps she had.

"Did you notice that she called you Nancy?" I asked. "Does she often do that?"

"Now and then, yes. I suppose she has me confused with someone from the past."

"She must be thinking of Nancy Harris, who was her maid for years. They were good friends, actually. I have often wondered why Nancy and her husband, Michael, ever left."

Jane looked at me sharply. She said slowly, "When I came it was clear that there had been a good deal of changing around. I think your uncle had his hands full, trying to get the household organized. He seemed very relieved when Miss Clark offered to take charge." Her broad face assumed that indulgent expression that so many women wore when they spoke of Uncle John. "Mr. Ryder isn't really the type to concern himself with servants and bill-paying, is he?"

"No, unfortunately he isn't." I heard the tartness of my tone, and saw that Jane suddenly looked amused. We were in agreement on Gillian Clark; I knew it, even though we were being so careful not to say what we thought. Jane must be full of bottled-up resentment by now, and grateful to have me around to share it.

She said, "Are you sure you can stay until seven?"

She was really asking me if I thought I could sit tight in the face of Gillian's takeover efforts, and I replied with more firmness than the question might have seemed to warrant that nothing in the world could budge me from the room except the arrival of Miss Nelson.

People who are accustomed to having their own way can be rendered surprisingly powerless when confronted by a worm that has decided to turn. Some instinct told me this, making me almost glad I had been easily manipulated by Gillian two evenings earlier so that now I could enjoy her bafflement.

Not that she allowed it to show, of course. It was only because I was so edgily defensive that I was able to detect in the slight twitch of her lips and the fixed, ceramic quality of her wide eyes that she was put off by my determination to stay at Granny's bedside. We were utterly courteous, facing each other with false, toothy smiles and speaking in near whispers so as not to disturb the sleeping woman. But when she finally backed reluctantly from the room I slumped in my chair, quite undone by the sudden release from tension.

Terry McGinnis found me like that when he entered a moment later. "I'm sorry. Did I wake you?" he said, and I quickly straightened up and shook my head.

"No, I'm just relaxing—and enjoying the fact that I stood my ground, for once." I couldn't help smiling at him. In his rumpled corduroy blazer, with his hair, as usual, slightly tousled and his cheeks bright with color, he looked like a schoolboy just in from the playground.

He smiled back at me. "Are you and Gillian having some kind of a contest?" he asked. "I passed her on the stairs. She's usually arriving about this time, not leaving."

I stood up saying, "I'm not sure I know the answer to that question. There is something I want to ask you, though, if you have a minute."

Terry raised his eyebrows inquiringly, then moved past me to the bed. He reached for Granny's wrist and stood for a minute taking her pulse, then he gently tucked her arm beneath the covers and turned to join me by the window.

"I've been thinking about that drug you give my grandmother when she is agitated." I saw a patient look come to his face, as if he were about to repeat the explanation he had given me before, and I quickly went on. "I understand the reason; it isn't that. What I'm curious about is the form of the dosage. Is this Haldol given in a pill or a powder, or is it an injection?"

"Usually we give it to Mrs. Ryder by injection," he said, "although Haldol may also be taken by mouth, in pill or powder form, when a patient is able."

"Then it has to be given by a nurse, of course. And where

is it kept? Is there a supply of it here in Granny's room somewhere?"

Terry was frowning down at me. He seemed about to object to my questioning, but after a moment he replied, "We keep disposable syringes, filled with the drug, in Mrs. Ryder's bathroom. In a locked cabinet, for which each of her nurses has a key." He paused, still studying my face intently. "Come, I'll show you."

I followed him across the room, past the foot of the bed, to where a door led to a dressing room and beyond it, Granny's bathroom. We passed through the dressing room, which was lined with drawers and closets, and opened the mirror-paneled door to the bathroom. Here were more mirrors, covering the walls from floor to ceiling, and the fronts of still more drawers and cupboards. Several of the latter had keyholes beneath their crystal handles, and Terry went over to the one nearest the marble wash basin and pulled a key chain from his pocket. After searching through the keys for a moment he found the proper one and unlocked the cupboard. I saw that it contained various familiar medications, such as aspirin and digestive aids, as well as eight or ten rectangular white boxes about six inches long.

Terry took one of these out and opened it to show me the syringe it contained, then he closed the box and replaced it in the cupboard. He stood regarding the neatly stacked containers for a moment, apparently counting them, for he turned to me and said, "I see that the supply of Haldol corresponds to the dosages entered on your grandmother's chart. There is no reason to think she is being given any that I have not ordered."

He spoke almost sternly, giving me the uncomfortable feeling that he thought I was something of a busybody. Still, there was something I had to know.

"I suppose you could tell if Granny had been given a shot

recently. I mean there would be a needle mark on her arm wouldn't there? Or a bruise?"

"Sally, I wish you would tell me what you are getting at. You seem to have some ugly suspicion on your mind. I am certain it is . . ." He stopped abruptly, and once again turned to run his eye over the containers of Haldol. "Here. Open these while I check on the others." He quickly handed me four of the narrow white boxes and took the remainder, and we silently opened each one to make sure it contained a syringe.

All the dosages appeared to be intact, and when we had returned them to the shelf Terry firmly closed the cupboard door and locked it. "When you mentioned needle marks it occurred to me . . ." He hesitated, then ran his fingers through his hair as he so often did. "We give Mrs. Ryder injections of vitamins to build up her strength, and of course she has the needle marks from those. It would be difficult to distinguish them from any others."

I said, "I know you think I'm being unbearably nosy, and I apologize. But there was such an amazing change in Granny yesterday. It seemed impossible that she could be so bright and lively most of the day and then so totally out of it by evening—without being drugged." I was pleading with him to understand, for I saw all at once how presumptuous I must appear. I said, "It was so terribly disappointing . . ." and as I spoke I felt the prickle of imminent tears. At that moment it would have been easy to give in to a fit of sobbing. Then Terry would stop looking at me so coldly; he would see that it was my love for Granny that made me weak and foolish.

I resisted the impulse, however. The honesty I sensed in him, the trustfulness, reached out to my own integrity.

"I didn't see Mrs. Ryder last night," he was saying, "but it would be natural for her to be tired after what was a very active day, for her."

"She was more than tired. It was impossible to wake her up—even when Uncle John was there."

"And yet Jane called this afternoon to tell me she was greatly improved."

He opened the dressing room door for me with what seemed exaggerated courtesy, but instead of preceding him through it I took a deep breath and said, "I'm sorry, Terry, but there is one more question I have to ask. Would an overdose of Haldol be fatal? To a weak, old person like Granny, I mean? An overdose could kill her, I should think."

Terry studied my face before replying, and I saw his own expression soften. He reached out to pat my shoulder reassuringly as he said, "I'm afraid you're allowing your imagination to run away with you. You're overtired, I suppose, and the situation is a sad one for you, of course." He smiled, then gave my shoulder a final squeeze and reached again for the door. "It would be impossible to administer Haldol in sufficient quantity to kill a person. Even frequent unauthorized doses would result in heavy sedation, not death. Please put such worries out of your mind, Sally. No one is trying to kill your grandmother, and if they were they would have to find some other means. Haldol simply wouldn't do it."

He stood peering down into my eyes, half-smiling in the manner of a kindly professor who hopes he has finally gotten a point across, but is, in any case, thoroughly tired of the subject.

He opened the door wider, and I plodded obediently through Granny's dressing room, feeling both defeated and confused. As we entered the bedroom the door to the hall was pushed open and Miss Nelson came in and quietly greeted us.

"Good evening, Dr. McGinnis. Good evening, Mrs. Templeton." She surveyed us coolly, removing her coat as she spoke, then placing it neatly over the back of the chair. "How is Mrs. Ryder today?" Her eyes raked the bed in a quick professional appraisal, then she glanced inquiringly at Terry.

He stepped over to the desk, where Granny's chart was kept, and Miss Nelson moved briskly to join him.

"I'll see you later," I said, and as I began edging toward the door they both looked up and said goodnight politely and in unison.

I felt cross and somehow resentful as I left the room and started down the stairs to the front hall. Terry and Miss Nelson seemed only too willing to dispense with my company; in fact, I had a most uncomfortable feeling of having been ousted.

Obviously, I had now established myself in Terry's mind as a confirmed troublemaker. I bitterly regretted that; however, I had found out one thing I desperately needed to know. For whatever purpose it might serve, Gillian Clark apparently had no more nefarious aim than to keep Granny mentally confused. She was not bent on murder.

So then, I told myself sternly, it was possible that all my suspicions were groundless. For how in the world could my grandmother's stuporous condition be useful to Gillian, who for so long had been looked upon as trusted lawyer and friend?

I had been too quick to join with Jane Kelly in what could be neurotic fantasies. After all, I barely knew the woman. Perhaps her plain appearance, combined with the restrictions of her way of life, had made her totally paranoid. If she truly believed Granny was in danger, why did she not press Terry to take some action? Since we had never discussed it openly, I had assumed that Jane was biding her time, waiting for some good, solid evidence with which to support any accusation.

My head had begun to ache intolerably, and I hurried downstairs, eager for distraction from my oppressive thoughts. I had left my fishing equipment on a chair in the hall, and now I scooped up my fly rod, my box of flies, and a small canvas creel and pushed open the heavy front door. Immediately the soft, fragrant air filled my nostrils. The sun had sunk low in the west and its long rays turned the pale budding branches of the trees to hazy, pink-tinged clouds. When I walked around to the back of the house I could see the water of the Sound in the distance, and it too glimmered rosily under the lowering sun.

Slipping a little on the damp young grass, I made my way slowly down the hill to the stream. My burden of worry and suspicion fell away as I went. The gentle spring evening was like the ones so long ago, when I would play out of doors every evening until dark, sometimes later if Nancy Harris forgot to call me in. I remembered the light, free sound of children's voices crying, "Ally, ally outs in free!" or "One, two, three, red light." I could almost hear them now on the cool, clear air.

Philip always went in early, but Tommy Harris stayed till the last, running after me on his chubby legs, and all too often giving away my hiding place. We played until the other children had drifted off to their houses in response to their mothers' distant, calling voices. Then all at once the air on my flushed cheeks would feel chilly and the lighted windows of the house seem to beckon with an irresistible invitation.

I sighed, content in the memory of those childhood days. I did not wish them back; it was enough to remember it all so vividly. As I drew near the stream a picture appeared in my mind of my grandmother lying still and shrunken in her quiet room. All my happy recollections were due to her. With the always capricious help of Uncle John, she had given Philip and me something approaching a normal childhood. Our debt to her could never be repaid; I must point that out to Philip when I saw him.

I tiptoed along the bank of the stream, with eyes and ears

alert for signs of rising trout. Soon I saw a small, agitated cloud of insects hovering above the surface of the water and I studied them closely, mentally running over the flies in my box to find a match. There was a sound as soft as a bubble popping, then a swirl that left a circle on the quiet water, and my heart gave a leap. A fish was feeding near the center of the stream, and if I got the proper fly tied onto my line soon enough, and if I managed to cast it well, rusty as I was, without getting snagged on any greenery, I just might provide a treat for Granny's breakfast.

I have never been good at doing things in a hurry, and I felt unbelievably clumsy as I attempted to thread the fly onto the gossamer nylon leader and knot it there. I had forgotten how difficult it was to see in the early evening light; and when I was finally ready to make my first cast I found I had forgotten how to do that as well. My line slapped roughly onto the water twenty feet short of my target, and I knew that any nearby fish would either flee or stay cautiously on the bottom until every last ripple had stilled.

I stepped out to a clear, grassy space to practice my casting, as I should have done in the first place. In a few minutes I had it back: the controlled lift of the rod, the pause for the line to straighten in the air behind me, the forward flick of the wrist to send it cleanly out onto the water. But by now the evening was closing in. The water, which had been a glimmering blue gray when I arrived, had turned black, with steely highlights. The pine trees and low shrubs that lined the opposite bank of the stream had become opaque, black shapes and the deep gray sky behind them would soon darken and blend with them.

I could see only a few small clouds high in the sky; the next day should be clear and bright, and since I had nothing to keep me up late that night, I decided I might as well get up early in the morning and come to the stream before breakfast.

It would save time if I could leave my rod set up, ready to go, so with that in mind I started off in the direction of the small wooden bridge that crossed the stream just before it reached the road. I remembered that a shed stood on the other side, reached by an access lane leading from the road. Garden tools were stored there, along with mowers and wheelbarrows and other bulky equipment. It would be a perfect place to leave my fishing gear. In fact, I might find a pair of waders there; I had looked in vain for some in the basement of the house.

It was almost dark when I crossed the bridge. The air had cooled, and I felt chilly and hungry, and anxious to put away my fishing rod and head for the house. The shed should be two or three hundred feet from the bridge, as I recalled; but since it stood behind a birch grove, one came upon it suddenly. Ahead I saw the dappled white trunks of the slender trees and as I came closer I made out the dark rectangle of the shed beyond.

I stepped in among the birches and turned slightly to the right to approach the shed from the front. Then I stopped, suddenly wary, for I saw a gleam, an unexpected contour. It was a car standing in the access road, close to the door of the shed. I stood very still, straining my eyes against the darkness. There was something about the shape of that car that nudged my memory; I could not think why.

I moved forward slowly, my sneakers silent on the damp, soft ground, and soon I head the murmur of voices through the open door of the shed. Perhaps it was the gardener, I thought, discussing the next day's chores with a helper; they worked long hours at this time of year. I was about to call out in hopes of getting a ride up to the house when I heard one of the speakers say, "It has got to stop, Michael. Mr. Ryder is reaching the end of his patience."

I could not mistake that firm, melodious voice, and hearing

it, I knew immediately why the outline of the car had seemed familiar to me. It was Gillian Clark there in the shed, unlikely as it seemed. In the next second I heard the low rumble of a voice replying and realized that the man she had been addressing was Michael Harris, Granny's former chauffeur and Tommy's father.

Nothing in my experience had prepared me for such an encounter, but as I stood there, frozen, scarcely breathing, it did not take long to weigh the options. I could stay very still until they went away; but that might be a long time off. What if I accidentally made some sound? It was appalling to think what an awkward situation would arise in that case. I could try to tiptoe silently away, but again, any slight sound would precipitate a scene of unimaginable embarrassment.

The only thing I could do was to start crashing around in the underbrush, then stride openly to the door of the shed, hoping to look as guileless and unsuspecting as a Girl Scout returning from a hike. I took a deep breath and composed my features in an expression of good-natured surprise. I was about to step forward when I heard Gillian's voice again and knew it was too late. For her words held me pinned in helpless fascination.

"You seem to think there is no limit to Mr. Ryder's financial resources," she was saying. "And in a way it's understandable." She laughed shortly, and I could picture her great, dark eyes narrowing as she went on. "I would like to have a look at your stock portfolio, Michael. You must have done very well for yourself over the last few years."

"I've earned it, every penny of it. Mr. Ryder must agree on that or he wouldn't have paid me—which he was doing quite willingly until you came along."

I felt monstrously confused. It didn't seem possible that these words were being spoken, in such a hard, calculating tone, by Michael, who had driven me to dentists and dancing

class and so often exchanged amiable banter with my grandmother on her drives in and out of New York. Granny had
always enjoyed his company, it had seemed to me, and trusted
him as she did her doctor or lawyer.

Her lawyer. This woman on whom I was eavesdropping was
her lawyer now. I wondered whether she was representing
the family interests in this little talk she was having with
Michael.

There was no way out now, I would have to stay and hear
more, so I very carefully crouched to a position that I thought I
could maintain comfortably for a while. The muscles of my arms
and legs had begun to ache from the strain of staying tensely
poised. I leaned against the wall of the shed, concealed from the
road by a clump of bayberry bushes. I was prepared for a long
siege, but apparently the two in the shed had run out of time.

They did not appear to have settled their differences, however. As they parted I heard Gillian say, "There will be no
more advances, is that understood?"

"Not by me it isn't, whatever you may think. You can tell
Mr. Ryder I'll be coming to see him in person. I've had enough
of talking to lady lawyers."

I fancied I heard an indignant gasp from Gillian, perhaps because that was the reaction I would expect. There was no mis-
taking the solid slam of her car door, however, or the angry roar
of the engine as she stepped on the ignition. Before the sound
of her tires had died away, crunching on the dirt road as she
turned the car around, I heard the impudent jingle of a bicycle
bell. I risked peeking over the bushes in time to see Michael
Harris wheel down the lane, and as I sank back against the shed
I was smiling shakily in the dark. However she might intimi-
date the rest of us, Gillian had apparently made little impression on Michael. Beauty, brains, law degrees—it took more than
that combination to shake the confidence of an Irishman.

CHAPTER 11

That night I dreamed again that I was passing through the rooms of the little house Joe and I had lived in when we were first married. As always, he was at my side, courteous but critical, and I was opening doors, searching for something. A person? A means of escape? It wasn't clear. This time the person who accompanied us was again my Uncle John. He seemed to hover just beyond my vision, beckoning from the room ahead or waiting outside a door I had not opened, and although I wanted to catch up with him, I felt desperately sad when I seemed to be coming near. The sadness made me want the dream to end, and I forced myself awake and lay peering anxiously into the darkness wondering what message lay concealed in that recurrent fantasy.

Always before the dream had left me feeling vaguely disturbed; this was the first time I had known such overwhelming sorrow, a bitter sorrow, as if mingled with disillusionment.

Dr. Zeigler had said he thought Joe represented—in dreams and in reality—the masculine force my life had lacked because of my father's death. My need for this had led me to marry

Joe, but I also needed more—a mentor or guide who would help me to become a complete person and not remain merely a protected little girl. In my dream this mentor, who was sometimes my mother and sometimes my former boss, had always been elusive, always unsatisfactorily placed just beyond my reach. This had left me baffled, but never until the mentor became Uncle John had I felt this surprising grief. I felt slow tears slipping down my temples, and sat up angrily to grope on the bedside table for a tissue. I had better see Dr. Zeigler once more when I returned to Los Angeles to move out of my apartment; if the dream was upsetting me this much we obviously needed to talk about it some more.

I had fallen asleep easily a few hours before, dozing off over my book, in fact, and I supposed my deliciously relaxed state was due to having a quiet evening alone for the first time that week. Now, however, I sat in bed hugging the blanket around my knees, my mind teeming with speculation about the events of the day before.

It had been astonishingly pleasant to see Betsy again, and wonderful to find her unchanged in the essentials. She'd retained the wry humor and the oblique point of view that had always made her such entertaining company. And it was obvious that beneath her sleek, big-city exterior her values were the same; they had to be for her to appreciate a man like Terry McGinnis.

Thinking of Terry, I felt once again the pang of regret I'd stifled when Betsy told me her amazing news. I could imagine the look on Dr. Zeigler's face if I were to tell him about that fleeting pang, then the tears I had just shed. I could hear him saying, "And although you saw Dr. McGinnis that same afternoon you did not congratulate him on his engagement to your friend?"

We were busy talking of other things, of course; and my

questions about Granny's medicine had placed an element of strain on what had looked like a ripening friendship. It seemed odd that I felt compelled to hammer away at the subject even though it threatened my relationship with Terry. Perhaps it was because of the honesty, the basic goodness in him, that I knew would welcome the truth from whatever source.

How did I know that with such certainty? Well, you see, Dr. Zeigler, I felt close to him the first time I met him. Somehow I knew he was a man with whom I could be totally myself, and what a rarity that is! I hadn't fallen in love with him, but I had sensed that the possibility existed, waiting in the wings like a shy child. And now that child would never step out in the open; I could not allow it.

Unless . . . No, recalling the light in Betsy's eyes and the softness of her voice when she spoke of her love for Terry, I felt certain it would take more than a disagreement about where to live to come between those two. They were mad about each other, and right to be, I was forced to admit. Terry's humanity, his genuineness, would counterbalance the artificiality and commercialism of Betsy's swift-paced career. That must have been part of the attraction, an unrecognized ingredient perhaps, but a compelling one; and he must have felt a similar need for the laughter and adventure Betsy would inject into the demanding life of a busy doctor.

I had no doubt they would work out a solution to their one problem. They were far too intelligent not to, and far too much in love. It was impossible for me not to envy Betsy; she had it all.

I shivered and slid down beneath the covers again. The room was slowly lightening; if I were to have any more sleep I should get up and pull the curtains, but I closed my eyes instead, determined to think of something that would push Terry McGinnis from my mind. Immediately I began wondering what he would have thought of that scene between Gillian Clark and Michael Harris, and then I was wide awake once more, for I saw that I had been postponing my own evaluation of the encounter. Now I must face it, lying sleepless in the gray dawn. My uncle had been annoyed at the suggestion of helping Tommy Harris because he was already giving money to his father, apparently on a regular basis. And if it weren't for Gillian's interference he would still be paying money to Michael. I could not imagine why. If he felt responsible for the Harrises he could have kept them in Granny's employ. There must be another reason, a devious one, I feared; but I had no chance of learning what it was while he stayed in his present state of mind. My first order of business must be to get back into Uncle John's good graces.

Moving slowly in my heavy rubber waders, I walked through the knee-high water to the edge of the stream where my uncle waited with his hand outstretched to help me up on the bank. Even with his assistance I staggered clumsily as I stepped out of the water. The boots I had found in the garden shed were meant for bigger feet than mine, and the size of their thick soles made it nearly impossible to walk in them on land.

I sat right down on the grass and pulled my feet out of them at once. Then I picked up my canvas creel and opened it to show Uncle John the two nice trout I had caught.

"Very good," he said. "I guess our practice session paid off."

"Yes, but why is it you never lose the knack?" I asked. "It's like sailing; boys seem to be born knowing how to handle a boat."

My uncle was rummaging in the picnic basket. "Maybe it's because my father started me on fishing when I was only around four," he said, "and I think you were at least six and a half before I got you out here." He opened a can of beer and handed it up to me from where he sat on the ground.

"You weren't fly-fishing at that age; you'd be too small." I pulled off my sweater and sat down on the sun-warmed grass. Except for the thinness of the foliage on the trees and bushes it could have been June instead of mid-April. Even a long-sleeved shirt was too hot, and I rolled up my sleeves as far as I could, then leaned back on my elbows with my face turned up to the sun.

My uncle had settled himself with his back against a rock, using his rolled sweater for padding. He too sat with his head back and his face tilted up, and I saw that the dark lashes of his half-closed eyes were still thick and long enough to incite envy in a movie star.

I told him so, and without changing his expression he replied lazily, "You're just trying to butter me up because you were so bad-tempered yesterday." He shifted his weight to one elbow and lifted his can of beer to his lips.

"I have never known a man who took compliments so calmly." Instead of being shaken by the fact that he had guessed so accurately how I felt, I found it reassuring. This was the good companion I remembered, who teased me like an older brother and never stayed out of sorts for long.

"Did you get anywhere looking for that Martin Josefson you were so curious about?" He had sat up and was taking sandwiches out of the picnic basket, trying to discover what they were without unwrapping them.

"Some are ham and cheese and some are chicken," I said, "and may I please have another beer?" He handed me a can, and I gave him the empty one to stow in the basket. "I tried looking up Martin Josefson in the Detroit phone book, but he wasn't listed."

"So you're dropping the matter?"

"Well, I'd hardly give up that easily, would I?" I held out my hand and Uncle John placed a wrapped sandwich in it. "I asked them to look in old directories from the early fifties. Around the time my mother brought us to stay with Granny. What year was it exactly; do you remember?"

"I'm pretty sure it was 1951." He sat scowling into the distance over his half-eaten sandwich. "Bill was killed in 1952, and I think he'd been overseas just about a year." There was a silence and then he said softly, "That was a rough time, with all of us going around in shock and Mother at the center, trying to keep up some semblance of normality for the sake of you and Phil."

"And yet she must have felt the shock as much as the rest of you—perhaps more. She had lost her son, after all."

"Yes, but if she ever went to pieces it must have been in private."

"What about my mother? Was she devastated?" As I asked the question I faced once again that period that existed in my memory as a dark, forbidding cloud. Dr. Zeigler had helped me probe within it, to feel the sadness it contained. To experience it would lead to healing, he had explained, but as I waited for my uncle's answer I felt the old, raw pain rise within me.

"Devastated. That's probably the right word." I waited for more. The lean, handsome face was grave, and in the unsparing noon brightness I could see the lines etched into his forehead and, more deeply, around his mouth. He did not look at me, but stared into the distance, and I sensed that he was recalling a memory I desperately needed to share—if only he would let me.

"Tell me about it," I breathed, hoping my quiet tone would sound in his mind as an inner urging.

He turned to face me. He said nothing, but in his eyes I

saw a look of assessment. He was on the point of telling me something that touched him deeply; I was certain of it and I did not move, but solemnly returned his regard. If only he would trust me . . .

But after a moment he sighed heavily and reached for my hand. He pressed it tightly as he said, "We all got through it somehow."

I quickly glanced away so that he would not see my disappointment. "I wouldn't say my mother got through it very well. A few weeks later she ran away." I'm sure I sounded as hopeless as I felt. Why was he so unwilling to tell me what I needed to know, I wondered? Had he something to hide, or was it the normal male reaction when feelings came uncomfortably close to the surface?

He said slowly, "She never meant to stay away. I'm sure she didn't." He tightened his grip on my hand and peered earnestly into my eyes. "As you said the other day, she couldn't help it that she was killed. I'm certain she meant to come back to you."

His voice was firm, almost harsh, with conviction. His fingers pressed painfully into my hand, but I welcomed the discomfort, for it seemed to convey a reassurance my uncle could not or would not put into words.

My spirits lifted. While it was not what I sought, that firm assurance was something I had never had before. Meanwhile, there was clearly nothing to be gained by pressing the issue at the moment. I bent to give him a light kiss on the cheek, then gently drew my hand from his grasp and sat back to finish my sandwich.

I said, "So then you made it your job to take the place of your brother." They were idle words, intended only to sustain the mood and keep him talking, but suddenly he looked stunned.

"I mean playing with Philip and me, taking us to the circus, settling our fights." I spoke soothingly, and gradually his face relaxed. "Maybe you weren't even aware of it, but I'll bet you were trying to make up to us for losing our father. I have wondered sometimes if that's why you never got married. So you wouldn't have children of your own to take you away from us." He was looking at me so strangely that I felt suddenly shy. My voice faltered as I added, "I know that's presuming a lot."

He continued to stare at me broodingly. Then he started to speak, but checked himself and gave a short laugh instead. "We're getting in pretty deep here, aren't we? I'm inclined to think I never married because I was never attracted to the wifely type."

"A lot of them seemed to feel pretty wifely around you." I raised my voice to a falsetto. " 'Oh, John, you simply must take your vitamins!' and 'Oh, John, that sweater is a disgrace; let me mend it for you.' It was disgusting!"

He was chuckling softly. "Yeah, and what's worse, it was boring." The old look of mischief flashed in his eyes as he went on in a confiding tone, "You know, Sally, I'm not as conceited as you may think. I never could see myself as some woman's life work."

"Maybe that's what attracts you to Gillian," I said. "She seems to have plenty of other things on her mind."

"You know, I've been meaning to talk to you about that note of sourness that creeps into your voice when you speak of her." His tone was still light, but the blue eyes were serious. "Gillian's a hell of a woman, Sal. She had to be to get that job working for Judge Parsons in the first place. She was just out of law school, but he told me she handled the clients better than any of the experienced lawyers on his staff. And then when he saw what a head she had for investments he began turning more and more accounts over to her."

My uncle wore a foolish, fond smile I found intensely ir-
ritating, and I said sharply, "I can see that she's very bright,
Uncle John. I've never questioned that."

"Well, if you're questioning her loyalty you're on the wrong
track. When the judge got sick and started losing his grip she
covered for him; fixed his mistakes, kept him from looking
foolish. While his associates were waiting for him to fold so
they could take over she made sure everything went as smoothly
as ever. None of his clients had any idea what bad shape he
was in when he finally had to stop going to the office. And
then every night Gillian took him some good soup or something he could enjoy eating, because his housekeeper wasn't
much of a cook. She was able to help him with his medication,
too. Her father was a doctor, and she seriously considered
medical school until she got fascinated with law." He looked
at me earnestly. "Gillian's not just an ambitious career woman,
Sally; I think that's what I'm trying to say. She really cares
about helping people."

I said, "So I gather. She was as puzzled as I was when you
got so annoyed at me for mentioning Tommy Harris."

A wry smile appeared on Uncle John's face as he said, "I
don't think Gillian was puzzled. She knows I can't stand that
kid."

I was shocked. "Why, I always thought you were fond of
Tommy. You taught him to fish; you used to take him along
with Phil and me." I paused. My uncle seemed relaxed; I saw
no sign of the anger that had erupted at the club, so I went
on. "It seems to me you used to give him some nice presents
too. Is that it? Do you feel you've done enough for him?"

"I suppose so. Although I don't like to think of myself as
mean-spirited." He frowned at the paper napkin he was twisting in his hands. "Michael hasn't hesitated to come to me
whenever he's short. I guess he thinks I owe him something

for all his years of service; but he was well compensated for that, very well indeed. And no lifetime guarantee went with the job."

"Still, a medical education is expensive, and Tommy seems so well qualified."

"I'm not so sure about that." The paper napkin was being torn into postage stamp-size bits. "I think he's finding it tougher than he expected. Nonetheless, I shouldn't get so annoyed with the Harrises, I know that; especially if I'm going to take it out on you."

Abruptly he scooped up the little pile of shredded paper, tossed it into the picnic basket, then got to his feet. "Come on, let's see if there are any more fish in that stream."

Again that afternoon I stayed with Granny between the two nurses' shifts, managing, as I had the day before, to get to her room ahead of Gillian Clark. Gillian arrived very soon after Jane Kelly had left, however, in the midst of a conversation between Granny and me that might almost have been called animated.

She was telling me how clever she had once been about her clothes, attending the showings of her favorite Paris designers but buying only one or two dresses each season.

"I loved going to Madame Grès the most," she said. "Her showings were like theatrical productions, with chamber music playing, lovely, tall candelabra about the room, and models who moved like dancers in those beautiful, flowing dresses." A reminiscent smile played about her lips and her blue eyes shone as she pictured the scene.

"You make it come alive for me, Granny," I said. "In fact, didn't you take me with you once? I seem to remember a big, gold room, with models walking on a platform."

"There were rows of spindly, little gilt chairs and all the

important buyers and fashion editors had to sit in them, no matter how fat they were." Lying back on her mountain of white pillows, Granny was going on as if I had not spoken. Perhaps she did not even see me, I thought, so real was her vision of that long-ago gathering in a Paris couture house.

Suddenly she was laughing. The sound was whispery and weak, but I recognized the musical lilt I had not heard for years, and it made me so happy that, without knowing why, I began laughing with her.

"They sat in the front row, those two. You know who I mean; they were very important in the fashion business, these two very fat women from New York." She stopped, and again I heard that soft, gay laughter. "They wore wonderful hats, to distract the eye from their fat bodies, I imagine, and when they sat in those little gold chairs they stuck out so on either side, I felt certain the chairs would collapse."

"I hope if they did you were there to see it."

"No, they never did, and do you know why?" The smiling blue eyes questioned me and I shook my head. "Miss Levy and Miss—I can't remember the other one—were always carefully guided to the same seats, halfway up the right side of the runway. It was a very desirable spot, and one year I was fortunate enough to be given a place behind them. Just before the two ladies arrived I looked closely at their chairs and I saw that under the legs and seats was a metal framework, bolted to the floor. Do you suppose they ever wondered why their chairs couldn't be moved?"

The whispery laugh came again, but only for an instant. Her eyes fluttered shut, and she slept against the fat pillows with her lips still slightly parted in a smile.

"What a delightful story!"

I turned to see Gillian coming forward from the shadows beyond the softly lighted area created by Granny's bedside lamp. Apparently she had entered while Granny was talking and had not wished to interrupt.

I smiled at her while inwardly warning myself that she was here for a purpose. Picturing the deceptively strong gilt chairs, I decided to cling to my position at Granny's bedside as staunchly as they had remained fixed to the floor of that golden Paris salon.

But to my surprise, Gillian did not try to take my place. "I stopped by to pick up the mail," she said, "and I like to look in on Mrs. Ryder when I'm here." Her smile was vibrant, her full lips and white teeth shining in the lamplight. "It's wonderful to see the effect you're having on her. We should have sent for you weeks ago."

"She has certainly been more alert the last two days; but I don't think I can take the credit. You have all been giving her such good care . . ."

Still smiling, she gave a modest little shake of her head and began moving toward the door. "I'm about to be late for an appointment," she said, "so I'll say goodnight. But I'll be glad to take over for you any time you want to get away. Tomorrow night, or any time, don't hesitate to ask me." With a friendly flutter of her fingers she was gone.

CHAPTER 12

Following Gillian's departure I felt oddly let down. I had geared myself for a struggle that never took place, and the unspent energy made it impossible to sit still. I got to my feet and prowled restlessly around the room, pausing only briefly to look at the photographs on the dresser, then quickly moving on to the window.

The bright, warm day was giving place to an evening of lambent beauty. Beyond the tender green tree tops, which trembled and nodded in the gently moving air, the sky was a velvety, rose-streaked mauve. Gazing out at it through the window, I began to feel caged. I went over to the french doors, quietly turned the brass handles, and stepped out onto the narrow balcony.

Leaning against the wrought iron railing and breathing in the cool, fragrant air, I thought of California and how different it was. There, in what was supposed to be the land of golden sun and healthy, natural living, my windows looked out upon a vista of cement, punctuated by tropical shrubs and palm trees that would always look plastic to me. The pastel stucco

houses, with their roofs of curved, russet tiles, were dwarfish
Spanish imitations, crowded close together on tiny plots of
land. It had surprised me from the first to find that in the
spacious West people were more confined than in New En-
gland. On my first visit to Granny after my marriage I had
rejoiced over the lush green trees and shrubs, the curving
country roads and picket fences, the rolling, wonderfully var-
ied hills and grassy fields.

"It's where you live, dear," she had gently pointed out.
"Some day you'll have a larger house, of course, and the kind
of grounds we have here."

I smiled, remembering how she had always assumed that
I would eventually live as she did, in a spacious, important
house with as many servants as I wanted. Intelligent as she
was, she did not seem to realize that women's lives were
changing. She could not see, I guess neither of us could at
that point, that my attempt to model my life on hers was part
of the reason I was so tense and unhappy. It was that and the
fact that Joe Templeton had apparently missed out on the
sixties. He hadn't happened to notice, or had chosen to ignore,
the rebellion that took place in attitudes toward politically
contrived wars, civil rights, education. He knew there were
young people called hippies, at least I assume he did. But he
didn't seem to know he had married one—probably because
I abandoned my flower-child image when we met. I changed
my style of dressing and pretty much gave up smoking pot.
It wasn't long before I had my hair cut a little shorter and
began wearing lipstick. But nothing could make my thinking
match that of an established businessman who was ten years
older.

I sighed in the sadness of the lilac-tinged twilight. Joe had
suffered too, but he had quickly remarried. Now he had the
babies we had wanted, two of them, and I had something

else: a profession, a skill I had honed, learning to make my natural facility with words fit the needs of the marketplace until I found myself in a surprising position. I had become one of the top copywriters in Los Angeles. I was assigned to the agency's most important accounts; some of my ads were used as teaching tools in vocational schools. My salary was substantial, and I never had to ask for a raise. And, sure sign of success, the other writers who had joined the agency when I did were beginning to look at me with hostility.

Until the day I casually announced that I was leaving. Then, as one by one they appeared in my office to express their shock, they looked so pleased and relieved that I was embarrassed for them. Even now, even with the prospect of a job that exceeded my most optimistic expectations, I found it hard to believe that my colleagues could have seen me as a threat to their ambitions. I could not seem to think of myself as a big shot.

It was nearly dark; the breeze had dropped and the outlines of the trees were still and black against the deep gray sky. I could not read the face of my watch, but I knew Miss Nelson would be arriving soon, so I pushed open the balcony doors and returned to Granny's bedroom.

I was delighted to see that she had awakened from her nap and was sitting up in her bed, peering inquisitively in the direction of the opening door.

"Come in, my dear," she said brightly, "and I'll send for some tea." At that moment Miss Nelson entered the room from the hall, and Granny extended a welcome to her as well. "Oh how nice; it's Miss—ah yes— Come right in and ring for Nancy. We'll have tea and some of those delicious little éclairs. Tell her to bring lots of those!"

I could not stay for tea because I had promised to get to Phil and Barbara's house in Larchmont before the baby's bedtime. As I drove onto the turnpike I wondered anxiously whether I had remembered to bring the stuffed rabbit I had bought for little Chip. When it was safe to glance around at the back seat I saw that indeed a pink and white package rested there, next to the shabby briefcase I had intended to leave behind.

The case contained my resumé, a portfolio containing samples of my work, and copies of the correspondence I had carried on with the Chicago agency where I hoped to start a new job. I would be an account supervisor, directing the campaign the agency had designed for a nationwide food chain. At least it appeared that I would be. I couldn't feel confident until I saw the offer confirmed in writing, with salary, starting date, and expense account all spelled out.

Speeding along the wide superhighway, I counted back to the day of the interview and was amazed to realize that I had been at Granny's for five days. I felt a twinge of anxiety. I had given the new agency my temporary address in the East. If they really wanted me perhaps I should have heard by now.

The president of the company had been sympathetic when I described Granny's situation and explained that I could not set a firm date for starting the job until I had fulfilled my obligations to her. Still, I knew he would not be reticent about ordering me to report for duty once he had decided to hire me. Perhaps I should call him next day and make it clear that my priorities coincided with his.

I turned off at the Larchmont exit and drove toward the center of town, carefully counting the stoplights until I reached the corner where I had been instructed to turn right. My brother's house was a Victorian located in the village, rather than in the more recently settled outskirts. There was a nice feeling about the area, an old-fashioned neighborliness. Most of the houses were wood, with pointy roofs and cupolas; many of them had swings on their wide front porches, and I thought how pleasant it would be to sit in one on a hot summer evening.

It surprised me a little to find that Phil and Barbara had chosen such a neighborhood instead of a more fashionable, country club environment, and as I pulled into their driveway I felt a heightened interest in the evening ahead. My footsteps echoed noisily on the wooden porch and after I had rung the doorbell I could hear a child's excited babbling within, and the patter of small, running feet.

The door opened to disclose Barbara, flushed and smiling as she bent to restrain her eager child. "Yes, it's Aunt Sally," she was saying, and then to me, "Chip has been waiting all day to see you. He's so excited . . ."

Faced with the reality, however, Chip had undergone a change of heart. I saw a look of dismay appear in the wide blue eyes that gazed up at me; then the round little face was buried in Barbara's skirt, while her knees were gripped so tightly she could not move.

Barbara looked chagrined as she tried to pry him loose. "But Chip, darling, it's Aunt Sally; remember how you wanted to see her? Really, Sally, I don't understand this . . ."

Some instinct made me sink to my heels beside them, holding the pink and white box in my hands. I waited, perfectly silent, and in a moment the little boy cautiously lifted his head. Still holding tight to his mother, he looked from my eyes, now on a level with his own, to the satin-tied package I held. He studied it and when he looked at me again the blue eyes held a clear question. I nodded, slowly proffering the box, but before he reached for it he looked up at his mother, as if for permission, and it was not until he received her affirmative smile that he returned his attention to me.

And that is how I happened to spend the first half hour of my first visit to my brother's house on the floor. I had not had much to do with small children since the nearly forgotten days of mothering Tommy Harris, and I can't say that I'd noticed any lack in my life. Occasionally I thought of how fiercely I had wanted a baby when I was married to Joe and recalled the battery of embarrassing tests we were put through to determine the problem; but in spite of that I felt confident that some day, when the man and the time were right, I would have children. Meanwhile, I seemed to have shelved the subject; I was occupied with other matters.

So I was not prepared for the impact of Chip, christened William Staunton Ryder II after my father. We settled on the hall carpet while he applied himself to opening the package, and when he could not untie the ribbon he held out the box to me wordlessly, as if we did this together every day. I loosened the knot, then returned the gift to him and watched expectantly while he pulled out the soft white bunny by its pink-velvet-lined ears. Slowly his face broke into a beaming smile. He looked over at me and said, "Bunny rabbit," then impulsively held the toy out for me to touch.

I was aware of Barbara uttering appreciative exclamations as she stood looking down on us. I knew I was expected to jump up and take an interest in her, the house, the dinner; but I was caught in a totally new enchantment. He was beautiful, this little boy, with his pink and ivory coloring and eyes such a clear, clean, and shining blue they took my breath away. When he looked down, his soft brown lashes seemed incredibly long against his rounded cheeks, and his blond hair curved about his head in silky disorder. The arms that clutched the rabbit were plump and satiny, with dimples at the elbows. I had to test the texture of that smooth, resilient skin, and when I placed my hand on his arm he did not draw away, but smiled confidingly into my eyes.

I looked up at Barbara and the wonder I felt must have

shown in my face, for she stopped twittering and her lips slowly curved in a smile that was somehow both shy and proud. For that instant she was my sister. I knew that beneath her fluttering, vapid manner, beneath whatever surface perception she had of me, we were joined in this.

"He's just wonderful," I whispered, my fingers still lightly stroking one small, warm arm. "I've never seen such a lovely child."

Her smile was suddenly tremulous. She bent and quickly squeezed my shoulder, then she said, "Play together for a while. I have one little chore in the kitchen."

As she hurried off a look of alarm appeared on Chip's face and he began to push himself to his feet. I said softly, "Can the bunny rabbit come too?" and he turned back, gave me a long, measuring glance, then picked up the toy again. He handed it to me, stood undecided for a moment, then stepped over and sank comfortably into my lap.

Phil found us there a few minutes later. I heard his car in the driveway, heard the kitchen door open, and the sound of his voice mingling with Barbara's. Then he was in the hall with us, and I saw his thin, anxious face relax in an expression of delight as Chip clambered out of my lap and ran to give him a joyous welcome. I felt an upwelling of tenderness for my brother as I watched him pick up his son and hold him tight, while the baby clung as hard as he could with his own plump arms and burrowed his face into his father's shoulder.

I got to my feet and waited, smiling, until Chip wriggled down from his father's arms and seized one hand to draw him over to the new rabbit and, incidentally, to me. As he approached, stooping slightly to grip his son's hand, Phil's face resumed the tense, harried look I had observed at Uncle John's. Though he glanced fondly from Chip to me, the happiness that had flashed so briefly was completely gone by the time he kissed my cheek, and looking into his bleak, exhausted eyes, I felt a stab of apprehension. The other night I had been too annoyed to worry about the cause of Phil's tight reserve. Now it struck me that a man with a son like Chip had no right to look so defeated. My brother must have a serious problem I did not know about.

"So I gather that the portion of Granny's estate that would have gone to our parents will be divided equally between you and me, with the other half going to Uncle John, of course." Phil reached for the bottle of Chablis we had been drinking with our dinner. I saw that his thin, long-fingered hand trembled slightly as he poured my glass half full, then, seeing Barbara give a negative shake of her head, tipped the last of the wine into his own glass.

"That seems logical," I said. "Have you any idea? Oh, I hate to be talking this way, but anyone would be curious . . ."

"The size of the estate? Naturally, we'd want to know, need to know." He paused, and it was as if Barbara's unspoken signal vibrated in the air. "I mean, how can a person plan his own affairs without knowing such things? But try to find out from Miss Gillian Clark. Goddamn it, Sally, you'd think I was some kind of conniving crook instead of Granny's lawful heir."

Barbara's face was smooth and untroubled; she appeared almost bored with the discussion, but I thought she seemed unnaturally still, and her untouched coffee was cooling in the cup.

"Won't Uncle John explain it all? I got the impression that the two of you were handling Granny's affairs together."

"He has that impression too." Phil's lips twitched sardonically and he darted a quick glance at his silent wife. "You know how he is, Sal; he doesn't really understand the financial world at all, which is a pity. Mr. dePew told me they had great hopes for Uncle John when he went to work for dePew and Reynolds that time. They all liked him, and of course the women customers had to be driven off with sticks, but he simply couldn't be bothered to learn the basics of the bond market."

Barbara turned to me then, and I saw the hint of a plea in her wide hazel eyes. "It's hard for someone like Philip, who is so immersed in the business world, to cope with your uncle's vagueness."

"It's not just the vagueness that worries me, Barbara, as you know very well; it's the idea that Uncle John and Gillian Clark between them can make a balls-up of Granny's estate. It would be ignorance on Uncle John's part, I'm sure of that; but I have an idea Gillian knows exactly what she's doing." He glared unseeingly down the length of the table. "I'd give anything to have a look at her account books."

"Well, can't you? Can't we? Maybe we should hire a lawyer if you think things are being mishandled."

"We can't do one goddamn thing!" Phil pushed back his chair and stood up. "Uncle John and Gillian Clark are coexecutors; they both have power of attorney. They can buy and sell any of Granny's property, as they see fit, and as long as they keep records that look businesslike nobody is going to question a few thousand here or there. You and I have no rights whatsoever except as heirs when Granny dies. Heirs to whatever happens to be left."

Abruptly, he threw down his napkin, turned, and strode from the room, leaving Barbara and me facing each other across the table. In the flickering candlelight I saw the pain in her hazel eyes, pain she was not attempting to conceal, and again I was aware of a bond between us.

I said, "I'm sorry I brought up the subject. I had no idea he felt so strongly about it."

She was not soothed by my words; instead she leaned forward tensely and whispered, "He has reason to feel strongly. Get him to tell you, Sally, right now while I make some fresh coffee. Go in the living room and tell him I said he's got to tell you everything. Somebody has to share it with us or he'll go crazy and so will I!"

It was not until much later that I was able to place the events of that evening in perspective and see the ironies that had surfaced, turning in the light of my awareness like the facets of a hard, cold jewel.

That I, from my prideful position as a successful career woman, had looked down on my sister-in-law as a silly and empty-minded housewife was both ironic and shameful. For it became clear to me that night that she was dealing with realities more stringent than any I had ever faced, and doing it with grace and sportsmanship.

There was another, more poignant irony in my complete capitulation to the charm of my nephew. I had pictured "dear little Chip" as spoiled, whining, warped already at two by his limited suburban environment. Instead, the child had been a revelation to me, not only because of his physical beauty, but because of the instant comradeship between us. I was amazed by the intensity of my feeling, and pleased to realize that it involved no envy of Barbara, but rather a strange mixture of gratitude and respect.

Phil's situation of course turned out to be the most desperately ironic element of all. We sat opposite each other before the cold, empty fireplace while he spelled out the harsh facts. He had been offered a partnership in his Wall Street firm, not as an honor, he was quick to explain, but because the company needed cash. Philip could invest in the firm, or he could leave to make room for another investor. The timing was bad. Wall Street was in a slump; it would be nearly impossible to find another job just then; yet Phil had put all his capital into his house and was carrying a sizable mortgage in addition.

"Barbara said right away that we should sell it, but how could I do that to her? She spent months sanding and painting and making curtains; she was almost as excited about this house as she was about the baby." Phil smiled wearily. He gazed into the bare hearth in silence, and I knew he was remembering a time of happy anticipation.

"I went to Granny about it; that was the only thing I could think to do, and as you might imagine, she was wonderful. Oh, of course there was some preliminary stalling. I could see she was trying to decide whether it would ruin my character if she gave me some money." Phil looked over at me sharply. "I told her it had to be a gift, Sal, against my future inheritance, because I couldn't afford to pay any more interest just then. She said in that case she would feel obliged to offer you the same amount. Remember how she always tried to be absolutely fair about things like that?"

I nodded. It was pleasant to realize that only a few months ago Granny had been alert enough to reason it out.

"We agreed on the amount, two hundred thousand, and then Granny said she would have to check with Gillian Clark and Uncle John. She said, 'Just as a courtesy, you understand. I'm training those two to take charge of my affairs when it becomes necessary—not a minute before!' I remember getting a funny, ominous feeling when she said that. I should have paid attention to it."

At that moment Barbara came into the room, carrying a small tray containing a coffee pot and cups. She glanced anxiously from my face to Phil's, and I saw his expression soften as he looked up at her. He rose to his feet and took the tray from her, and when she turned to leave us alone again, Phil said, "Join us, Barbs. You know I can't tell a story straight without your help."

I was amazed to hear such a flippant remark in the midst of what seemed to be shaping up into a grim story. Barbara too looked pleasantly startled as she settled herself on the sofa beside me.

"I think we need a little Cognac to get us through the rest of this explanation." Phil left the room almost jauntily, it seemed to me, and Barbara poured the coffee and handed me a cup.

"I can see what a relief it is for him to be telling you all this at last," she said, and from the way she sank back cosily against the sofa pillows it was apparent that a burden had been lifted from her as well. "It's been on his mind from the beginning; he dreaded having you find out, yet he knew you had to."

I was dumbfounded. I said, "Well, of course I still don't know what happened, but it's hard to imagine Phil worrying about my reaction to anything. He's always been the one who disapproved of me."

"Oh Sally, is that what you thought?" Barbara's face was bare of makeup and her curly brown hair a little rumpled. She looked like a tired child as she gazed earnestly into my eyes. "Why, Philip has bragged about you since the moment I met him. His beautiful big sister, who was always so popular, so bright and independent. He said he was often tongue-tied around you and your friends because he felt so insignificant in comparison."

Before I could respond to this astonishing disclosure Philip was back with a bottle of Cognac. He stood before me holding it poised in the air while I hastily took a few sips from my full coffee cup. Then he added brandy to the brim. While he did the same for the unprotesting Barbara I stared numbly at his face, as if to reidentify this suddenly strange man as my brother. Phil's straight, narrow nose was like mine, and I saw a resemblance too in the curving jaw line and slightly pointed chin. But my eyes were wide and dark blue like our mother's, while Philip had the hooded pale eyes that looked out from our father's photographs. Now that his face was so thin and his light brown hair so sparse he looked like the father of that boy in uniform.

But Barbara was right. Phil did seem relieved all at once. I found it hard to believe that confiding in me could make such a difference in him, but his face had relaxed, and there was an almost reckless air in the way he topped off his own coffee cup, then sank into his chair across from us.

"I imagine you can guess what happened. Only a few days later Granny lost her grip. It was so sudden I couldn't believe it. Uncle John thought she must have had a stroke, but Terry McGinnis said no, it was senile dementia, which usually comes on gradually, but not always." Philip's mouth twisted bitterly. "It seemed like a cruel joke. I'd been feeling quite relieved, thinking that it really made good sense for Granny to disperse some of her funds this way because it might save on estate taxes later. I'd told Bill Watkins I would be able to accept the partnership offer, and we were having heavy conferences about restructuring the office setup."

"But Phil, surely Uncle John would honor any agreement Granny had made with you. Did you tell him about your situation?"

"You can believe I did, but it took nerve. I waited a few days, and I had several chats with Terry about the chances of Granny's coming out of it. He said she would probably be up and down, but might never be her old self again, and clearly Uncle John would have to handle her affairs. So I went to see him." Phil reached for his cup and took a sip of the brandy-laced coffee. "I was praying Granny had mentioned something about the money to Uncle John before her mind went fuzzy, because it seemed so tactless to ask for it right then, but no such luck. He was sympathetic, though. I think he believed me when I told him Granny had agreed to advance me the money so recently that she hadn't had a chance to mention it to him. He said he didn't see how it could be any problem, but he didn't know exactly how to handle it and would have to consult Gillian."

Now Barbara pulled herself from the depths of the sofa to pick up her own coffee cup. "What I've learned from all this is the importance of timing," she said. "If Gillian hadn't left town at that point . . ."

"She was only supposed to be gone overnight, just long enough for the closing on the Palm Beach house; but there was some kind of a snag. As it turned out, the deal fell through, but Gillian was gone for several days." Phil paused. He looked over at me solemnly. "I want you to understand that what I did wasn't stealing, Sally. It was more like a loan, an unauthorized loan, of course." Again his lips twisted bitterly, and he glanced at Barbara, as if for confirmation.

She spoke up at once. "It's so complicated, but you see, Philip holds many securities for his clients, so he can clip the coupons and all that. It's done in every investment firm."

"Bill Watkins came to me that Monday morning and said he had a hot prospect to join the firm if I was having any problem raising the money. Some kid out of Harvard Business School whose father wanted him to get off to a good start. He couldn't keep him waiting, so could I let him have my check the next day? Otherwise, regretfully, the partnership would go to young Smithers or Smathers or something. I was too panicky to get it straight."

"Panic is exactly what it was, Sally." Barbara's eyes were

enormous in her white face as she leaned toward me intently. "Philip never would have dreamed of doing such a thing if he hadn't been in the grip of absolute panic."

"So you took two hundred thousand dollars worth of somebody's bonds," I said.

"I didn't take them; it wasn't that. I simply borrowed them for a few days to use as collateral against a loan." The words were out, and Phil sighed, then reached once more for his coffee cup. "I don't know if I can make you see how easy it was and how harmless it seemed. I mean, I'm dealing with huge amounts of money every day, and so much of it goes on by telephone and telex that you begin to forget there are any real dollars involved. I simply meant to stall for time, until Gillian could get back and give me the money Granny had promised. The bonds never actually left the premises. Nothing really happened, except on paper."

My head was spinning. I reached for my coffee cup and was surprised to find only a pale trace of liquid in the bottom. Phil's was gone too, apparently, for he suddenly sprang to his feet, saying, "Don't say anything yet, Sal; let me make you a real drink and then I'll tell you the rest of it."

Barbara jumped up too and began gathering the cups so hastily that it seemed clear she was determined to accompany Phil to the kitchen. To reassure him, I wondered? Or to avoid hearing a condemnatory outburst from me the minute he left the room?

Little did she know how incapable I was of such a thing at that moment. When they left me I sat staring numbly at the jumble of magazines on the coffee table, remembering how neatly they had been arranged at the beginning of the evening. I had given up smoking six months earlier, but I suddenly hungered for a cigarette. And above the confusion in my aching head I saw a small face, with wide blue eyes that smiled trustingly into mine. That child would be hurt by this. His father's reasons for doing what he had might be twisted and unclear, but there would be no uncertainty about the damage; it would slash like a laser into the lives of his wife and son.

CHAPTER 13

I left at midnight, though I was tempted to stay as they urged me to, if only to have a few minutes with Chip in the morning. I needed to get away, to separate myself from Phil and Barbara and their shocking predicament in order to gain some kind of perspective. Theirs was totally lost; the problem held them in a paralyzing grip, partly because they had gone over it so many times without discovering any fresh answers, and partly because they were in fact immobilized. There was nothing they could do, quite literally.

When Gillian Clark had returned from Florida she had been amazed to find that Uncle John and Phil expected her to turn over two hundred thousand dollars of Granny's money. She had patiently explained that it was out of the question, that Granny's accounts would be more closely scrutinized now than when she had been in charge of them herself. Gillian would try to think of some way to transfer the funds to Philip, but it would take time. It would be best if Phil looked for another resource.

This was a stunning blow. Where only days before losing

his job had looked like the worst thing that could happen, now Phil was in danger of total disgrace.

He was reluctant to confide in Uncle John, partly out of pride, partly because he felt Uncle John's tendency to sympathize would undoubtedly be overridden by his confidence in Gillian's judgment. So, hoping for a miracle, Phil made a clean breast of it to his boss, Bill Watkins.

Predictably, there had been no miracle; still, Watkins had acted quite decently. Following hours of tense, miserable meetings with the firm's lawyers, it had been decided that Phil would be given six months in which to raise the money, during which time the company would substitute its own collateral for the loan he had incurred, and would not expose him. Meanwhile, his assets were frozen. While auditors studied his accounts he could not buy or sell any property, for himself or his clients, and was prohibited from traveling outside the country. The one thing he was allowed, in fact urged, to do was look for another job. Phil had smiled at the irony of that.

I drove through the dark streets of the village and easily found the entrance to the turnpike. In spite of the drinks I had had, my mind seemed to be ticking like a computer. I felt unnaturally alert; there must be a way out for Phil, and if he couldn't think of it I would. I didn't feel anxious or upset, but stimulated by the challenge, and I began to whistle as I drove through the night.

It wasn't until I turned off the turnpike and began threading my way along the winding roads that led to Granny's that I turned my thoughts from Phil's predicament to Phil himself. In my strange state of clarity I realized that I had liked him better that night than almost ever before in my life. It was the discovery of his fallibility, I decided; apparently I could better relate to weakness than to strength. I wondered what that said about my own character. Whatever the reason, my brother had become a human being to me that night, as had his wife and son, and I felt a closeness to them now that precluded any moral judgments.

I pulled into Granny's drive to find lights glowing in the tall carriage lamps beside the front door. As I maneuvered the car into its parking spot I saw the curtains part briefly in a window above the kitchen, and when I reached the door it was pulled open before I could insert my key in the lock.

Mrs. Berger stood there in her light blue quilted wrapper, looking so relieved to see me that I felt remorseful.

"I'm so sorry," I said as I stepped past her into the hall. "I hope you haven't been waiting up for me."

A wan smile flickered on her pale, tired face. "Well yes, actually, but there's no way you could have known. Your grandmother wants to see you."

"Now? It's long after midnight. Surely she has gone to sleep by now."

Mrs. Berger shook her head, and looking down at her I thought how small and defenseless she appeared in her shapeless robe, with her gray hair falling to her shoulders instead of being smoothly pinned up as she wore it in the daytime.

"Mrs. Ryder has been turned around today. She slept most of the afternoon and early evening, but she's been wide awake all night. I just took her a bowl of soup and a sandwich so Miss Nelson could have a rest."

"Oh my," I breathed. "Lunch at midnight. You are good to Granny, Mrs. Berger. I hope she appreciates it."

"Sometimes she does." I heard no resentment in her tone, but what seemed mature acceptance of a less than enviable situation. "She really has you on her mind tonight, though. Keeps asking if you've come in, and telling us to be sure and send you directly to her when you do. So you'd better go up and see what it's about."

I said, "Please go to bed now. Miss Nelson and I can cope for the rest of the night."

Mrs. Berger switched off the outside lights, then said good night and left me. I took off my raincoat, hung it in the coat closet, gave my hair a hasty brushing at the hall mirror, then mounted the stairs to the floor above. Before I had reached the top I could see the triangle of light at Granny's partly open door. The door to the next room along the hall opened at the sound of my step and Miss Nelson peered out to see who was approaching.

She stared impassively while I whispered, "Go back to sleep. I'll stay with Granny for a while." Then she gave a matter-of-fact nod, and disappeared inside the room.

I tiptoed over to Granny's open door, hoping I might find that she had fallen asleep, thereby giving the household a few hours' reprieve from attending to her suddenly unreasonable demands. In the doorway I stood very still; I was barely breathing as I looked over at the bed. Then I blinked in astonishment. The bed was empty. The lamplight fell on the usual mountainous heap of pillows, but no fluffy white head rested there, and the blankets were thrown back from an expanse of smooth, white emptiness.

I slowly entered the room and at the same moment the door to the dressing room swung open and Granny stepped out. She was an arresting sight, for she had put on a white lace dressing gown that was far removed in spirit from the sensible wool wrappers I'd seen on her since my arrival. Originally she must have worn the robe with high-heeled mules, for the hem trailed behind her, catching on the thick carpet. The ruffled sleeves fell over her hands, and she shook them back impatiently as she reached for the arm of one of her little

French chairs to steady herself in her progress toward the bed. I was fascinated to see that she carried a navy blue wool dress draped over one arm and a pair of navy pumps in the same hand.

She saw me at once. "Oh, there you are," she said, giving me the quick, perfunctory smile of a busy person. "I hope you are ready to go. I told Michael we would be leaving at two."

"I seem to be readier than you are." I said the first words that came to mind, going along with her game partly because I didn't wish to upset her and partly to find out what the game was.

She did not respond, but placed the shoes on the floor and the dress on the bed, carefully spreading out the skirt and sleeves and smoothing away the wrinkles. Then with a little sigh of satisfaction she turned and sat down on the bed facing me.

"I'm quite worn out with all these preparations." She sat there smiling, as if at her own inadequacy; then as she gazed at me a playful glint appeared in her eyes. Keeping them fixed on mine, she fumbled in the pocket of her robe and slowly brought out an object that she held dangling in the air before me. "Look what I found," she said.

I did not need to come closer to see what it was, for it sparkled as it turned in her hand, sending forth stabs of brilliance that contrasted with the smooth lustrous glow of pearls. It was a bracelet—four strands of creamy pearls clasped with two delicately wrought diamond flowers. I knew instantly where I had seen it before, and I glanced toward Granny's dresser in confirmation. It was the bracelet my mother had worn with her wedding dress. I could not see it clearly from where I stood, but I knew it circled her slim wrist as it lay against the shining satin of her skirt. Studying the picture, I had wondered whether the bracelet had been Granny's gift to her son's bride; now perhaps I was about to find out.

Granny seemed eager to have me take it from her, but I felt extremely hesitant. "Take it," she said almost sternly. "It's time you started wearing some of your nice things."

I sat down beside her on the bed and slowly took the bracelet from her hand. "It's beautiful," I said softly, turning it to watch the diamonds blaze up when the lamplight touched them.

"It's no wonder you've forgotten; you haven't had it on since your wedding day." Again I heard the sternness that I remembered from childhood, and I remembered too how that firm tone had always been tempered with fondness, as indeed it was now. But to whom was that gruff affection directed in Granny's present sphere of reality?

"That was an unforgettable day," I said, feeling pleased with the ambivalence of the remark.

"But you must put that day behind you." My grandmother seized my hand and I felt her thin fingers press into mine with surprising strength. Her eyes were misted with tears, but as she gazed at me intently the lively, deep blue color shone through. "You must not dwell on the past, Kitty. I never thought a mother could say what I am saying, but you must try to forget my son. Bill is dead. I will always miss him, always love him, and so will you; but you owe it to yourself and your children to build a new life."

My eyes too were wet with tears and my throat so tight that it was a moment before I could manage to speak. "And that's why you want me to go to New York," I whispered.

Granny nodded, her eyes still fixed on mine. "It is time," she said firmly. "I know it has been only a few weeks, but you must make an effort, dear. Your grief is affecting your health; I can see it. You eat almost nothing; you must have lost ten pounds. I'm sure you will feel better if you have a change. I really think you should get a job."

On the last words her voice lifted as if the idea had taken her by surprise. She narrowed her eyes and studied me thoughtfully.

"Of course, I can't imagine what you are fitted to do, but I'm sure you could find something. How about decorating? You have good taste. Would you like me to speak to Esther Madsden? She's done all my houses, you know."

"What about the children?" It was my first truly deceitful remark. I had been careful, so far, not to lead Granny on; but I'd gotten caught up in the game, and now I was so utterly fascinated that I had to spin it out.

"Let's see how it goes these next few days while you're in the city. The children are used to being here with me, and if they don't miss you too much you can work during the week and spend weekends here with them." I was aware all at once that she had begun to slump against me, and that her voice had taken on the frail, hollow tone of fatigue. "We can hire a nurse, and of course they'll soon be in school."

Her head had dropped to my shoulder, but in a moment she pulled herself up and sighed heavily. "Tell Michael to come back in an hour, will you, dear?" she said. "I think I'll have a little rest before we leave."

I said nothing, but carefully rose to my feet, drawing Granny with me. With my arm around her for support, I gently removed her lacy robe. Then I helped her into the bed, pulling up the blankets and arranging the pillows to make her comfortable.

I switched off the bedside lamp and stood staring into the darkness of the silent high-ceilinged room. Again I had the unnatural sense of clarity I had felt on my way home from Phil's. It was so obvious all at once. I was not going to learn about my mother by questioning Granny; I would learn what she had to tell me by *being* my mother. And in no sense would it be a deception, for I had not assumed the role, but only accepted what Granny had thrust upon me. I should have been perceptive enough to see that, in keeping with her code of family loyalty, my grandmother would discuss the affairs of Kitty Ryder with no one but Kitty Ryder herself.

The next morning when I awoke my eyes went instantly to the bedside table. The pearl and diamond bracelet lay there, spread on the embroidered linen table cover as I had lovingly arranged it before I went to sleep. A shaft of morning sunlight glanced sparks from the diamond clasp and caressed the lustrous surface of the perfectly matched pearls. I smiled and snuggled comfortably against my pillow, wondering dreamily whether my mother had lain like this enjoying the sight of that bracelet on the morning after it had been given to her. Perhaps it was her wedding day, and she had wakened early because of the excitement.

My mother's wedding day had never occupied my thoughts before, but now I wondered what her mood had been when that long ago morning dawned. I wondered how she felt about sex. Had she been apprehensive about "giving herself to a man," as they used to call it in books, or did she confidently anticipate years of a pleasure she had already frequently enjoyed—possibly as recently as the night before? Perhaps Kitty Lewis and Bill Ryder had crept into this very bed on the eve of their wedding, smothering their laughter over the risk they were taking, with Bill's parents sleeping only a few doors away.

The notion delighted me. I loved thinking of my parents as young and passionate and impulsive. I wondered why it had never before occurred to me that my mother might have enjoyed sex as much as I did. The thought was like a firm brush stroke applied to the picture of her that was growing in my consciousness. From a dim jumble of childhood impressions she was slowly emerging as a person, and not because of what other people told me about her, but because remembering her brought their feelings close to the surface. Uncle John's wistful longing when he recalled her youthful vitality, my grandmother's loving concern for her in her grief; these emotions were felt for a real and vital person. I felt a surge of elation as I realized how well I could relate to my mother as a passionate young bride, greedy for pleasure, or even as a widow facing a future that stretched bleak and empty before her. I knew how she would feel, how lonely and bored and powerless, living there with her children in the home of her strong-minded mother-in-law. Imagining it, I felt a connectedness with her that was almost eerie, and I was filled with gratitude to Granny for inadvertently having forged the connection.

I thought of Dr. Zeigler then, picturing his reaction when I told him I had impersonated my mother. It would not be a matter of my passively accepting the part Granny had forced me to play; oh no, not to Dr. Zeigler. I suddenly felt thankful for the thousands of miles that lay between us. I would handle this particular bit of craziness in my own way, and he could shake his head all he liked when it was over.

There was one question he would be sure to ask. Did I think that scene had actually taken place between my mother and my grandmother? I asked it now of myself. Was Granny playing out with me a confrontation that had occurred—or in the light of later events had she always regretted not persuading my mother to go to New York and build a new life? Perhaps it was necessary for her to say before she died the words she so bitterly regretted omitting when the time was right.

Suddenly restless, I threw back the covers and climbed out of bed. Although I had slept for only a few hours, I was not

tired. The sense of coming closer to my mother was invigo-
rating; all I wanted was to see Granny again, to learn more
each time we played our poignant game until at last I knew
the truth.

When I stepped into the shower and felt the warm spray
strike me I realized that Phil's problem had been pushed
completely out of my mind. As I considered it freshly I felt
ashamed of the brisk confidence I had felt the night before.
I had no magic solution to bestow on my bumbling younger
brother. I could not even consult my uncle about it, for that
would be a betrayal of Phil's confidence. And yet Uncle John
was in a way at the heart of Phil's trouble, for if he had not
carelessly assured him that he could produce the money Phil
needed, Phil would not have "borrowed" his client's bonds.

Out of the shower, I toweled myself dry, then distractedly
puffed up a cloud of bath powder that made the steamy bathroom so foggy I had to grope for the door handle. In my room
I pulled a shirt from a hanger in my closet and stared unseeingly into the mirror while I put it on and buttoned it up.

It was unsettling to think that my charming, attractive uncle, who had asked only pleasure of life, could be partially
responsible for Phil's unhappy situation. It was a worse than
unhappy situation, in fact; what faced Phil and Barbara was
no less than tragedy, the wreckage of their lives. Suddenly it
was all too much for me. I felt caged.

As I hurried downstairs for breakfast I consulted my watch.
It was nine-fifteen, an hour earlier in Chicago. In forty-five
minutes I would call the agency. Today was Thursday, the
weekend was approaching, and I couldn't bear to wait any
longer to hear their decision.

They wanted me! Before I could get to the telephone, before I had even finished breakfast, the call came to say the
job was mine, provided the ad director of the food conglom-

erate was as impressed with me as they were at the agency. It was almost a formality, but would I mind making one more quick trip to Chicago to meet the client? And if by some quirk of personal chemistry we didn't hit it off, they had another account in mind for me. They didn't want me to get away.

I was almost purring with self-satisfaction when I hung up after assuring them that I'd fly out on Monday. The president of the agency had switched me to his secretary, who had a schedule of morning flights for me to choose from. I would be met by a company car and could use a company apartment if I wished to stay over and look for a place to live. A dinner would be arranged so that I could meet some of the other account people.

It was heady stuff. I felt like a balloon that might rise into the air any minute. I quickly dialed my uncle; I had to share the news. His line was busy, so I tried Barbara, but there was no answer. Briefly I pictured Phil gamely commuting to his office, keeping up a front but stripped of responsibilities; then I suppressed the thought of that dismal charade. I thought of Betsy; I might go into town to meet her for lunch. Why not? But before I could run upstairs to get her office number from my handbag the telephone rang again.

I picked it up eagerly, hoping it was Uncle John, but instead I heard the velvety voice of the helpful lady at the telephone company. After she had made certain that she was indeed speaking to Sally Templeton, she told me that in a back issue of the Detroit telephone directory she had found a listing for a Martin Josefson, M.D. Could that possibly be the person I was looking for? I heard a faint note of reproach as she gently pointed out that I had neglected to tell her that Martin Josefson was a doctor. It would have saved time.

I assured her that I had not known Martin Josefson's profession. I asked her whether the listing indicated what kind of medicine he practiced, and she said it did not. There were fewer specialists twenty years ago.

Twenty years ago? Yes, that was the most recent listing for Dr. Josefson, though he had been in Detroit for ten years before that. I added it up: ten years of practice, plus twenty, and he must have been twenty-five or older before he finished his education. Martin Josefson was at least fifty-five by now, if it was safe to assume that he had started practice in Detroit immediately after earning his degree. It wasn't safe to assume that, of course. He might have gone to Detroit at the end of his career, not the beginning. He might be dead by now.

Somewhat hopelessly, I asked whether there was any record of a forwarding address or a telephone number in another city, then listened in amazement while the dulcet voice, now unmistakably triumphant, reported that Dr. Josefson had moved, in 1964, to Grand Rapids, Michigan, where he still conducted a practice at 345 Bayside Road. She then gave me listings for his office and his home and I had the impression that if I had needed to know more—his wife's favorite color, for example—she could have provided it instantly. The woman was not only cheerful and polite, she was a miracle of efficiency, and I stifled an impulse to ask her if she would like to move to Chicago. Instead, I thanked her and hung up, reflecting that if the day continued as it had begun, I might have all the problems that had been nagging at me solved by noon.

I sat thinking for a moment before I dialed Martin Josefson in Grand Rapids. I was using the phone in the library, but I had left the door open to the hall and I could hear the familiar morning sounds of the household: the hesitant voice of Mrs. Berger as she greeted the maid, Jenny, followed by Jenny's cheerful response, then the high-pitched hum of the vacuum cleaner. Someone opened the front door and a gust of air rustled the pages of a magazine lying on a table near the window. I rose and went to close the door, then returned to the comfortable old green leather desk chair. That chair must have been there during my father's childhood. I wondered if his father had sat in it when he lectured him about his behavior.

I was stalling, of course, because I was uncertain what to say to Martin Josefson, M.D. Doctors had many restrictions when it came to passing out information about their patients. I wondered if being the patient's daughter carried any weight, or the fact that the patient was no longer alive. Terry could tell me, of course.

I called his office and was told that he would be at the hospital until early afternoon. I knew I should wait and talk to him before I called Dr. Josefson, but I could not. I was too keyed up, too excited at the prospect of finding out what this man had meant to my mother.

So with trembling fingers I dialed the number of Martin Josefson's office in Grand Rapids. I had such a sense of reaching back into another time that I felt a shock when a brisk, young woman answered and said Dr. Josefson could speak to me immediately. It was too quick, I wasn't ready; my throat went dry and I stammered as I gave her my name.

Then the doctor was on the phone, and I launched into my explanation. It was more difficult than I had anticipated. Dr. Josefson had not had the mystery of my mother's disappearance taunting him for thirty years; my query must have been totally unexpected.

"Just who is this calling?" he asked, and I told him again that I was Kitty Ryder's daughter, that my mother had died when I was a child, that I had unearthed his name and was anxious to know why it had been in her possession.

"I believe your mother did come to me for treatment, yes.

But it was many years ago." He paused, then he said slowly, "Catherine Ryder. Just what are you trying to find out about her?" His voice was deep and he spoke with the deliberation of age. I pictured a white-haired, kindly old gent, like a doctor in a TV commerical, and it helped me continue.

I said, "Well you see, Dr. Josefson, I have never known exactly what happened to my mother." I had to stop. It was happening again: the tight, choked-up throat, the tears misting my vision so I could hardly make out the number I had jotted down.

Dr. Josefson cleared his throat. No doubt a doctor with his backlog of experience could detect my emotional state over the telephone. He said gently, "Do you mean you don't know how your mother died?"

"I do know how she died, yes." The need to explain clearly helped me to recover my poise. I told him in a few words about my mother's death in an automobile accident and what a shock it had been. "But a year before that she had gone away and left my brother and me, and that was a more damaging shock somehow. I have always had a desperate need to know why she did that, and when I found your name in her desk . . ."

"I see. Yes, I can understand why it would bother you, but I'm afraid . . ."

I interrupted. "I know you may not be able to tell me anything; I don't know what the rules are about that sort of thing. But if you can . . . if you wouldn't mind looking up your records to see what you treated her for it might give me a clue as to why she went away when she did. It is terribly important to me. I feel I must pursue every avenue, and there are so few."

There was a silence, and when he spoke he sounded so cool I feared my insistence had offended him. He said, "I will do what I can, Mrs. Templeton, but please don't expect too much. Now, give me your mother's name and her address at the time. And her date of birth."

I felt absurdly elated as I spelled it all out for him. It was as if he had promised me an answer, but of course he had not committed himself to a thing. He said he would call me as soon as he had checked his old records and I thanked him effusively.

It wasn't until we hung up that I realized I had neglected to ask whether he was a specialist in a particular field of medicine. The question could wait, I decided, until our next conversation. I had taken up enough of his time that morning.

CHAPTER 14

Tapping sounded on the french door that gave onto the terrace and I turned, startled out of the reverie into which I had fallen after my call to Dr. Josefson. Peering uncertainly, I crossed the room, then as I reached the door saw that it was Tommy Harris standing there.

The door stuck and as I pulled and pushed and jiggled the key in the lock, I wondered why I had not thought to call Tommy when I had failed to reach Terry McGinnis. Surely a medical student would know how much information a doctor could give a relative of one of his patients. Tommy was gesturing that he would go around to the front when the door flew open, throwing me off balance, and Tommy quickly reached out to steady me.

"I'm glad to see you," I said breathlessly. "Come on in. I'll get some coffee."

"No coffee, thanks," he said as he entered the library, stooping to clear the door frame. When he straightened he seemed even taller, here in a confined space, than he had out of doors.

I grinned up at him. "I remember when you looked up

to me," I said. "Now it looks like I have to treat you with respect."

"I'd die of the shock." He smiled, a slow, lazy smile, and his blue eyes held my gaze in a way that I recognized. He was accustomed to women's admiration, was our Tommy. He sought it automatically, even from me. Well, there was no rule that said idealistic young doctors had to be unattractive. Still, I felt vaguely uncomfortable as I sank onto a small chintz-covered sofa and indicated a nearby chair for him.

"Have you made any headway with your father?"

Tommy did not reply immediately, nor did he sit in the chair I had meant him to occupy. Instead, he stood staring down at me with that lazy, knowing grin still fixed on his face, then stepped forward and lowered himself to the sofa beside me. It was a very small sofa, a loveseat actually, and Tommy's long body took up at least two-thirds of it. He wore well-aged blue corduroy pants, and when he bent his legs I saw that the bones of his knees fit comfortably into the thin, faded spots they had worn in the fabric.

He leaned toward me, studying my face intently, and I was amazed to find myself pressing my spine against the cushions like a cornered animal. We were so close that I could feel the warmth of his body and smell the faintly musty scent of his thick wool sweater. His eyes were a deep, deep blue; I had not noticed the other day how blue they were, nor how thick and long the dark lashes that rimmed them. They were Irish eyes, of course, the sort I had thought of enviously as Catholic eyes at my convent school. And the high color in his face was typical Irish too, a fine healthy flush that ran along his high cheekbones and down to his firm, square jaw. To complete the picture, he should have had jet black hair like Michael's, but Tommy's was brown with auburn glints and it curved against his head in soft disorder, with short, curling tendrils at ears and neck.

He said softly, "It's wonderful to see you again, Sally. I didn't even know how much I'd missed you." He reached out with one hand and gently pushed my hair back from my cheek, the blue eyes still intent. Then his hand slowly moved to the back of my head, drawing it close, and I felt his firm, warm lips on mine. It was a brief kiss, but authoritative, controlled, and when he drew back he smiled gravely, as if to show that he was deeply moved.

I too was moved, totally shaken, in fact, at the idea of sitting on that sofa in the middle of the morning, kissing Tommy Harris. I scrambled out of it, awkwardly climbing over his long, imprisoning legs.

"Tommy, for God's sake!" I laughed, and it sounded like a loud, artificial cackle. "I'm glad to see you too, but take it easy."

I knew I looked ridiculous, standing there breathlessly straightening my skirt and smoothing my rumpled hair, but instead of loathing myself I felt enormously angry with Tommy. How dare he cause me to lose my poise? How dare he sit regarding me with an insufferable expression of appraisal— this boy I had known since his babyhood? Why, I had practically brought him up; but today I saw no vestige of the toddler who had once dogged my steps, nor of the medical student I had met at the trout stream. This person seemed cool and detached; my discomfort appeared to have no affect on him. He watched me in silence, his features passive, the fine blue eyes fixed and unblinking. It wasn't right, that nearly catatonic stare; I realized it with a surge of apprehension that must have shown in my face, for his expression softened and he said, "Hey, Sally, I didn't mean anything, you know." He got to his feet and, placing one hand lightly on my shoulder, smiled down into my eyes. "We're old buddies, aren't we? Come on. Sit down and tell me what's been going on with you all these years."

"Are you sure you won't have some coffee?" I asked, settling myself on the sofa once again. I would not give him the satisfaction of seeing me take refuge in the chair. This was Tommy Harris, after all.

He shook his head impatiently before my words were out. "No coffee." Then, with a quick upward glance he went on, "How's your grandmother? What's her mental state these days?"

Some callousness in his tone made me weigh my words. "Granny is doing much better," I said evenly. "I've seen an amazing improvement in her since I've been here. I really think she's going to pull out of this."

Tommy had folded himself into the chair across from me and was once again studying me intently. He no longer wore that fixed and somehow predatory stare, however, but seemed to be concentrating on my words as if they carried great import.

He leaned forward, resting his forearms on his knees, and began questioning me in the routine manner of a doctor gathering a medical history. I answered in the same terse way, giving him the facts of Granny's diet, her wakeful periods, her ability to comprehend, her forays out of bed. When he asked about medication I was vague, intimating that it had never occurred to me to inquire, and I thought I saw a flash of skepticism appear in the steady blue eyes. It was suppressed with such calculated speed that I felt a twinge of uneasiness. I continued talking, but in the back of my mind I reviewed what I had already disclosed. Nothing meaningful, I decided. I hadn't revealed anything about Granny that would be useful, even to a doctor. And with that quick mental scanning I realized I was protecting Granny. Protecting her from Tommy? I felt dizzy in my confusion. What was going on with Tommy? Where was the eager, dedicated scientist I had longed to help? Had he been putting on a skillful performance that day at the stream, or was he performing now, hoping to impress me with his professionalism?

Well, I wasn't impressed. I didn't like this interrogation, and I didn't like the suspicion I was beginning to feel about Tommy's reasons for conducting it.

"What is this?" I asked abruptly. "You've been around here longer than I have, Tommy. I'm sure Terry McGinnis would allow you to examine Granny if he knew you were so interested. Have you thought of asking him?"

I heard the coldness in my voice, but Tommy seemed untroubled by it. "I would like to check her out; that's a good idea," he said, still speaking in the flat, mechanical manner of his questioning. Then he was silent, staring at the floor in front of his chair so fixedly that I began to fidget. I was about to jump up and send him on his way when he slowly raised his eyes to mine and smiled, almost shyly. "Of course geriatrics isn't my field. I told you that. But I'll be glad to take a look at Mrs. Ryder if you want me to."

For a moment I was speechless. I had seen movies where swift personality changes took place, and had always considered it a cheap dramatic device, but that was exactly what appeared to have happened before my eyes. For the old Tommy Harris was back again; I saw it in his face, which was once again young, vulnerable, confiding. The ruthless inquisitor of a moment ago had been replaced by an old friend offering to help. His innate kindness had come to the fore; even his eyes had changed, had lost the stony glint that was somehow familiar to me, though I could not remember why.

Now it was I who reached for him. As if to keep my friend from slipping away again, I bent forward and placed my hand on his arm. I had to ask him for an explanation, but I must be tactful.

That was our situation when Terry came into the room: Tommy and I, knees touching, gazing absorbedly into each other's eyes, too preoccupied to hear the opening of the door. And then when Terry spoke I started in consternation, feeling the hot blood rise to my face.

"No, no, don't let me interrupt you. Sorry!" Terry was just as flustered. He nodded at Tommy; apparently they had met. But Terry was backing toward the door even as I hurried over to drag him back, if necessary.

"I thought you were at the hospital," I blurted.

"I was. But I wanted to see your grandmother before I left for Vermont." Terry was grinning now, at my confusion I assumed, but I was wrong. "I don't know what you've done to your granny, but keep it up," he said. "She's making big plans; I think you're going to have an interesting weekend."

With that, he was gone.

Tommy did not linger, which was a good thing, for that brief visit of Terry's had quite shattered our tenuous rapport. And I didn't want to examine his strange behavior just then; I was far more concerned about Terry's impression of us. Damn! What must he have thought? And again, damn, because what did it matter? If he was going off to Vermont for the long Easter weekend Betsy would be with him, I knew that. There was no point in calling her just to hear it confirmed. They would have an idyllic three days in the mountains, planning their future life together, while I moped around waiting for Monday and my trip to Chicago. I went over to close the french door, and glared out at the sparkling spring day. I hadn't had a chance to tell one single soul about my new job. All these people were completely wrapped up in themselves.

Then I thought of Jane Kelly, pictured her plain face lighting with sincere pleasure at the news of my good fortune.

Suddenly it seemed ages since I had seen her; it had been two days, in fact, and a good deal had happened. I ran it all over in my mind as I made my way through the hall and up the stairs. Of course I couldn't tell Jane about Phil's problem, but she would love the description of Granny preparing to go to New York at one o'clock in the morning.

And Granny. I stopped before her partly open door to prepare myself for our encounter. In her mind who would be stepping into her bedroom this morning, Sally Templeton or Kitty Ryder? I took a deep breath, fixed a friendly smile on my face, and entered the room. I moved quietly, in case Granny was sleeping, but instead of finding the hushed, dimly lighted scene I half-expected, I saw that the room was flooded with sunlight, the bed was empty with the covers thrown back in disarray, and several dresser drawers had been pulled open and left that way. The door to the dressing room and bath stood ajar, and I could hear animated voices from within. It was exactly the sort of scene I had often come upon during my childhood when Granny was packing for a journey. Even if she merely intended to spend a few days in New York, her preparations were tumultuous, always including some crisis concerning an undelivered dress or hat or a complication caused by me or my brother. I smiled, remembering the relief everyone had felt when at last Michael headed the big black car down the drive toward the road, with Granny's handkerchief fluttering at the rear window.

I waited uncertainly, unwilling to add my presence to whatever problems were already occupying Jane Kelly, and in a moment the sound of the two women's voices grew louder. They were returning to the bedroom, and I braced myself in anticipation of my grandmother's greeting. Nothing could have prepared me for it, however; most certainly not the loving demeanor she had displayed in the early hours of the dawn.

She still seemed to have a trip to New York in her mind; that much had carried over, for in the dressing room she paused to say to Jane, "I want all of these closets cleaned and my dresses aired. You will have plenty of time to do it while I am in the city."

She sounded so exactly like her old self that I automatically glanced toward the mirror to make sure my hair was tidy and my denim skirt hanging straight. Granny could not abide uneven hemlines.

She appeared in the doorway wearing the lacy white dressing gown of the night before, but with high-heeled slippers on her feet now, so that the ruffled skirt swung gracefully instead of dragging on the floor. She and Jane must have been working on her hair, for it was piled smoothly on her head; the unruly white halo had been firmly pinned and sprayed to stay in place. She did not see me at once, for she had turned her head to speak to Jane. The words were never spoken, however, for when I said a tentative, "Good morning," Granny froze. She stayed motionless for an instant, then slowly swung around to face me.

The blue eyes that fixed mine in a level gaze held no slightest gleam of warmth, nor did they waver as Granny said without turning, "You may leave, Nancy."

Jane Kelly stood in the door now, just behind my grandmother, looking comically undecided about how to respond to the unexpected order. At last she slipped past Granny's still figure and made her way to the bedroom door. She smiled at me reassuringly before she went through it to the hall, and I knew she would wait there in case I needed her.

"I am surprised to see you this morning," Granny said, her words cold and distinct. "As far as I am concerned, we have said all there is to be said."

Ah then, I was Kitty and Kitty was decidedly out of favor.

But how could she have offended her mother-in-law so deeply in only a few hours? I soon realized that in the shadowy recesses of my grandmother's mind a good many more than a few hours had passed.

"Are you going to tell me you have changed your mind?" Her voice was heavy with sarcasm. "Surely you have not been influenced by my wishes, or by your children's need to have you with them at this time?"

I could not imagine how to respond, so I said nothing. I prayed that she would give some clue to the cause of her anger before my silence goaded her to even greater fury. My heart was pounding, for I sensed that this confrontation contained an important key to my mother's disappearance. Indeed my grandmother's next words made this a certainty, and I had to reach for a chair to steady myself.

"Well, will you answer me, Kitty? I have a forgiving heart, as you know. If you have decided to give up your selfish plan and stay here where you belong, I will not hold your momentary weakness against you."

I do not know to this day what inspired me to cry out, "I can't help it if the time is wrong. I have to go now!" My voice trembled with passion. I was amazed at my own conviction, and frightened by it as well.

Granny was staring at me wide-eyed, and I struggled for control of my sudden wild emotion. I dared not frighten her into reality before I had learned all I could.

Making my voice soft and level, I took a chance. I said, "You told me I should build a new life, and now that I have gathered the courage to try . . ."

"A new life, yes. But in New York; that's the place for you. What makes you think you can learn more in some godforsaken town in Michigan than you can in New York? Why, New York is the center of everything, all the arts, every important business . . ." Now it was her voice that shook with intensity.

I groped for the meaning of her words. Michigan. Kitty was going to Michigan. That did not surprise me; the interesting discovery was that Granny had known it too. She had known Kitty's destination, but not her reason for going there, and indeed it was a baffling choice. I knew my mother had lived near Detroit for a few years of her childhood. Perhaps she had old friends there who had offered her a job. But Granny was right; New York was the city of opportunity. New York had everything. Except Dr. Martin Josefson. Were they lovers, was that it? Or could she have had some obscure illness that only Martin Josefson was qualified to treat?

Granny had lowered herself into one of her small French armchairs. The morning's unusual activity was taking its toll. But the anger that blazed within must have given her strength. Her spine was rigid as she sat composedly facing me; her eyes flashed with the cold brilliance of diamonds, and the rosy flush along her fine, high cheekbones had nothing to do with the rouge pot on her dressing table. Even as I searched desperately for the right words I was aware in another part of my mind that Granny had probably never in her life looked handsomer or more imposing. She was like a great actress playing her most dramatic role.

I said tentatively, "I will come back, of course." But my words did nothing to ease the situation.

Granny seemed to hold her head even higher as she replied, "That is the most maddening aspect of this whole affair: your refusal to say exactly how long you will stay in that place, that insignificant town in Michigan." The contempt with which she pronounced the final word would have brought tears to the eyes of any native of that state. "It is as if you have been mesmerized, Kitty, you are so changed. I thought I knew you well, but suddenly you are a stranger to me—stubborn, intractable, with no feeling, it seems, for me or your children. And what a time you have chosen to draw away from us. I can only assume that your grief has unbalanced your mind. Won't you do as I have asked and see a good doctor before you go?"

Her voice had softened, and I sensed the compassion, indeed the love, she was extending to her recalcitrant daughter-in-law. This only increased my bewilderment, for it was hard to believe that my mother, in her fresh bereavement, would have rejected such kindness and emotional support. I felt so strongly what a wrench it must have been that I went to Granny's chair and knelt, grasping her hands tightly in mine.

Again words seem to come of their own volition. My voice was husky as I said earnestly, "I don't want to leave you. And it breaks my heart to go away from the children. But I must go, and I must do it now. I can only trust that some day you will understand and forgive me."

"When I know the reason?" I heard the challenge in the question. Granny had not pulled her hands away, but they were so stiff and unyielding they might have been carved of wood.

"Even if you never know the reason." My lips were trembling as I spoke. My whole being yearned for her understanding so intensely that I did not ask myself why I sought it. I was Kitty at that instant. Ignorant as I was of the secret that tore at her, for the pulse of a second I was my mother.

Granny too must have felt that throb of authenticity, for all at once her hands were clutching mine and as she bent forward to look into my eyes I saw that the hardness had gone from hers. She was not pleading with me, but stating a fact as she said, "We need each other now as we never did before. I know how it hurts you to leave the children and I know you would never trust them to anyone but me. So I must believe you have a good reason. Anyway, I have no choice." A quick, wry smile briefly twisted her lips. Then she sighed and her eyes were suddenly old and weary and full of wisdom. "Something tells me you do have to go now. It isn't just stubbornness I'm facing; you would not be so adamant without a compelling reason. But Kitty, you must know that I have loved you like a daughter, not only as the wife of my son. So I think a part of my anger is fear of losing you, as I have just lost Bill. You will not let that happen, will you Kitty? No matter what?"

The beautiful, carved features were crumbling, her mouth was shaking uncontrollably, and her anguished eyes brimmed with tears.

A sob rose in my throat as I put my arms around her. "No matter what," I murmured, rocking her gently as our tears mingled. With no idea of the meaning of my words, I said them over and over: "Never, never, never. No matter what."

CHAPTER 15

Wheeling my little red car along the winding road to Uncle John's house, I had no attention to spare for the shimmering beauty of the bright spring day. I would find my uncle, confront him with the facts I had learned, and drag the rest of my mother's story out of him. I had had enough of his hedging. After the dramatic scene between Granny and "Kitty" it was clear to me that my uncle had been deliberately evasive. Kitty's departure had shaken the whole family. Granny had fought it; my brother and I must have wept over it. Undoubtedly Uncle John had been ordered to stop her; he must have known something of her reason for being so stubborn, even if she could not confide it to Granny.

As I swung around the curves in his driveway, I closed my eyes for a second, sending up a wordless prayer that I would not find Gillian's car parked before the door. I was in the mood to order her out if I found her there, and I shuddered to think of the scene that would follow. But when I rounded the final curve I saw that the gravel expanse was empty. The garage door stood open and I could see Uncle John's car

parked beside an empty space that was no doubt often occupied by Gillian's. Several garden tools had been propped
beside the door: a rake, a hoe, a pair of long-handled clippers.
It appeared that my uncle was about to embark on the spring
cleanup he had been postponing.

I parked and climbed out of my car just as Uncle John
emerged from the rear of the garage, pushing a wheelbarrow.
He wore faded old denim jeans, his familiar patched cashmere
sweater, and a straw hat that bore a look more of the Caribbean
than the farmyard. When he saw me he lowered the wheelbarrow to the ground, dusted his hands on the seat of his
pants, and ambled toward me with a smile of welcome spreading across his face.

"I thought you'd never get here," he said, bending to kiss
my cheek. He straightened and indicated the equipment lined
up outside the garage. "It was a near thing, as you can see.
Come on in and have some coffee."

At any other time I would have been amused by his delight
in having his chores interrupted. But I was still vibrating from
the scene between Granny and "Kitty." I felt I was very close
to learning what I had always so desperately needed to know;
surely Uncle John could put the last piece of the puzzle in
place. But would he? I suddenly remembered how balky he
had been when I wanted him to help me find Martin Josefson,
and I realized that I should have given some thought to how
I would handle him.

I believe it was his unusually rugged appearance that guided
me to the right approach; that and the fact that I honestly felt
like a little girl on the verge of tears. It had been a very
emotional morning, after all.

There was a genuine quaver in my voice as I said, "Wait,
Uncle John. What I really need right now is a hug."

I moved close to him, nestling my face against the shabby

old sweater as I had so many times before, and instantly his arms were around me. He held me gently, stroking my hair with one hand, crooning the same kind of comforting words I had so recently used with Granny.

"Didn't you get the Chicago job?" he finally asked, holding me off to look at my face. "Is that the trouble?"

I shook my head. "No. I just heard that they want me. That's OK, better than I expected in fact. But I've just had the most amazing scene with Granny. Amazing and upsetting. She thought I was Kitty."

As I spoke, I saw my uncle's expression tighten as it always seemed to when we talked about my mother.

His hands dropped from my shoulders and he turned toward the house. I followed, but I could not see his face as he said, "What do you mean she thought you were Kitty? What did she say to you?"

For the next fifteen minutes we sat drinking coffee at the kitchen table while I described the two occasions on which I had played the role of my mother. I explained my theory that if Granny chose to speak to me as Kitty I saw no harm in it, but a possibility of finding the answer to the question that had hounded me for so long.

"Granny seems to want it," I said slowly. "That's the only way I can explain it. She apparently has a need to relive the period just after my father was killed and before Mother went away. It's as if she never got it straight in her mind and she needs to . . . before she dies."

My uncle had propped his head on one hand while he stared down at his coffee cup. I wondered uncomfortably whether his silence indicated that he was deeply moved by my story or whether he was restraining his irritation at my simple-mindedness.

"It does sound kind of crazy, I know." I was squirming. I

longed for him to look up so I could see his reaction. "I suppose it was sort of like a séance, though I don't know exactly how those things work. But at least twice I found myself saying words that meant absolutely nothing to me. Where did they come from if not from my mother?"

Now he did look up, fixing his gaze on a point beyond my head. "But these things you said seemed to mean something to Mother?"

"Yes, they did. That's why it was so unnerving. I didn't know what I was talking about, but Granny did. And not only that; I had the impression that in Granny's mind a certain amount of time had passed between the two scenes. She and Mother had obviously been arguing about this trip to Michigan for several days, maybe longer." I leaned forward eagerly. "I can hardly wait for our next session. The reason for it all is bound to come out the next time Granny has a talk with 'Kitty.' If she does, of course. I'm certainly not going very far from her between now and Monday morning."

"Sally." Uncle John peered into his coffee cup, found it empty, and got up to get the pot from the stove. I waited impatiently while he filled my cup, then his own, and resumed his place at the table. "Sally, you're a smart girl, and yet you're telling me that you believe your poor old grandmother, who is obviously not in her right mind, makes sense when she thinks she is talking to your mother?" He was shaking his head sadly as he stirred his coffee. "I'm just as anxious to believe it as you are. I'd welcome any sign that Mother was regaining her mental capacity. But there's no truth in it, you see. I can't explain why she is inventing this fantasy, but I'll bet Terry can. Ask him." My uncle's deep blue eyes were brooding as he studied my face in silence for a moment. "You do resemble your mother. It's startling to anyone who knew her when she was your age. It's easy to see why your grandmother might be confused and think she was talking to her."

The disappointment was like a rock lying heavily upon my chest. "But so much of it really happened! My father was killed. Granny's reaction to that seems very normal, and so does her concern for my mother. And my mother did go away, with no explanation that I've ever head."

"To Michigan?" He did not attempt to hide his scorn. "That's where the craziness comes in, Sally. Nothing in the world would have taken your mother to Michigan. That's out of the blue."

It was then I realized that Uncle John knew nothing of my success in tracking down Martin Josefson. I opened my mouth to tell him, and I could feel my face flushing with excitement. Wait until he heard that I had actually talked to Martin Josefson, that he was a doctor and might at this very moment be looking up my mother's records! But as I looked across the table at my uncle's face I felt a chill. I had seen that expression of weary regret before, the sorrowfully crinkled brows and the faint, rueful smile. It had often amused me to see how he could use his handsome face with an actor's skill to deceive others—women usually—about his true feelings, but never before had he practiced his art on me. Somehow the saddest thing about it was his unawareness that I would see through him.

My throat was so tight I could not speak, but it did not matter, for there was nothing more to be said. I sank back in my chair and gave all my attention to finishing my coffee so I could be gone from there.

If I had driven straight home from Uncle John's everything might have worked out differently. Still I have never blamed myself, for when I saw Nancy Harris in the drugstore what could have been more natural than to invite her to have a sandwich with me? It was late, after one o'clock by then, and I was famished. I was also overjoyed to see the woman who had been Granny's servant and friend for so many years, and who had been so kind to me when I was a lonely little girl.

Nancy seemed equally pleased to see me. We hugged each other with real warmth; it was not the falsely affectionate greeting women usually exchange, and when we drew apart I saw that Nancy's wide hazel eyes were misted with tears.

"I wondered when I would see you," she said. "Tommy said you were here, and I've been on the point of calling you so many times. But something stopped me." She was groping in her bag for a handkerchief, and when she had wiped her eyes she gripped my arm and said anxiously, "How is your grandmother, Sally? I think of her every day. I wish I could do something . . ."

I smiled and patted her hand. "You could come and see her, Nancy. I know she would love that."

Nancy had always been a pretty woman, with a gentle, caring manner. When I was little I had sensed her vulnerability, without knowing the word for it. When Granny was short with her I had seen the hurt in her eyes, and admired the way she often covered it with a laugh or forced some teasing rejoinder. I think Granny saw it, too, and sometimes regretted her sharp tongue, although of course she never apologized.

Nancy glanced quickly around the busy shop before replying to me. "I'm not sure of the reception I might get if I went to see Mrs. Ryder." She smiled as if at her own foolishness. "Maybe I'm imagining things, but I don't think Miss Clark would be pleased to find me there."

There were several small, round tables near the soda fountain at the back of the store, one of them just being vacated by two girls who probably worked in a nearby office. I said, "Come on, Nancy," and started in the direction of the empty table. "Let's have a sandwich while we talk. I'm starving."

Nancy claimed to have had her lunch, so I urged her to indulge in a chocolate sundae. "You can use a pound or two," I said as we settled ourselves at the table.

The truth was that Nancy was too thin, almost gaunt. I didn't like the empty look of her crisp, printed cotton dress, the roominess of the sleeves from which her slender arms protruded. And I saw that her anxious expression lingered even when we were not discussing my grandmother.

When we had ordered I said carefully, "Tommy came to see me this morning. I was fascinated to hear about the medical career he has planned." I paused, but Nancy remained silent. "It's a shame he has to take time out," I continued.

She nodded slowly. She did not look at me, but concentrated on rearranging her silverware as she replied, "Yes, I guess it is."

I was astonished. I had thought I was tactfully providing an opening so that she might vent the anger she must feel over the circumstances that were slowing Tommy's education. I said, "I'm surprised, Nancy. You don't seem very upset about it."

She looked up with a flash of anger, and I feared I had gone too far. But her expression softened immediately, and she reached over to pat my hand. "You're still defending Tommy, just the way you always did. It's nice of you, Sally, but the situation is more complicated than it looks." Again she busied herself with her knife and fork. "Michael and I aren't sure medical school is the best place for Tommy right now."

"Oh, I see. Then it's not just a matter of money. Uncle John hinted that Tommy might be having a difficult time with his studies. Is that it?"

"Your uncle suggested that?" Nancy smiled, slowly shaking her head. "I know how you've always worshiped him, Sally, but I have to say John Ryder isn't one to go into things very deep, is he? He's gone around in blinders most of his life, that man." At once she seemed to think better of her words. "Not that there's any reason he should get worked up about our Tommy, of course."

"No, except he was always fond of Tommy. At least I thought he was." I bent over the table and lowered my voice. "I can be frank with you, can't I, Nancy? I hoped I could get Uncle John to lend Tommy some money, and he was anything but receptive to the idea. He doesn't seem too pleased with him at the moment."

Again Nancy smiled and this time I saw bitterness in it. "You've been frank; I'll be the same. I haven't always agreed with Michael about his handling of Tommy. Michael's a different sort from Tommy. He's stubborn and cautious; he's tight with money and it's not surprising, considering what's happened in Ireland. Tommy calls him greedy, and maybe he is." She clamped her lips tight for a moment, then glanced up sharply. "I'm in between, you can see that."

"Well, Michael must have handled Tommy the right way, or he wouldn't have turned out so well. He's been tops all the way through school, he's won every honor, and everyone looks up to him. However you two disagreed, you seem to have done a super job."

There was silence while I attended to my tuna fish salad and Nancy toyed with her ice cream. I sensed the tension that had been building in her. It was like the old days, when I knew she was nearing the end of her patience and wasn't certain whether or not I wanted to push her the rest of the way. The explosion would be enthralling, I remembered thinking—if I felt equal to it.

Abruptly Nancy looked across at me and said, "How was Tommy when you saw him this morning?" Before I could reply she went on. "Did he seem all right? Perfectly normal?"

I took a minute, I didn't want to overreact. "Well, of course I haven't seen much of him lately. I don't know what 'normal' is for Tommy these days." I smiled nervously, but Nancy's face was still and set as she waited for me to stop hedging. "Oh hell, Nancy, the truth is I thought he was very strange. At first anyway. Then after we'd been talking for a few minutes he began to seem like himself again. I wanted to ask him about it, but Terry McGinnis came in—Granny's doctor— and I didn't have a chance."

Certain faces are not suited for displaying anger. Nancy's, with its short, turned-up nose and piquant curve of lips and chin, was molded for love and merriment. Even with her jaw grimly set and a cold, bleak light in her eyes it was hard to believe she was really disturbed, and I had an instant's understanding of why it is sometimes difficult for men to take pretty women seriously.

She stared at me thoughtfully, and I knew she was asking herself whether she could trust me. It had been a long time, after all. She sighed, shut her eyes tight for a second, then opened them, and in an even, unemotional tone told me she feared Tommy was addicted to drugs.

"It happens sometimes with medical students," she said. "The pressure, the long hours of concentration, and for many the constant worry over money, puts them under more stress than they can handle. Or think they can handle." The hazel eyes glinted in a way I remembered. "I happen to believe they could take it, most of them anyway; but they're learning about the effects of all kinds of drugs, discussing them all the time. And they have access to them, there's no use saying they don't. It's a dangerous combination."

Adopting her matter-of-fact approach, I asked quietly, "What drug is he hooked on? Do you know?"

"It's not heroin; he's sworn that, and we believe him.

Otherwise he would be in a treatment center right now."
Again the hazel eyes sparked dangerously. "You can imagine
Michael Harris's reaction to all this, can't you? He was ready
to turn him over to the police, but Tommy said give him six
months and if he hadn't cured himself by then he would get
help voluntarily."

"Whew," I breathed. "The atmosphere at your house must
be simply lovely these days."

Nancy managed a faint smile. "Luckily, they don't see much
of each other. Between his two jobs Tommy is too worn out
to do much but sleep when he's home, and Michael has never
been one to hang around. He can't relax, though. Keeps asking
me where Tommy is and what I've seen. I hear him prowling
around in his room and I know he's looking for signs of drugs,
even though he doesn't know exactly what to look for. And I
know while he's in Tommy's room he sees the trophies, the
high school pictures . . ." Her voice faltered to a stop.

I longed to take her hand, to offer some silent comfort, but
I knew she did not want to break down in a public place, so
instead I beckoned the waitress and requested more coffee.
Then I said, "I gather Tommy is certain he can lick the problem. That must mean he isn't taking the most addictive kinds
of drugs."

"They're all addictive. Even the coffee in this cup has an
addictive drug in it, and so do cigarettes. You go up the scale
from there." Her face was set and grim again. "Tommy won't
say exactly what he takes. It's some combination of things.
He says it's too complicated to explain the way they work
together. You have to go to an expensive medical school to
learn that. Medical school! I wish Tommy had wanted to be
plumber!"

I chuckled, then I did reach out and pat her hand; she
seemed safely under control. "I can't tell you how I admire
you, Nancy. You must be worried sick, but you haven't lost

your fighting spirit, that's obvious. And it seems to me you're handling Tommy the best possible way."

She said earnestly, "Do you really think so? It's so hard to be sure. He's a fine boy, we all know that. He's going through something, that's what it is, and I think he'll come out of it and be the wonderful person he's capable of being." She set down her cup and sat gazing at it. "Of course I have to believe that, don't I?"

"I believe it too," I said, "I only wish I could help somehow. I could talk to him; tell him I'm rooting for him . . . ." But Nancy was shaking her head.

"I think he'd be very upset if he thought you knew. And upsetting him is what we want to avoid. Thanks anyway, Sally. It's good to know we have your support."

She was getting to her feet, and I did the same. It was after three; Granny might have awakened from her nap by now. I was about to urge Nancy to come along to see her when I stifled the impulse. If I should happen to find Granny in another of her talkative moods I wanted her all to myself.

On the way home I thought about Tommy and the six months he had allotted himself for a cure. Looking back at those of my friends who had gotten involved with heavy drugs, I wished him luck. Of course, that had been during the sixties. People were better informed now; certainly a medical student should know what he was up against. Six months. How strange it was that both Phil and Tommy faced six-month deadlines. I shuddered. Theirs were genuine deadlines, in the most sinister sense of the word. But I was suddenly appalled to realize that I had neglected to ask Phil what would happen if he did not come up with two hundred thousand dollars in the allotted time. As of course, barring some miracle, he would not.

Uncle John would have to be told, that was the only hope.

I pulled the car to a stop at the side of the road while I tried to think what to do. My palms were wet and my heart was pounding, not from anxiety alone, but because of anger over my own negligence. Why, I hadn't even asked Phil how much of the six-month period remained to him. I should know that before I appealed to Uncle John, that and the nature of Phil's penalty if he did not produce the money.

Let's see. I could call Phil the minute I got to Granny's, then hurry over to my uncle's house. Or perhaps it would be better to find a public phone. And what if Phil continued to insist on hiding his predicament from Uncle John? Did I tell him anyway? My mental confusion might have amused an observer—especially one who knew of the responsible job I had just accepted. It didn't amuse me, however; I hadn't felt such helpless panic since the final months of my marriage.

Sternly I ordered myself to be calm. It was very simple. I would not call Phil; I would go and tell Uncle John the problem and with family pride at stake he would, of course, arrange to borrow the money from Granny's funds. He had power of attorney; it would be very businesslike, a matter of giving Phil part of his inheritance in advance. If necessary, I would offer my share as well. Then, with Uncle John and me presenting a united front, Phil would be forced to accept our solution.

I felt better as I looked up and down the road to see if it was safe to change my course and swing around in the direction of Uncle John's house. Only one car was approaching; as soon as it passed I could pull out. Then as it came nearer I saw that it was Gillian Clark, headed the way I had meant to go, toward Uncle John's.

I reconsidered my plan. Although she might not be going directly to his house, if I wanted to see my uncle alone it would be safest to go home first and telephone him.

The car swept past and I glimpsed Gillian's intent face at

the wheel. It was somehow disturbing to realize that she might have just left Granny's house. There was nothing wrong with that, I told myself as I turned into the road. She looked in almost every day. But I felt a flutter of apprehension as I drove the short remaining distance and turned into Granny's drive.

I hastily parked my car and hurried up the steps, only to find that I was without my door key. I rang the bell and stood fidgeting for what seemed an interminable wait before Mrs. Berger opened the door. She was flushed and breathless, and as she stepped back to admit me she apologized for her delay in answering the bell.

"I was up with your grandmother," she said, the habitual nervous smile trembling on her lips. "Miss Clark asked me to stay with her until you or Miss Nelson arrived."

"But where is Jane Kelly?" I asked. "Isn't she here?"

"Well, no. She left around one, shortly after Miss Clark arrived." A look of alarm appeared in her pale eyes as she saw the consternation in my face. "Is something wrong, Mrs. Templeton? Your grandmother hasn't been alone for a minute. She's quite all right . . . ."

But I was halfway up the stairs before she finished. And when I entered Granny's room I was not surprised to find her sleeping peacefully. The curtains had been drawn, and in the soft lamplight she looked exactly as she had when I had entered that same room six days earlier.

CHAPTER 16

"Miss Clark said you were on your way over, and that your uncle had asked her to make sure you were left alone with your grandmother."

Jane Kelly's voice was unwavering. If not for the bright color in her cheeks I would have thought she had been unmoved by my angry outburst. For of course I had been waiting when she entered Granny's room that morning, and had immediately accused her of deserting her post on the previous afternoon. She had not been intimidated, however, and now as I listened she continued her explanation without apology.

"She said your uncle was greatly encouraged by the way Mrs. Ryder had reacted to your visits. She was close to tears when she talked about the beautiful relationship you had established. And I've got to admit I was taken in; probably because I agreed with her. It has been very touching to see you and your grandmother together lately." Jane's gaze was as level as her tone; she was not attempting to play on my emotions as Gillian Clark had on hers.

I simply nodded. My worry and anger had given me a terrible night's sleep. I had visited Granny's room repeatedly, and each time Miss Nelson's expression of cool inquiry as she looked up from her book had pushed me closer to the edge of hysteria. Finally I had gone downstairs and helped myself from the brandy decanter in the library, with the result that I now had a piercing headache in addition to demolished nerves. It was small wonder I had lashed out at Jane Kelly, and although the manner she had adopted was ameliorative, I was not yet ready to forgive her.

I said, "I know we've never spelled out how we feel about Gillian Clark; I didn't think we needed to. I thought I had made it clear that I didn't want Granny left alone with her ever, under any circumstances."

"That is true. But you must remember that Miss Clark has been in charge of this household for some time now, obviously with the full approval of your uncle."

"My uncle, ah yes . . ."

"Mrs. Templeton, before you say any more will you please let me finish?" Jane did not wait for a reply, but pulled a chair closer, watched as I automatically sank into it, then seated herself opposite me. Again I was reminded of the day of my arrival, when I had so imperiously demanded an explanation of my grandmother's condition, and she continued her story with the same poise she had displayed on that occasion.

"Before I could think of a plausible reason for preventing her, Miss Clark walked into the bedroom—we had been talking just outside the door—and your grandmother gave her a warm welcome. Miss Clark exclaimed over how well she seemed, and asked if she wouldn't love to have a cosy visit with her, just like they used to. And of course Mrs. Ryder said she would. It is not as easy to control the situation when Mrs. Ryder is alert; surely you can see that."

I said, "Yes, of course. You were in a spot, no question about it."

"Even so, I'm sure I could have found a way to stay if Miss

Clark hadn't said you were right behind her and would be here any minute."

I jumped to my feet, almost tipping over the little brocade chair I'd been sitting in. "That woman is incredible! It's diabolical the way she manipulates people. Uncle John—Granny—maybe even my brother." I paused, struck by the notion that Gillian's contribution to Phil's disaster might not have been as passive as it seemed.

Jane waited calmly. She had rested her case and, given the skillful nature of her opponent, I did not see how she could have acted any differently. I said, "I'm sorry, Jane. I apologize for blowing up at you, but it's very upsetting for me to see Granny in this state again. It was so wonderful the way she was opening up, coming back to life, it seemed. And I was learning so many things I'd never known about my mother . . ." I stopped, and we both looked bleakly over at the bed.

Granny had barely moved since the day before. Only the gentle rise and fall of the counterpane and the faint color in her cheeks indicated that she still lived. Her condition was worse than when I had arrived, for now she would eat nothing. Both Miss Nelson and Jane had found it impossible to make her swallow anything, even a sip of water.

I strode to the bedside and studied her peaceful face, then I turned to Jane. "How long do we let this go on before we call Dr. McGinnis?"

Jane came to stand beside me. "We should tell him immediately. He'll have to put her on IV if she continues to refuse any nourishment at all. Otherwise she'll become dehydrated."

I said, "Some other doctor must be covering for him this weekend. It would be quicker to get him than to track down Terry in Vermont."

"I'll call the office right now." Jane walked over to Granny's desk. With the telephone in her hand she hesitated. "Before the doctor comes I think there is something we should do."

Our eyes met in total understanding, and I nodded. "Yes. As soon as you make that call we'll check on the supply of Haldol."

Twenty-four hours later Terry McGinnis stood there with us in Granny's bedroom, listening to Jane report on the mixture and administration of the IV solution, and on the patient's continued unresponsive state.

I wondered whether she would touch on the matter of the Haldol syringes and, recalling Terry's disapproval of my earlier suspicions, fervently hoped she would not think it necessary. As in a way it was not; for when we had unlocked the medicine cabinet in Granny's bathroom we had seen the slim white boxes piled neatly as before. Jane had consulted the chart to discover that the number of remaining syringes corresponded with the recorded dosages, and when we opened the boxes, one after the other, we found that each contained a full, unused syringe.

I sat at Granny's desk while Terry and Jane conferred. I waited for them to be finished so I could ask the question on my mind, idly observing as I waited that it was too warm in the room and that beyond the closed window the silently tossing branches of the trees glistened in the sunlight. The leaves, which had been pale and tender a week ago, were fully developed now and had deepened in color to a vibrant green. I could imagine how firm and smooth one of them would feel in my fingers and the crisp snap with which it would break if I folded it sharply.

Yet on this day of almost unbearable spring beauty Terry and Betsy had cut short their weekend in Vermont, returning a day earlier than they had planned, without receiving word of Granny's changed condition.

It seemed to me as I watched him study the chart that Terry's usual aura of life-giving vitality was somewhat dimmed. There was compassion in the warm brown eyes when he turned them toward my grandmother's still figure, and when he touched her hands and her throat I knew his fingers were gentle, as always. But he seemed subdued, softened, like a photograph slightly out of focus; and when he approached me I saw an abstracted sadness in his face that seemed unconnected with the sickroom.

He brought a chair close to mine and sat down, and as I had several times before, I restrained an urge to reach out to him in tenderness. "I'm so glad you're here," I said softly. "Of course I'm sure Dr. Wilson did all the right things, but you're the one Granny responds to."

He smiled fleetingly. "No, you're the miracle worker. But I must tell you, Sally, there may not be much that either of us can do for her now."

I swallowed hard, blinking back the tears that instantly filled my eyes. I felt Terry's warm hand close on mine, and I grasped it tightly. "Hearing you say that makes it so . . . definite."

"I know. I'm sorry."

We sat in silence for a minute, not looking at each other, his hand firmly clasping mine. His closeness made my heart rise to my throat. The touch of his strong fingers meant so much to me that I abruptly pulled my hand free and sat back in my chair.

I said, "I've been waiting to ask you whether or not I should go to Chicago Monday, as I had planned. I don't suppose you can predict . . ."

"Your grandmother may remain in this state for a long time; or she may go tomorrow." He paused, frowning in the direction of the bed. "If she were conscious I would say your presence could be very helpful. As it is, though, I think it would be better for you to get away. How long will it be? A few days?"

I explained the reason for my trip and saw his grave expression brighten. We had never talked about my profession, and now I could see that he was regarding me in a new light, trying to place me in a role other than attentive granddaughter.

"This interview is important to me," I said, "but if Granny needs me it can wait. There are other jobs."

"But this sounds like the one you want." He said thoughtfully, "You're making a clean break with the past, aren't you? That takes real courage."

I must have looked startled, for he quickly added, "I think I told you that Mrs. Ryder used to read me your letters. I got the impression from them of someone who was fighting to solve her problems, trying to grow without becoming hard or bitter." His voice trailed off, and again I saw sadness in the brown eyes that studied me. "Your grandmother felt it too," he went on. "She always read from your letters herself, and often when she had finished there would be a particular look on her face. I'd say it was a mixture of disapproval of what she considered your mismanagement, and great affection and pride—tremendous pride. Because she could see that you weren't letting yourself be defeated, any more than she would have."

"Thank you for telling me that." I got to my feet and stood looking down at him. "Thank you even more for seeing it."

I walked over to the bed, where Granny lay in her stillness. She looked much as she had during the past week, yet I fancied a serenity in her features I had not seen before. In my thoughts I spoke to her. You needed to give me something and you did, I silently told her. You found a way to tell me what my mother was like. You made me feel what she felt. You caused me to weep with her tears. No one else in the world could have made that happen, and I will thank you for it as long as I live.

I turned away then and went out of the room and down the hall to pack for my trip.

In spite of Terry's reassurance I did not leave for Chicago until I had secured Jane Kelly's promise that she would provide no opportunity for Gillian Clark to be alone with Granny. The damage was done, apparently, for Terry held out little hope that Granny might emerge from what appeared to be a deeply comatose state. And, I reminded myself, my suspicions about Gillian were just that, suspicions only. I had no shred of proof that she had drugged my grandmother. Indeed, all indications pointed away from such an act, including lack of any motive that I could imagine.

On the plane I went over and over it in my mind. Certainly Gillian was madly in love with Uncle John. That much was clear in every look, every gesture, even the restraint I sometimes sensed when they were together. That he reciprocated with equal passion was, well, doubtful. I smiled to myself, recalling the consistently one-sided nature of my uncle's love affairs.

Their relationship was quite probably being bolstered by whatever funny business they were involved in with Michael Harris. It would take time and tact, but I felt confident that eventually I would winkle the details out of Uncle John. He had always been honest with me in the past, even when his stories shocked me. As soon as we got back on our old comfortable footing he would take me into his confidence again. Even so, I could imagine no way that Michael Harris could

benefit by Granny's being kept sedated. Nor Uncle John, nor
Gillian. And certainly not Philip, who stood at the brink of
ruin because of her condition.

My speculations made the flight seem short, and when I
reported to the headquarters of the company I was to work
for I realized that all that time spent thinking about Granny's
situation had been of inestimable value in another way. It had
given me the detachment I needed to keep from being overwhelmed by the scope of my new job.

This was a big agency, one of the top three in the country.
I had known that, of course, but it was sobering to think that
the five floors of offices in a lakefront tower now belonged
partly to me, along with the limousine that had met me at
the airport. I felt an odd sense of responsibility as I greeted
the pretty receptionist, and observed her smart silk dress and
heavy gold bracelet. She might have to make an unwelcome
change in her shopping habits if my work did not come up
to snuff.

The thought was more amusing than frightening, however,
and the same unexpected ironies continued to strike me
throughout my visit. The reception area was tasteful in the
extreme; all gray silk and wool, with the thick carpeting continuing up the walls to the ceiling, as if someone had neglected
to tell the installers where to stop. I had barely settled into
a pale leather chair when a second beautifully dressed young
woman, whom I remembered as the secretary to the president, appeared and invited me to accompany her to a lounge
for female executives, where I might freshen my hair and
makeup.

There I found silk-paneled walls and velvet-covered chairs
and a smiling maid, who gently removed my jacket and brushed
it while I sat at the mirrored dressing table. I was tempted
to remark that I no longer needed the job—this was all the

luxury I could handle in one lifetime; but the pride I saw in the two women's faces kept me silent.

The agency's president, Michael Alwyn, was a legendary figure in advertising, and his awareness of this was evident in the determined informality of his manner. He greeted me in shirtsleeves, and after he had kissed my cheek he flung one arm casually about my shoulders and led me to a sagging old leather sofa that faced the fireplace on the wall opposite his desk. On my first visit I had been impressed by the simplicity of his office, without taking in the details. Today I saw it as the stage set it surely was. The patches on the sofa were artfully placed; the colors of the rumpled rag rug were perfectly keyed to the heavy linen draperies. The brass coal scuttle, the antique Windsor chairs, the pine table littered with papers and ledgers, all added up to an effect of disarming folksiness. And when I saw Mike, as I had been urged to call him, sink onto the sofa and put his feet up on the low table, I realized that he was the key fixture in the display.

He was watching my reaction to his setting, it was clear, for he drawled, "Good old, straight-from-the shoulder midwestern honesty, that's what we're featurin' here, Miss Sally."

I was appalled until I saw the sparkle in his wise blue eyes. His face was alight with a virile intelligence that matched the strength I sensed in his powerful body. He was in his early fifties, I judged, and he took good care of himself. His skin had a ruddy glow, his stockiness seemed more muscle than fat, and though he sat quietly beside me he exuded an effect of restless energy, briefly restrained.

"You saw it right away, I could tell," he said, dropping the farmboy twang. "That's why I know we're going to hit it off. I don't have to spell out for you what a prospective client thinks when he passes through the rest of this fancy place and finds me here looking like the corner grocer. I'm a holdout, he thinks, defending what may be the last bastion of honest, square-shooting Americanism."

"God help us if you ever go into politics," I said; then as a smile began to spread across his face I went on, "Of course it's been suggested. And of course you can do more behind the scenes. I won't ask which party gets the benefit."

"It'll all come out in time." Ignoring the untidy heap of papers on the table before us, he got to his feet and went to his desk, beckoning me to follow. One folder lay on its uncluttered top, and when he handed it to me I saw that it was labeled Comprehensive Foods—Sally Templeton.

"We'll be meeting the client for lunch in an hour." Still standing behind his desk, Mike reached out and pressed a button. "I suggest that you study the contents of this folder to prepare yourself. Miss Parker will take you to an office you can use."

His eyes focused on a point behind me, and I turned to see that his secretary had entered as silently as she had materialized earlier in the reception room.

I held out my hand to Mike. "Thank you. I hope I can absorb enough of this to make some sense at lunch."

"I'm not worried about it, and don't you be." He shook my hand firmly and in his level gaze I actually did think I read "straight-from-the-shoulder midwestern honesty." "You're not taking some final exam today, Sally. I want you here; it's just a question of meeting the rest of the gang, that's all."

It went like that for two days; everyone was friendly, welcoming, eager to say how impressed they were by what they'd heard of me. We lunched and dined splendidly, in restaurants that could have been in New York, London, or Paris. When it came to mealtimes there was no pretense of folksy simplicity. Nor indeed did I see it displayed anywhere after that initial greeting in Mike's office.

There was nothing regional about the men and women I met, no characteristics of speech or dress that marked them as midwesterners. They would have been comfortable anywhere in the world. Their clothes, their casual good manners, as well as their good-humored intelligence stamped them as creatures of breeding and education—top executive material. They kept any insecurity or aggression well concealed, for the moment. I knew I would meet it eventually; it was interesting to speculate about whose would surface first.

Meanwhile we were an attractively assorted group of men and women, and I had more a sense of having been accepted as a member of an exclusive club than of being hired to do a job. When job talk was interjected it came in offhand, amusing references that seemed to reduce the selling of cornflakes and cake mixes to a task so enjoyable it might qualify as recreation. But the lighthearted aplomb was a skillful cover, for it was obvious, looking around the table, that such a battery of well-trained minds had not been assembled in the name of sociability. The pale young man who headed the client's advertising department had millions of dollars to dispense. That cold fact lay close beneath the veneer of easy cordiality. I knew that none of the people around me could forget it for an instant, while I, in my still peripheral connection, was able to see that there was something horrible about a cookie maker, however successful, wielding such power over the lives of talented men and women.

Perhaps that was why I reached the afternoon of the second day in a state of maladjustment. I didn't feel properly awed and grateful at the prospect of my glorious opportunity. Instead I kept thinking of wry asides I would have liked to share with Betsy. And would share, I vowed. She was the only person I knew who would understand the anomalies of the situation, with all its rich possibilities for future conflict.

Mike Alwyn maintained the mood he had established, avoiding any crass commercial references, but I observed a sharpening of his attention when I replied to a question or offered some comment. He was not with me all the time, but joined the various groupings for brief periods, like a considerate host making certain his guest was well cared for. Somehow, though, his manner implied that this tender treatment was only temporary, for soon I would not be a guest, but a member of the family, with duties and responsibilities to match those of my colleagues.

It was taken for granted in his mind. Any questions concerned when, not whether, and by the end of our second lunch the date was settled for me to report for work, and it had been decided which office I would occupy and who would be my secretary. Mike had suggested a nice young man for the job, and seemed surprised when the office manager told him I had chosen a woman instead.

He swung around in his chair and regarded me with raised eyebrows, his expression saying, Oh ho, what have we here, some semiliberated dame who hasn't the courage to take the power that God and I have offered her? Perhaps it was as a final act of independence that I refrained from explaining that I simply liked the girl better.

In the car going back to the office Mike asked whether I planned to stay until the next day and look for a place to live. Miss Parker had contacted a real estate broker who could show me some available apartments.

I hesitated. It was the sensible thing to do, while I had the use of the company flat and no urgent demands on my time. But I found myself saying that I must make several phone calls before I could decide. There was some family business

I might have to attend to; it would depend on my grandmother's condition. As I spoke I saw in my mind's eye the airline map I had examined on the plane, the short, straight line that went from Chicago to Grand Rapids.

In my temporary office at the agency I placed a call to Granny's house and heard, without surprise, that her condition was unchanged. She had not opened her eyes, nor spoken a word, and was still being given nourishment intravenously. Mrs. Berger said that Dr. McGinnis had been there twice on the preceding day, and that Philip and Uncle John had also come to see Granny, as had Gillian Clark.

I was pleased to hear of Phil's attentiveness; it gave me a warm glow to think he was filling in for me. He must have shared the new sense of closeness I had felt after our intimate talk that night at his house.

There was only one telephone message for me: Betsy Marsh would like me to call as soon as I returned. No word, then, from Martin Josefson, M.D., although six days had passed since our conversation. Another call from me was surely justified, especially since I found myself so unexpectedly in his part of the country.

Punching in the number on the sleek telephone, I thought of the scorn Granny had expressed at the idea of Kitty Ryder finding it necessary to go to Michigan. Clearly she had been wounded by my mother's refusal to tell her the reason. Perhaps I would soon be able to; and perhaps, like a fairy-tale princess, she would awaken when the right words were spoken.

As before, I was quickly connected to Martin Josefson—so quickly it made me wonder about his patient load—but this time I heard warm recognition in his voice.

"I have been remiss," he said slowly, "and I apologize. But, I felt my call would only increase your frustration because there is really nothing I can tell you over the phone."

"Over the phone," I repeated numbly. "You mean you did find my mother's records? You did treat her, but you can't tell me for what?"

There was a silence, then the doctor said carefully, "I did find records on a patient named Catherine Ryder, yes. Whether or not she was your mother is another question."

"Well, of course she was my mother. Why else would I have found your name in her desk? Why in the world would I be calling you . . . ?"

His voice was gentle but firm as he said, "Excuse me, Mrs. Templeton, but it is a matter of identity. You can see, can't you, that anyone might claim to be Catherine Ryder's daughter on the telephone? Before I can disclose any information regarding a patient I must be certain that the recipient is legally entitled to it."

"Then if I were to come to see you in person, with proof of my relationship . . . ?" My thoughts were darting about frantically. My birth certificate—where was it? I could not remember.

"If you came in person? With proof of identity? Yes, but it is quite a distance, Mrs. Templeton."

"Not at the moment, Dr. Josefson." I explained then about my visit to Chicago. "I can be in Grand Rapids in a few hours; that's no problem. But I can't think what I can offer in the way of an identifying document." As I spoke something nagged at my memory, some very recent occasion when I had listed my mother's name.

I spun out the conversation as best I could while mentally groping for that elusive moment. I remembered a long list of questions on a pale green sheet . . . my job application, that was it!

It came to me in a rush. I remembered how I had looked up in astonishment at being asked to give my mother's maiden name. Of what possible use could it be? And I recalled being told that this was a new tool for identification. In today's computerized archives there might be several Sally Templetons. There was likely to be only one whose mother was born Catherine Lewis, however. It was a refinement made necessary by the ever-increasing number of listings in which one person's name might be found.

"I've got it! I can do it; I just figured it out." I explained that I would get on the first available flight to Grand Rapids, and unless I was delayed until evening would take a taxi directly to his office. He said he would be glad to see me any time before seven, and gave me his home number in case I arrived later.

I hurried to Miss Parker's office to tell her my plans and ask her to call the airline for me. In minutes she had booked me a seat, ordered a car to take me to the airport, and instructed the personnel department to prepare a copy of my application form immediately. She also gave me the welcome news that Mike Alwyn was closeted with an important client and could not be disturbed. She would tell him good-bye and thank him for me; she didn't think I should take time to write a note; they would all be waiting eagerly for my return. And then I was in the elevator wondering why, as I plummeted toward the earth in that tight, enclosed space, my spirits seemed to be soaring like those of a bird released from its cage.

CHAPTER 17

Martin Josefson looked nothing like the kindly family physician I had pictured. He was small and wiry and Semitic. His narrow face was deeply creased; the black eyes that peered from behind rimless spectacles were shrewd and assessing. When he spoke it was a shock to hear the mellow voice I knew from our phone conversations; it did not seem to fit his appearance.

"You're Catherine Ryder's daughter, there's no question about it now that I see you." The dark eyes shone as he studied my face. Then he dropped my hand and held the chair before his desk until I had seated myself. He went around to the other side and sat down, and I saw that a manila folder rested on the surface of the desk. He folded his hands on top of it as he peered curiously across at me. "I am very sorry to hear that your mother died in such a tragic way."

I nodded. "Thank you." I had opened my handbag and was carefully extracting the job application bearing my mother's name. "I'm so glad I thought of bringing this. It saved me a trip to Connecticut and back."

I handed it to him, but he did not immediately examine it. The intelligent black eyes were still fixed on my face as he said, "I've never forgotten your mother, Mrs. Templeton. She was a delightful person."

"It's very nice to hear that. I was so young when she died, and then of course a child sees its mother differently. I suppose that's one reason I am so driven to learn all I can about her; I want to know her as an adult would." I was surprised to find myself discussing my mother without the usual overwhelming sorrow. Face to face with Dr. Josefson, I was stripped of all feeling except anticipation. My heart was knocking in my chest and I had poised myself so stiffly on the edge of the chair that my knees began to shake. I forced myself to sit back.

"Exactly how much do you know about your mother's . . . departure?" Dr. Josefson asked.

I told him, and he listened attentively, all the while keeping his hands folded on my mother's medical file in what seemed a protective attitude. He questioned me closely about my uncle's reluctance to give me any solid information, then shrugged and said, "Maybe he doesn't know the truth. It's altogether possible."

I waited, but he gestured for me to continue and so, feeling slightly defensive, I described the two occasions on which Granny had apparently taken me to be my mother. The doctor was fascinated as I described my momentary illusion of actually speaking with my mother's voice. I was anxious about his reaction; if he thought I was a spiritualistic nut he might think it best to give me no more fuel for fantasy.

But when I expressed that fear he shook his head energetically. "No, no, my dear. I can tell by the way you describe them that those episodes with your grandmother were very real and moving to you." He sat back with a faint, reflective smile on his face. "It's not true, of course, that only women are gifted with intuition; many men have it too. But I think this is a case of two especially intuitive people, you and your grandmother, each with a special need at this point in life, communicating in a totally instinctive way. Thinking she is speaking to your mother, your grandmother seeks answers she has always wanted. You cannot give the answers in words because you do not know them; but you reply with your feelings, and because your grandmother has so convincingly cast you in the role of your mother the feelings you express ring true."

My mouth was dry. I sat staring at him, speechless because he had found the way to say so precisely what I had sensed. It was as if he had reached into my mind and put my thoughts in order.

I saw the dark eyes narrow as he watched me, then he pushed back his chair and got to his feet. "I'm going to offer you a drink," he said, starting over to a cabinet that stood against the wall. When he reached it he turned and smiled at me. "I'll have one with you, I believe. This is proving a good deal more dramatic than I had anticipated."

I accepted the glass he brought me with gratitude. If I was already such a wreck, what would happen when he told me what I had come to learn?

We sipped our drinks while he offered to get me a hotel reservation for that night, then picked up the phone and did so. He hung up the phone and leaned forward to open my mother's folder. He sat with his eyes fixed on the top sheet in a way that told me he was not reading it, but thinking about what he would say. Finally he cleared his throat and looked up.

"You know that in 1953 a woman's life was very different from what it is, or can be, today." He looked at me inquiringly, and I nodded. "Particularly in sexual matters," he went on, "as I, of course, have especially good reason to know."

I started. His specialty—I had not even asked, and suddenly did not need to. I glanced from his face to the framed diplomas on the wall and there it was: obstetrics and gynecology.

"There is no reason to go into my philosophy at the moment, except to say that I have always been a liberal. A 'flaming liberal,' I remember my conservative friends calling me. It always amused me. Because of my outspoken defense of various unfashionable policies, such as women's rights, my colleagues sometimes referred cases to me that they were unwilling to undertake themselves." He paused and his black eyes held mine sternly, "Your mother came to me to request an abortion."

Certain words and phrases strike a woman with an impact that I think would not be felt by a man. I did not know then that one day the words "You are pregnant," would hit me with the solid body blow of Dr. Josefson's "abortion." It must go back before language, to a woman's primitive sense of responsibility for the ongoing stream of life.

It was especially jarring to link my own mother with the idea of abortion. That was bizarre, negative, an option available to me or my friends, if necessary, but inconceivable for our mothers.

I must have been shaking my head in denial, for I heard Dr. Josefson say, "That's right. In those days abortion was against the law unless the pregnancy imperiled the mother's life. Even then it was a weighty, risky matter, and women did not consider it unless they were desperate." He paused and sat watching me expectantly; I could not think why. He was the one with the story to tell.

"Did you perform an abortion on my mother?"

Dr. Josefson slowly shook his head. "No. She was mistaken in thinking I was one of those who, for a price, would skirt the law. I suggested an alternative, which she finally brought herself to accept: that she have her baby and immediately give it up for adoption."

Again I saw expectancy in his face. He was waiting for some response from me, but I was laboriously trying to adapt the picture of my mother that had formed in my mind to the surprising fact of her third pregnancy. It was an unwelcome pregnancy, that was clear, or she would not have gone to such lengths; but she was married, there was no disgrace. Then I gasped. Dates began to whirl about in my head until it felt like a computer gone wild. I gazed openmouthed at Dr. Josefson and saw his eyes soften with compassion as he watched me work it out.

"It wasn't my father's baby. It was several weeks after he was killed that she came to you, and he hadn't been home for . . ." I could not remember the last time I had seen my father. Of course I hadn't known it was going to be the last time; but I couldn't even recall seeing him in uniform. Had he come home at all, once he was in the army? How funny that I didn't know.

Dr. Josefson was speaking, and I gave him my attention. "I have been waiting for you to ask why your mother was unwilling to have her baby." He picked up the first page of her file once more, and this time I saw him skim rapidly over its contents. "Your mother was distraught at finding herself pregnant. She was almost suicidal. If it hadn't been for you and your brother I think she would have done harm to herself. She felt overwhelmed with guilt. She was so physically run down, between guilt and grief over your father's death, that it is surprising she didn't miscarry. She told me over and over that your father's death was her punishment."

I didn't realize that my face was streaming with tears until I felt them fall on my clenched hands. "She must have thought he would be alive if she hadn't . . . she must have thought she killed him. Oh, my poor mother, how awful. How she must have suffered . . . did you help her? What did you say to her?"

My hands were shaking so that I had difficulty opening my handbag to find a handkerchief, and Dr. Josefson quickly got to his feet and handed me a box of tissues. Just like Dr. Zeigler, I thought as I mopped my eyes and tried to compose myself. And indeed he seemed to have something of my therapist's empathy, for he said, "This is especially painful to you, I'm sure, because of those talks with your grandmother—that strong connection you felt."

"I suppose so," I replied. "But I think I could always have imagined how she would feel about this."

The doctor did not return to his seat behind the desk, but stood by the window toying with the cord of the blind as he went on, "I was moved by her situation, deeply moved. I felt your mother was as much a casualty of the war as was your father, and although I could not help her in the way she wished, I determined to do all I could to erase the guilt that was tormenting her so." He turned to me then and I saw on his face an almost boyish look of shyness and pride. He said, "I think I did help her with that, Mrs. Templeton. My wife and I together. My wife, who died two years ago, was a clinical psychologist. When she saw how disturbed I was by your mother's plight she insisted that I bring her to dinner. A real friendship developed between them."

"I'm so glad. I'm very glad she came to you. I wonder who gave her your name?"

"She told me; let me see." Dr. Josefson walked back to his desk, and I observed for the first time that he moved stiffly and that the long, slender fingers with which he picked up my mother's file were slightly bent from arthritis. He glanced again at the first page of her records, then smiled at me. "One of those conservative colleagues I mentioned gave my name to a friend of hers who lived in a suburb of Detroit. A childhood friend, I believe she told me." He examined the sheet of paper more closely, then replaced it. "Unfortunately, I did not record the name of her friend, only the physician."

"Did she live here then, until the baby was born?"

"Not here, Mrs. Templeton. I was practicing in Detroit at that time, and my wife found a furnished apartment for your mother, only a few blocks from the office."

"She must have been so lonely." I could see it, a cramped apartment filled with horrible furniture, orange and brown probably, and ghastly lampshades. How depressing it must have been, compared to Granny's beautiful house.

Dr. Josefson sat down in his desk chair. His face was reflective as he said, "Yes, she was lonely; but it was also a period of inner growth for her, I believe. It often happens to people who are forced to step out of their normal life pattern for a time, soldiers in the army, for example. My wife gave her some books to study, and I persuaded her to work as a volunteer in one of the hospitals—in the pediatrics ward. She missed you terribly, and it was good for her to be with children."

"I seem to remember letters from her. I wish now that I had saved them."

"I know she wrote to you frequently; less often to your grandmother, of course. There was so little she could tell her."

"And yet I think Granny would have understood. At least Granny as I have seen her recently; maybe not as she was then."

"While her grief for your father was so fresh?" Dr. Josefson wore again his faint, thoughtful smile. "It would have been very surprising if your mother had taken the chance."

"So then the baby was born, but my mother still didn't

come home. I guess. I only remember one visit, but maybe that was right after. Maybe she stayed longer than I think. It's hard to get it straight."

"You were very little—only five, is that right?" I nodded, and he continued, "Your memory is correct, however, at least as far as my knowledge goes. You see, the baby, a boy, was born with a rare malformation of the digestive tract. He could not be fed in the normal way, and there was very little hope that he could live for more than a few months."

"What did she do?" I whispered the words. My mother was turning into a tragic figure of awesome dimensions.

"The baby could not be put up for adoption, of course, nor could your mother bring herself to abandon him. It was a dilemma, but one that should have been of brief duration, for no one expected the child to survive." Dr. Josefson's dark eyes glinted behind his glasses. "He was a tough little fellow, though, and after three months he was not only alive, but growing and developing normally in other ways. Kitty was beginning to hope."

And while my mother lived through what was probably the most dramatic chapter of her life, what was I doing? Missing her a good deal at certain times, I supposed, but I must have been mainly preoccupied with normal five-year-old activities: playing in my sandbox, fighting with my brother. I was too little even to wonder very much about her absence, and when she returned for that brief visit I doubt that I questioned her. It was not until I was old enough to realize how strange it was that the torment began.

"A few weeks after the baby's birth I read of a surgeon at New York Hospital who had developed a technique for correcting tracheo-esophageal fistula. He had operated on ten children, with varying degrees of success. Some appeared to be able to live normal lives; others were being kept alive longer than expected, but still being fed tubally. I said nothing to Kitty about this. It seemed unkind to build her hopes, when even if this man could take her baby's case the outcome was unpredictable. But then . . ." Again Dr. Josefson consulted the file before him; he had gotten to the fourth page by now. He looked up at me and smiled. "Every time I saw Kitty she questioned me closely about the baby's chances, and soon I realized that she was reading medical books, talking to pediatricians, educating herself in every way she could. She was not ready to give up."

I grinned at him. "Bully for her," I said softly.

"Bully for her is exactly what I was saying to myself. Not only that; I was becoming infected with her optimism. Without saying anything to her I examined the baby carefully and found him to be in excellent condition, except of course, for the malformation that would make it impossible for him to grow up. He was strong and alert, obviously intelligent; physically and mentally he was in much better shape than the other babies in the ward who had similar disabilities."

"So you called the doctor in New York." As Dr. Josefson talked I was getting very excited about the little baby. He was more than my mother's problem now; he was a person I wanted to live.

"Yes, I did; and after receiving the data on the case, the X rays and so forth, he agreed to perform the operation. I didn't say a word to Kitty until then."

"What a good friend you were to her," I said. "And your wife too. She must have been involved in all this."

"Indeed she was. And when Kitty and the baby left for New York we gave them quite a send-off." He was silent then, staring dreamily into space for so long that I couldn't stand it.

"What happened? What was the outcome? Did the baby survive?"

The doctor's lean face turned somber. Once again he consulted my mother's file, and I saw that he had reached the last page. "The operation was successful. Kitty called to tell me, and I never heard such joy in anyone's voice. She seemed to have forgotten all her fears of scandal and disgrace, and of course I didn't spoil her happiness by pointing out that her dilemma had worsened—because now she was strongly attached to the child."

I too had put aside the fact of the baby's illegitimacy; it seemed a trivial point. "Of course she couldn't put him up for adoption, after all she'd been through. But what . . . ?"

"That is almost all I know." Dr. Josefson spoke so gently I could tell he felt he was letting me down. "Your mother and I talked again on the day before the baby was to leave the hospital. She said she had worked out a temporary arrangement, and would let me know when she had decided where she would go from there. I got the impression that she intended to take you and your brother and start a new life, with the baby of course. But she had to handle it carefully, she said, because of your grandmother. It was going to take a little time."

"And then she was killed."

"Yes, but I never knew that until you telephoned me. There was simply silence." The doctor sighed. He closed the folder containing my mother's records, and when he looked across at me I fancied that the creases in his lean face were carved deeper. "Naturally I checked with the surgeon, but he was as baffled as I. You see, Kitty had given him a fictitious address. Somewhere in Yonkers, I believe; it turned out to be a warehouse."

"But didn't she have to bring the baby in for a checkup?"

"She did that, once at least. And it must have been shortly afterward that she was killed."

"So, after all you had done for her, all you had gone through together, you never knew what became of her?"

He nodded silently. "It happens often. Physicians become caught up in their patients' problems and never learn the outcome." He pulled off his wire-rimmed spectacles and held them dangling in one hand. He looked strangely vulnerable without them, "It's one of the things I've never become used to. Many patients don't even complete their course of treatment. When they begin feeling better they push the whole episode from their minds. But Kitty, poor Kitty had a reason."

He rubbed his eyes with one hand, firmly, almost as if he were pushing back tears he would not allow himself to shed. It had gotten dark, I realized, and I felt a wave of remorse. I'd put this kind man through an exhausting session, and he had probably had a long, busy day before I arrived. I pushed back my chair and stood up.

"I'm sorry, Dr. Josefson; I didn't realize how late it was."

He too got to his feet and put his glasses on, his gnarled fingers delicately adjusting the wire temples over his ears. "Just let me put this away," he said, indicating the folder on his desk, "and I'll give you a ride to your hotel."

"If you can stand it, I have one more question," I said; then, seeing him begin to shake his head slowly, I knew that he could not give me the answer.

"She never told me. In all the months before and after the baby's birth, she never gave my wife or me the slightest clue." He sighed. "I begged her to put the name on the birth certificate for the child's sake, but she refused. In the space where the father's name should appear we had to say 'unknown.' "

CHAPTER 18

For the flight to New York I was given a window seat, and since the one beside me remained unoccupied, I was spared the task of making conversation. This was wonderful luck, for I desperately needed a period of suspended time, the sort that is found only in travel, when one is cut off from telephones, doorbells, desks, and papers, all the paraphernalia of an active life. In the humming aircraft, which seemed to hang motionless amid banks of soft white clouds, I felt separated from the world. I could give myself over completely to imagining what it must have been like for my mother to live through the poignant events Dr. Josefson had described.

I felt humbled by her story. Coming as it had on the heels of my Chicago trip, with all its implications of personal success, it was as if a ghostly hand had taken me by the shoulder and firmly turned me away from a fantasy vision to take a look at reality. So proud I was, or had been; so sure and smug with my handsome new office, my secretary, my impressive salary. And how trivial it seemed now, compared to the elemental truths that had governed my mother's life. I applied my energies to finding clever approaches to selling merchandise; she had given her mind and heart to loving, nurturing, grieving. Like a swimmer who plunges into a turbulent stream, she had involved herself with the raw stuff of life; while I, fearing the swift current, had busied myself on the safe and comfortable banks. I pictured my mother's torment when she had to separate herself from Philip and me in order to give birth to an infant she must instantly give away. To have that baby born with a deformity must have seemed a cruel joke, for then she was trapped. Whichever way she turned lay suffering, but she did not shrink from it. The thought made me proud.

I felt suddenly as though the one meaningful theme in my life had been the quest to know my mother. Now I had been rewarded in a way I could not have foreseen, for her tragic story had touched a wellspring deep within me, a source of truth and strength I had not known I possessed.

I would have done what she did; I knew it with absolute certainty. I could easily imagine being swept into an affair if I were a bored and lonely young mother. I could also see myself accepting the consequences as my mother had done; and after paying such a heavy price in the months of separation from her children, I could sense her joy when the doctors told her the baby's operation had been successful. It was worth every minute of her suffering if her baby was to live. And if the child had lived, as Dr. Josefson thought, what had become of him after my mother died?

Again I had the sense that my attention was directed by an unseen hand. I had been amazingly slow to see that it was important for me to consider the fate of that child, for he was my brother; or at least my half-brother. If he had survived my mother, where was he? Kitty had told Dr. Josefson that she had made temporary arrangements; fine, but what happened to the child after her death?

Clearly, neither her doctor nor the baby's surgeon knew anything about the arrangements or they would have communicated on the subject of the child's health. But Kitty must have confided in someone; she was not likely to have placed a convalescing infant in the care of total strangers. I tried to project myself into my mother's mind, but I could not capture the sense of oneness I had experienced before. That had simply come to me, I recalled, when the emotional climate was right; I had never deliberately sought it, and I soon gave up trying in order to consider another, equally tantalizing, question: the identity of the baby's father. Who was Kitty Ryder's lover? Now I squeezed my eyes shut, and concentrated on my hazy recollections of the time before my mother went away. I searched my memory for the figure of a man—a man in uniform? Probably.

The image I conjured up was ludicrous: Michael Harris in his dark suit and chauffeur's cap. Impatiently I pushed it aside, then my eyes flew open as I thought, wait a minute, it's a possibility. Was Michael Harris attractive? Perhaps he had been thirty years ago; especially to a lonely young woman enduring a long, tension-filled separation from her husband.

But even as the notion grew more logical I found myself discarding it. Although I had concluded (gratuitously) that my mother was a passionate woman who enjoyed sex, I did not see her as being lightly unfaithful—especially with a man in Michael's position. He was too close to the family; an affair between them would be uncomfortable, almost bizarre.

Uncle John? Equally bizarre; but I disqualified him for practical reasons, not on the obvious moral grounds. Ethics had never stood in the way of his desires, but he had not been around to take advantage of his brother's absence. His photograph stood among the others on Granny's dresser top. Like my father, he was in uniform and I had often observed the contrast between the two soldiers. John's expression of confident sophistication seemed to mock the earnest idealism I saw in William's face.

My uncle would know something though; that was clear to me now. Perhaps it was to him Kitty had confided her story, knowing that because of his fondness for her he might take an interest in the welfare of her baby; knowing, too, that he was likely to be more amused than shocked when he learned of her infidelity.

I glanced at my watch and my heart began to pound with excitement. The plane should be landing in thirty minutes; in less than two hours I could be in Connecticut getting the rest of my mother's story from Uncle John. When he heard what Dr. Josefson had told me he would see there was no longer any reason to keep his secret.

I spent the remainder of the flight in happy anticipation. Once the truth stood plain between us, my uncle and I could resume our former close, confiding relationship. I no longer felt angry because of his evasions; he had been protecting my mother, after all. I felt my heart swell with appreciation of his loyalty. Never again would I be so quick to condemn.

I was so preoccupied with thoughts of my uncle as the plane made its landing that when I stepped off the escalator and saw him standing inside the door of the terminal I felt dazed. I looked behind me for a face I might recognize. Uncle John would not have come out to La Guardia Airport to meet me.

I hurried forward, smiling with the fun of surprising him, but as I drew near my smile faded and my step slowed. Uncle John was not searching the crowd of arrivals. He wore an expression of unutterable sorrow as he watched me approach and I knew before I reached him and wordlessly grasped his hands that my grandmother was dead.

Granny's death was the first bereavement I suffered as an adult, and it taught me the complexity of grief. I remembered the period following my mother's death as a black abyss from which I gradually emerged into the bright years of childhood. Granny's loss brought forth a mixture of conflicting emotions. After the first tears I felt enormously grateful that in our few days together I had learned to know her as a personality distinct from the authoritarian figure of my childhood. I couldn't recall loving that stern autocrat as I had come to love the spirited old lady who, when she was able, had displayed such endearing originality of mind. Was it a fault in me that I had not seen her earlier for the person she was? I told myself that a child could not be expected to appreciate the subtleties of Granny's character, and then was swept with regret for the years we had spent apart after I had grown up and married. If only I had been near enough to see her on a frequent, casual basis, how my life might have been enhanced!

I felt certain, however, that until her own mental confusion allowed it she could never have given me the intimate understanding of my mother I now possessed. When she was healthy and alert she would have been too guarded; she would have protected Kitty's secret to the end. For I was convinced, as I reconstructed our scenes together, that Granny had guessed a good deal more about Kitty's predicament than she would reveal. I saw that she had pressed my mother only so far, sensing that to know the truth might destroy a structure that was precious to her beyond any other. She needed to know that Kitty would return; and she needed Kitty to know of the love that would always await her. Anything more than that might be better left unspoken, but she could not always suppress the anger she felt because this was so.

Dear Granny, I thought; it must have been so difficult to hold her tongue and try to keep her temper, to assume the burden of two small children with some semblance of good will. It must have seemed that the world she knew had shattered with the death of her son. I regretted that I had never seen that before, had never expressed any admiration for her strength.

I wandered into her room when I felt remorseful, as if in that setting where we had been close my feelings might have a chance of reaching her. I would stand at her dresser, idly touching her silver brushes, studying the familiar photographs in their gleaming frames. These things belonged to me now, I supposed; some of them, at least. No doubt they would be distributed among Uncle John, Philip, and me. I wondered how such matters were decided, and resolved in the same instant that I, of course, was to have my mother's picture.

I was amazed to feel a hot wave of anger at the notion that Phil might demand it for himself. I felt tempted to take the photograph to my room on the spot, but I was too uncertain about the legalities, and I did not wish to seem grabby. I did feel like punishing my brother, however, for I had been hurt and baffled to find on my return that he had again adopted the cold, pompous manner that had kept us such poor friends all our lives.

I could hardly believe that he was the same person who had confided his troubles to me only a few days earlier. That had been an evening of exhausting emotion, but it had shown me another side of my brother; it had opened a possibility of affection between us, which he now seemed determined to deny. Perhaps he had exerted himself to please me that night in some wild hope that I might find a solution to his problem. And now of course his problem was solved. His inheritance from Granny would more than take care of the debt he owed his firm. I winced as I thought of my noble intention to give him my share of Granny's estate if necessary, and to persuade Uncle John to help him. Now it was unlikely that my uncle would ever even know of Philip's foolish misjudgment.

* * *

Both my uncle and my brother spent a surprising amount of time at Granny's in the days between her death and her funeral. Surprising, at least, in contrast to the rarity of their visits during the final weeks of her life. It startled me to come upon one of them using the telephone in the library or talking with Mrs. Berger, and I realized that during the first week of my visit I had grown accustomed to having the house to myself, except for the staff.

That was when a sick old lady needed the care of women and doctors. Now that there were more worldly matters to be handled, such as obituary notices, funeral arrangements, and the disposition of a large estate, the male members of the family stood ready to lend the required authority. With the tactful assistance, of course, of Miss Gillian Clark.

It appeared to me that Granny's lawyer had taken on a sheen, that her always gleaming dark eyes had gained an electric sparkle, her smooth black hair more luster; when she smiled even the dazzling whiteness of her teeth seemed to have increased.

I was in a position to observe these details because Gillian too was a constant presence in the house. I seemed always to be interrupting her in conference with Uncle John or Philip, or both together. They would courteously make room for me and then resume their discussion of Granny's affairs: her stocks and bonds, her real estate investments, the taxes that would be levied by the state and federal governments. Gillian's voice throbbed on softly, endlessly, her long white fingers with the rosy nails flipping efficiently through sheafs of legal-size paper or swiftly penciling columns of figures on a ruled yellow pad. In her slim hand the pencil flew over the paper with a velvet touch. It was mesmerizing to watch, and when I wrenched my eyes away I saw that Phil and Uncle John appeared equally fascinated.

Or perhaps it was the meaning of the numbers Gillian was juggling that kept them staring so fixedly. My uncle's lips moved occasionally as he silently repeated a sum to himself, and Philip now and then asked Gillian to verify the notes he was taking on a yellow pad of his own. Clearly, both men were having a wonderful time, which I told myself was understandable in view of the fact that they were about to become quite rich. Of course my share of Granny's estate would be equal to Phil's and, I found myself reflecting nastily, I won't have to pay out two hundred thousand of it the minute I get it.

As the sheets of figures and lists of holdings were passed from hand to hand it became increasingly evident that Gillian actually had done a superb job of managing Granny's finances. In listing the stocks and bonds Gillian had noted their worth at the time she took over as well as their current values, and it was clear that she had bought and sold with almost uncanny perception. I saw Phil blink in astonishment as he glanced over the figures, and he then launched a series of questions that seemed to me embarrassingly like a cross-examination.

Gillian was not at all offended by this, but seemed almost to welcome Phil's astute queries. She sat up very straight, giving quick, sure answers in her smoothly modulated voice, and I saw her glance flash frequently toward Uncle John, as if to insure that he too recognized the extent to which her stewardship had benefited Granny's estate.

Oddly, my uncle did not respond as I would have expected, but sat frowning at his own copy of the figures, only occasionally looking up with a faint, abstracted smile. The poor dear doesn't really understand, I decided, and he's not going to ask any questions that might give him away. I was mistaken in this analysis, as it turned out. His indifference to Gillian's bids for attention had quite another basis, but it was to be some time before I understood that.

My own grasp of all the fiscal terminology was somewhat fuzzy, but I gathered that the estate was worth several million dollars, perhaps five or six including the proceeds from the sale of Granny's house and furniture. Taxes would take a goodly chunk, and of what remained half would go to Uncle John, with the other half split between Phil and me.

It was nice to know that I would be comfortably fixed, whether I worked or not. But better not think like that, I cautioned myself; and heaven help me if Mike Alwyn found out. He would picture incentive running out of me like sawdust out of a doll.

It was also nice to hear of the generous provisions Granny had made for Mrs. Berger and the other servants. Even Michael and Nancy Harris had been left a legacy of thirty thousand dollars; surprisingly large, I thought, considering that they had left Granny's service five years earlier. Tommy now would have added incentive for curing himself of his addiction. His father could easily afford to pay his tuition, and when he was able Tommy could resume his education without the need to hold an outside job. I wondered how many months remained of the six he had allotted himself. And Phil's six months. I had never asked where he stood on that ominous timetable, but of course it did not matter now.

After the first day I gave up trying to corner Uncle John so that I could question him about the whereabouts of my half-brother. It was impossible to catch him alone for more than a moment. When he was not conferring with Gillian he was involved in funeral arrangements. I wanted his full attention when I told him what I had learned from Dr. Josefson, and for that I would simply have to wait.

Meanwhile I was growing restless. I had called Betsy's office and been told that she had gone to Sardinia to see the Aga Khan. Neither Jane Kelly nor Terry McGinnis had come to the house since my return, and I missed them. We had been collaborators, in a sense, the three of us caring about Granny in a way that separated us from the others who were close to her. We wanted her to live—really wanted it, while Phil and Uncle John and even the ardently protesting Gillian appeared to have accepted the inevitability of her death. It increased my sense of loss to realize that Terry and Jane and I were no longer bound together. Our lives now would take us in different directions, and indeed if I ever saw Terry again it would probably be as Betsy's husband. One look at his face then would tell me whether he had paid too high a price to get her, either in forcing himself to conform to the demands of a Manhattan practice or in sensing the discontent Betsy would attempt to conceal in her role as country housewife.

Seeking distraction from such thoughts, I went to the library on the afternoon of the second day to get something to read. The door stood ajar, and I could hear the murmur of my uncle's voice from within, so I hesitated, then knocked lightly before I pushed the door open and entered the room.

Uncle John was seated at the desk, one hand resting on the telephone, which apparently he had just hung up. He was frowning thoughtfully into space, and when I greeted him he did not respond in kind, but said, "I've just had the darnedest talk with Terry McGinnis. He's ordering an autopsy to determine the exact cause of Mother's death. There's some reason to think . . ." He shook his head as if to clear it. "God, Sal, I can't believe this, but he says the circumstances are somewhat suspicious."

"An autopsy!" The thought of Granny's frail body being dissected by a team of doctors was so unpleasant that for a moment I was unable to react to the more shocking notion of foul play. Then it hit me. Terry had found reason to suspect that someone had taken a hand in Granny's death. Or Jane had found it. That seemed more likely. I recalled how on that first night I had found her shrinking into the shadows as she listened outside Granny's door. She had been protecting her then; she probably regarded the ordering of an autopsy as a final act of protection.

But surely her suspicions were groundless, a result of what I now saw to be her obsessive hatred of Gillian Clark. Jane had become so convinced that Gillian was drugging my grandmother that when Granny died Jane fantasized that it was Gillian's fault.

My uncle was speaking. "Apparently there was something strange about the intravenous solution. I don't know whether it was Terry or one of the nurses who discovered it . . . ."

I nodded, moving around the desk to the telephone. "It was Jane Kelly, I'm sure. I'll explain later why I'm so certain, but right now I've got to call her and see if we can stop this thing."

"Wait a minute, Sally, will you? It's too late to get it stopped. They sent the remaining IV solution to a lab for what Terry called toxic screening."

"Toxic? Are you saying they found that it was poisoned?"

"Not exactly." Uncle John picked up a pad on which he had penciled some notes. "It seems there was an imbalance in the liquid remaining in the bottle. What they were giving Mother was a mixture of salt, glucose, vitamins, and potassium. I guess that's the standard formula for someone in her condition." He peered more closely at his notes. "The potassium is necessary to balance the solution, if I've got it straight, but an overdose can be lethal. I remember that was explained to us when Father was dying." He looked up at me grimly. "Terry said the percentage of potassium in the liquid remaining in Mother's IV bottle was three hundred times what it should have been."

"But who would do such a thing? Why do that to a sick old

lady who is already dying? What in God's name would be the point?"

My uncle shrugged. "I can't imagine. It has to be the work of an unbalanced mentality. Maybe someone who wanted to put an end to her suffering? Do you suppose that was it?"

He looked suddenly hopeful. Certainly if someone had hastened Granny's death this theory would be the easiest to accept.

"But she wasn't suffering. You know that, Uncle John. She was in no pain; she was perfectly serene. It was only a question of time . . . ." I was trembling as I reached for the telephone. "I'm going to get hold of Jane Kelly and ask for an explanation of all this. Where was she while someone was tampering with the intravenous equipment? She or Miss Nelson should have prevented any opportunity . . ."

"You don't have to call her; she's upstairs now." I slowly replaced the telephone, staring wide-eyed at my uncle. "She came in about an hour ago, to go over the records or something. But you can't accuse her . . ."

I was out of the room before he completed the sentence. As I started up the stairs I heard him call to me from the open door of the library, but I did not turn. Muttering angrily, he pursued me up the steps, and outside Granny's partly open door he roughly seized my arm to stop me.

We faced each other, both panting. I managed a tremulous smile as I said softly, "Don't worry, Uncle John. Jane and I are good friends. I won't accuse her of anything." Very gently I removed his hand from my arm. "But I think it would be better if I talked to her alone, OK? I promise I will be tactful."

Reluctantly, with an uncertain frown gathering on his face, he stepped back and allowed me to enter Granny's bedroom myself.

CHAPTER 19

It was our first encounter since Granny's death; the first time we had been together in that pale, silken bedroom without the need to lower our voices. Even so, we could not speak at first, but embraced each other wordlessly and when we stepped apart our eyes were wet.

I dabbed at mine with my handkerchief, then took Jane's hand and drew her to a chair. I pulled another close and sat down in it myself, then I said, "Do you really think it's possible that someone deliberately added something to Granny's intravenous solution in order to kill her?" My fingers tightened on my damp, crumpled handkerchief. "God, Jane, I can hardly say the words. How could anyone actually do it? Especially to Granny?"

Jane's face contorted, she tightened her trembling lips before she spoke, "It does seem inconceivable," she said. "Mrs. Ryder was so . . . it is hard to imagine anyone taking any liberties, much less . . ."

"I know exactly what you're trying to say. But apparently there is someone who doesn't feel that way." I paused. "Don't be offended, Jane, please; but are you positive the potassium was in the right bottle? The one that was actually being used when . . . when she died?"

"Yes, I'm absolutely certain it was the right bottle. Dr. McGinnis was here when I disconnected it—I called him the instant it happened, of course—and there is no possibility of a mistake of that kind."

"Well, what made you suspect that someone might have tampered with the IV solution?"

Jane glanced nervously toward the empty bed, as if it were her duty to guard it still. "When Mrs. Ryder died so suddenly, in spite of what seemed her stabilized condition, I knew the time had come to tell Dr. McGinnis about my suspicions regarding the Haldol injections. He immediately ordered the IV bottle sent to the lab for screening. Then he questioned me very closely, as you might imagine."

I said, "I never understood why you didn't tell him as soon as you suspected someone was giving her extra injections of Haldol."

Jane's healthy, peasant face suddenly looked pinched. "I'll never be sure I did the right thing. I go over and over it in my mind. But, you see, I never found any solid evidence. I couldn't make any accusations when I had no proof that anyone was giving unauthorized medication."

"How about Granny's condition? The way she was when Gillian Clark visited her every day and the change in her when we managed to keep Gillian away. Are you saying that was coincidence?"

Jane sighed. "I don't know what to think any more, I'm so shocked by all this." She looked over at me wearily. "I made that same point to Dr. McGinnis, and I must say he became very thoughtful. But he said the kind of ups and downs she had are part of the pattern of the disease. He mentioned the

time you checked the Haldol supply together. Whoever wanted
to give an extra injection would have had to bring his own,
and that seems very unlikely, doesn't it?"

I said softly. "Gillian Clark's father was a doctor; did you
know that?"

Jane's hazel eyes widened briefly, then she said slowly, "No,
I didn't; but it doesn't take any medical training to add potassium to an IV solution. You simply inject it into the bottle."

"But it can't be widely known that potassium can kill a
person, or I should think I'd have heard of it myself. How
does it work, Jane? Why should it be beneficial in one amount
and lethal in another?"

"It's a matter of maintaining the balance necessary for the
functioning of the body's electrical system." She paused to
collect her thoughts, then said slowly, "Let's see how far back
I should go. You probably know that the heartbeat, along with
the action of other muscles, is regulated by a system of electrical conduction."

I shook my head. "No, I don't think that was ever explained
to me."

"Well, you've heard of the process of metabolism, of course."
I nodded and she went on. "The metabolic process requires
a precise balance in the body between sodium and potassium
to supply the electrical voltage necessary for excitation of the
brain and the muscles. When these electrolytes are in order,
an electrical current is propagated along the membranes; in
the heart muscle this causes the contraction needed for pump-
ing blood. The impulse starts in the sinus node . . ." She
stopped and looked over at me hopefully. "I can draw a dia-
gram if you like."

I smiled at her enthusiasm. "I get the general idea, thanks,
but what happens when there is too much of one of these
elements? How can that cause death?"

"An excessive amount of potassium in the system destroys

the delicate interchange necessary to create electrical voltage. The result is a change in the contraction of the heart muscle, an arrhythmia, sometimes a cessation. Obviously that causes death."

The implications of what Jane told me were appalling. It would be easy for any conscienceless person to dispatch a patient who was being kept alive with intravenous feeding. And if there existed no reason for suspicion, no autopsy would be performed; the crime would go undetected.

The thought made me edgy. I got to my feet and started for the french doors saying, "I think we need some air in here, don't you?"

I pulled the doors open and the thin embroidered curtains hanging beside them billowed up on the breeze that danced into the room. How sad to die in spring, I thought as I stepped out onto Granny's small balcony. Jane followed me and we stood in silence watching a tractor mower move slowly along the shrubs at the edge of the lawn. The pungent scent of fresh-clipped grass came to us and we both sniffed appreciatively.

I said slowly, "This is a crazy thought, I guess, but people must be pretty decent after all, or there would be very few old ladies left alive—few rich ones, at any rate."

Jane looked slightly shocked. "Human beings aren't really programmed to kill," she said. "Look at all the controversy over euthanasia. Even when a patient is enduring agonizing pain, there's a respect for life, for a higher authority . . ." She stopped, then went on thoughtfully, "You're right, of course; it does mean there is some goodness, or at least humility, in most of us."

"Or ignorance," I said, and again saw a flicker of dismay on Jane's earnest face. "These chemical reactions aren't widely known, quite obviously. Now who of the people around Granny would be that well informed? You, of course, and Terry, and

Miss Nelson, and, I'm sorry, but again I have to point out that Gillian's father was a doctor."

Jane said slowly, "As I recall, Miss Clark visited your grandmother just once while you were away, and that was to look in for only a moment. I was here the whole time."

"But she might have come again when you were off duty; isn't that possible?" Jane nodded in silence, and I continued, "What about other visitors? When I called from Chicago Mrs. Berger told me my brother had come to see Granny, and so had my uncle. It pleased me because they had been around so little, as you know."

Jane's brief, humorless smile told me our thoughts were now in perfect accord. She said, "Yes, they were very attentive. Your uncle came every day, and your brother was here more than once on Tuesday."

"Twice in one day? Oh, but that was the day she died."

"Mr. Ryder said he was having his car repaired here in town, so he stopped by in the morning to arrange for Mrs. Berger to pick him up at the garage. He was in and out most of the day."

"I suppose Mrs. Berger came in occasionally herself. And how about Nancy Harris? I saw her just before I left, and I urged her to come to see Granny."

The lawn mower had completed its outer circuit and begun the second sweep, which brought it closer to the house. Jane waited impatiently for the noisy machine to pass, then she exclaimed, "I knew there was something I'd forgotten to tell you. Nancy Harris hasn't been here, but her son, Tommy, came to see Mrs. Ryder. He's a medical student, you know."

"Yes, I know. In fact he told me that he would like to examine Granny, but I'm afraid I never mentioned it to you. I'm sorry. I don't suppose you allowed it, since you were so unprepared."

"Well, Dr. McGinnis had called and told me it would be all right. He met Tom Harris here so they could discuss your grandmother's condition, but the examination—a cursory one—was finished by the time he arrived." She smiled reminiscently. "He's a lovely young man, that Tom Harris, and he was wonderfully gentle with Mrs. Ryder. He'll make a fine doctor, I'm sure."

Then Tommy must have been at his best. It was little to go on, but mentally I crossed my fingers.

"What about the supplies for Granny's IV injections: the potassium, especially. Where was all that kept?"

Jane frowned. "It was right here in the bedroom. I set up a little dispensary over there on Mrs. Ryder's desk. No one was using it, you see; so I kept the chart and the medications on it and the boxes of supplies piled on the floor next to it."

"And I suppose everything was clearly labeled?"

"Oh yes, it has to be, to save time."

The lawn mower was approaching once more. I started to speak, then shrugged helplessly as its determined whir grew steadily louder. When the machine had come within fifty feet of the house the noise was unbearable. I started to go back into Granny's bedroom, gesturing for Jane to follow me, when suddenly the mower fell silent. Its engine had gone dead, and in the abrupt, unexpected quiet I heard another sound, the unmistakable harsh tones of voices raised in argument: a man's and a woman's, coming through the open french doors of the library below.

"I do not have to account to you for one thing!" That was Gillian Clark, her throaty contralto pulsing with outrage.

In reply, more hotly furious than I had ever heard it, came the voice of my brother saying, "I'll have my own lawyers look into that."

They too must have become aware of the silence, for I

heard fast, hurrying steps, then the sound of the doors being pulled shut. The argument continued, however. Bending over the balcony rail as far as I dared, I could hear the angry throb of their voices, though I could no longer make out the words.

The mower started up again, and Jane and I quickly entered the bedroom and closed the balcony doors behind us. I stood uncertainly just inside, my eyes fixed on Jane's, which were bright with speculation. She had heard the voices too, of course. We stayed like that for half a minute, then I whispered, "I'm going downstairs to listen."

Jane nodded, sharply, just once. Her lips were parted in excitement, but she said nothing, just watched without moving as I walked quietly out into the hall.

The library door was solid walnut. I remembered how fruitlessly Philip and I had listened there when we were children, hoping to overhear some discussion of our Christmas presents. Now, because Phil's and Gillian's voices were raised in anger, I could distinguish a few words and phrases. I heard the name Harris spoken by one of them, then the other. Why would they argue about the Harrises? Then I was astonished to hear Gillian spit my uncle's name, John Ryder, in a tone of utter contempt.

"If you knew; if you were smart enough to see what's right before your eyes . . ." The resonant voice drummed on, but I could not make out her next words.

They were quickly cut off, in any case, by an inaudible outburst from Philip, ending with the suddenly distinct phrase, "This family is finished with you."

When Gillian spoke, her voice had gone an octave higher. "Ask John Ryder about the Harris boy. See how he stalls you off. He's a past master at stalling, that . . ."

The rest was lost in the sound of the ubiquitous power

mower, its relentless drone now pouring through the open front door.

Cursing, I ran to close it. I had just slammed it shut when the library doors were flung open. Gillian Clark stalked into the hall, her high heels striking the floor with a firm, metallic sound, her arms swinging like a soldier's. Her head was held high, her chin pointed forward, and although her dark eyes blazed as she marched toward me, she did not seem to see me there against the door. I knew what it was to be invisible as I moved aside so she could reach the knob, then watched her walk through the doorway and down the flagstone steps to the gravel drive.

I heard a rasping intake of breath and turned to see my brother emerging from the library. He was a shocking sight. His face was bone white, the skin stretched taut against the sharp planes of jaw and cheekbones, his pale eyes glittering. He did not seem to see me either, but strode across the hall and through the door, no doubt to deliver a final riposte. But as he reached the first of the flagstone steps I heard the roar of an engine, followed instantly by a shower of gravel, and Gillian's powerful car shot, swaying, past the house.

Phil stumbled down the first two steps as if he meant to run after his escaping adversary, then he stopped, reaching out to steady himself on the black iron railing. In a moment he slowly turned and I saw that the anger had left his tense, white face to be replaced by the most heartbreaking look of defeat. I ran to him and seized him by the shoulders. He sagged against me and, clutching awkwardly at his shirt, I pulled him down to sit beside me on the step.

"What is it? Phil, what were you fighting about? What has she done?" I was helplessly patting at him as I spoke, straightening his shirt, touching his hair. His pale face had acquired a frightening sheen of perspiration.

"She's crazy," he muttered, "she must be. Or Uncle John is; maybe both. They're in some crazy plot . . ." He did not look at me, but into the distance, fumbling his words as he tried to think.

"Tell me, Phil. What started it? What did she tell you that was so shocking? Why are you so upset?"

He turned to me then, seeming at last to realize who I was. "I simply asked her when we would get our money, our share of Granny's estate, and she went absolutely bonkers." Phil took a deep breath. He reached up as if to smooth his hair, then forgot his purpose and lowered his hand uncertainly. He said wonderingly, "I think Uncle John must have given her the air. That's the only way I can account for it."

I stood up and took Phil's hand to pull him to his feet. "Let's go in," I said, "and get you some coffee or a drink. You look as if you're about to collapse."

He did not protest, but followed me almost meekly into the library. He was back, the brother who needed my love and protection. If only he could be this human when things were going well for him, I thought fleetingly. I mixed him a stiff gin and tonic and one for myself as well, then I opened the french doors to refresh the hate-charged atmosphere of the room. Phil paced slowly back and forth, sipping his drink, while I sat down in the desk chair to hear his story.

He said, "You know I had good reason to ask about the money." Then he swung around and glared at me angrily. "But who wouldn't want to know? It seems natural to me to wonder when you're going to collect an inheritance."

I nodded. "I don't see anything wrong with the question, even if you didn't need it so desperately." I remembered then what I had meant for so long to ask him. "What is your deadline for raising the money, Phil? You never told me."

His face seemed to go a shade whiter. It was once more stark and skeletal as he replied, "The deadline was Wednesday, April fourteenth. I'll never forget that date as long as I live."

"The day Granny died," I murmured.

I regretted my words instantly, for I saw Phil's whole body droop. He sank into a chair, placing his glass on the table beside it so shakily that some of the drink splashed out and ran down the side. He lowered his face into his hands and his shoulders quivered convulsively.

I jumped up and hurried over to him. "Oh, Phil, I'm sorry. What a time to remind you—after that awful scene with Gillian—and the strain you've been under."

I tried to put my arms around him, but he pushed me away. He straightened and fumbled in his pocket for a handkerchief, and I turned away to allow him to regain his composure.

He drew a long sigh, then mustered the quivering semblance of a smile as he looked over at me. He said, "The old nerves are pretty shot, I guess," and I had to restrain myself from running over to comfort him again.

Instead I said softly, "I'm glad to see you weep for Granny, Phil. You've always been so good at hiding your feelings, unlike me. I think it's made a distance between us."

He did not reply directly, but the tremulous smile slowly left his face. He stared at me broodingly, and I thought perhaps he was searching for a way to tell me how he felt, but when he spoke it was once again on the subject of Gillian. "Well, anyway, she refused to give me any kind of rational answer, and when I pressed her, told her I had a real need to know, she started yelling about how greedy we all were in this family. Greedy and stupid, both. And how if it weren't for her Granny's fortune might have been totally wiped out. By Uncle John, I gathered."

"I heard her say something about Uncle John and the Harris boy. What's the connection there?"

"God, Sally, you won't believe it. This is what made me

think she really had lost her mind." Phil shook his head in wonderment. "She claims Tommy Harris is related to us somehow. That's one way she protected our interests, she said, because if Granny had known she would have left a big chunk of her estate to him. Now, I ask you, how could Tommy be related to us and Granny not know? It doesn't make any goddamn sense."

As he spoke I slowly got to my feet. I might have been a puppet, so mindlessly did I start for the door. I said nothing. I simply glided past my brother like a sleepwalker, out of the room, through the hall where I automatically picked up my handbag from the table, then out the front door and down the steps to my car. As I climbed into it I heard Phil calling to me. I was aware of his bewilderment, but I had no time to spare. It was imperative for me to get to my uncle before Gillian Clark. Not to protect him from her rage, but to hear from the lips of the one person who knew it, the full truth about my mother.

CHAPTER 20

I am not the avenging angel type. I'm too slight physically and I'm also too uncertain; my emotions are close to the surface and I'm easily swayed to tears or laughter. When in a professional situation I managed a display of authority I always felt like a fraud. So when I thought of it afterward I felt pleased with the way I faced Uncle John that day. I wasn't shrill; I didn't cry; I didn't coax. When he tried to draw me to him for a hug I quietly stepped back a pace.

He hadn't answered the door, so I had gone around the house and found him sitting on the screened porch reading a magazine. He jumped up, delighted and surprised to see me, and I simply watched him in silence until he finally realized this was not an ordinary visit and stopped exclaiming.

His guard went up at the same time; I saw it in his eyes, but it didn't worry me.

I said in a level tone, "I have seen Dr. Josefson and he has told me that my mother had a baby a few months before she died." I paused. Even now Uncle John was assuming an expression of puzzlement, as if he had no idea what I was talking about.

He said, "Josefson? Is that the fellow you were trying to track down?"

"You know very well it is, Uncle John, and now I know why you were, shall we say, less than helpful?"

"I can't imagine what any Dr. Josefson has to do with me." He turned away and reached for a glass of iced tea that stood on the table. "Can I give you some tea, Sal? Or a drink?"

"Please, Uncle John, can't you understand that I know almost the whole story? I didn't until today." He looked around, frowning, and I said, "I'm afraid it was your friend, Gillian, who filled in the gaps for me. Without meaning to, of course."

"Gillian told you some absurd story? Well, that's understandable, I guess." He smiled at me, the old rueful grin, then he sank into a chair, indicating the one opposite for me.

I stayed on my feet, "You've split up with her, I gather. I must say, it seems like strange timing, with Granny's estate to be settled."

"These matters are not always easy to control, you know." He was looking up at me with the naughty-little-boy twinkle that usually proved so effective. "Sit down, Sal," he said, "and I'll explain Gillian Clark to you."

I did take the chair; it was too awkward to stand peering down into his face, but he got no chummy, gossipy response from me. "I don't need Gillian Clark explained," I said gravely. "A child could see that she's wild about you, that she's been counting on marrying you, and that you've apparently just made it clear that you have no such intention. I don't know why she was surprised, it's the way you always treat women, though I had thought Gillian Clark might be an exception because she's been so useful to you."

His expression remained quizzical as he studied my face. "I'm afraid the business world has hardened you, Sally. I hadn't seen it before. It's an unattractive trait in a woman, you know."

"Yes, well, sorry. Now what are unattractive traits in men, do you suppose? Vanity? Selfishness? Dishonesty?" His slender fingers tightened on the sweating tea glass; the smile was fading from his lean, handsome face. "How about adultery? How about seducing your brother's wife? How does that rate—attractive or unattractive?"

On the last words I had risen to my feet and so had my uncle. For the first time ever I saw his face turn white, and I thought I detected a flicker of fear in the naked anger that flared in his eyes.

"What the hell are you talking about?"

"You and my mother, that's what I'm talking about. You had an affair while my father was overseas. She had a baby; that's why she went away and left me. And when she was killed the Harrises raised her baby. Everybody thinks he is their son." I had to stop; I was gasping for breath. Putting it into words made it so real, so overwhelming, that I thought I might faint. I would not faint, though; I had work to do. I gritted my teeth and dug my nails into my palms.

My uncle was shaking his head disgustedly. "You must have lost your mind. I should have realized you were headed for trouble when you told me about those conversations you had with Mother—or thought you had. You'd better get some help, Sally."

I said, "Where were you stationed during the Korean War?"

His eyes narrowed as he said slowly, "Several places. Why?"

"Were you overseas when my father was?"

"Part of the time."

"And part of the time you were based near New York, perhaps?"

"Sally, you're torturing yourself. You're putting together a fantasy in your mind—trying to make the facts fit the story you've concocted." He reached out, rather tentatively, I noticed, and gently squeezed my shoulder. "You're only going to make yourself miserable if you go on with this, you know."

I did not move. I looked into his eyes and said, "I've always thought you were the most attractive, the most lovable man in the world. If you weren't my uncle I could easily imagine falling in love with you. And I've learned enough about my mother now to see that she probably felt the same way." My uncle dropped his hand from my shoulder and turned away. I went on talking; I couldn't seem to stop. "Not while my father was around, of course. I gather they grew up in love. He must have monopolized her completely. But when he had been away for months, their first real separation; when she was even lonelier than most war widows because she had had his devoted attention ever since childhood; and when you turned up looking a little like him, but different too, fascinatingly different . . ."

"I did nothing! We did nothing when I came home on leave, and we were there in the house with every opportunity. Not a word, not a touch . . . nothing!" He had swung around and his eyes bored into mine with savage insistence. For a moment he was devoid of artifice; but would an honest man make such a point of it, I wondered? Would those days of forbearance have seemed so noteworthy if they had not been followed by others he recalled less virtuously?

"When you were there in the house, yes, I can believe you made the effort. Granny was there, after all; and Philip and I were running around. My father's picture was on the piano, probably the same one that's there now. I can imagine you in your room at night and my mother in hers, trying to fall asleep, thinking of each other . . ."

My uncle had slowly lowered himself into a chair as I talked on in a soothing monotone.

"You had never had her to yourself before," I said. "Bill had always been there, and you would see their closeness, and the way she looked at him. . . . Was she really the prettiest girl in town, Uncle John? That's what you told me once." My voice had dropped almost to a whisper, for I could see that he had fallen into a reverie. Without knowing what I was doing I had woven a mood and he was lost in it.

When he spoke his voice was gentle. "It wasn't just beauty that Kitty had. Even when she was a child there was something about her that caught me and made me want to watch her face, to make her laugh. Later, in sports . . . if I made a touchdown or a goal I would hope she was watching. Even though she was always with Bill; that was all right because I thought we'd be together someday. He kept her close to us, and eventually she would see me, really see *me*. I felt sure it would happen, almost up to their wedding."

"And meanwhile you had girls of your own, plenty of them, I'm sure."

"Oh yes, I had a good time; it was impossible not to in those days. Living here, all of us going to nearby schools, meeting in New York during vacations, using our families' clubs and summer houses and boats, with no worries about drugs or wars or politics . . . all that was in the future, your future, as it turned out." He sighed. "I suppose everyone feels nostalgic about that time of life, but I really do think it was better for our generation—until the war, of course."

"Did you and my father enlist at the same time?"

"I joined the army the minute we entered the war, but Bill stalled as long as he could. He had you and Phil by then, and he didn't want to leave Kitty." He frowned, going over it in his mind. "I think I had finished a tour of duty in Korea about the time Bill signed up. They sent me home for training on some new artillery, so I was stationed at Fort Dix when he went overseas."

"I hadn't thought of that. I just assumed you were both away at the same time, I guess because I don't remember seeing you around here. But I was so little . . ."

"After that first time I stayed away. It was too difficult to be in the same house with Kitty, so I spent my leaves in New York. Often Mother would come in to see me. I wonder if she ever guessed why I didn't go out to the house."

"I have a feeling she did. At least after my father was killed. Did she ever press you for a reason?" Uncle John shook his head. A faint smile appeared on his face, and I knew he was enjoying the memory of his mother's tact.

"It must have been tough for her, Sal, not to say anything all those years. There were lots of clues: I always had pictures of Kitty and Bill in my room; I always asked about them, both of them of course, when I called home from school." His eyes crinkled shut as if he were suddenly in pain. "Gosh, before I went away I even used to write poems about her, or to her. Mother must have seen them in my room. Sometimes I'd come home from a date and Bill would still be out, and I would try to write it all down. I suppose I thought something would happen to me and she would find these wonderful poems and realize at last . . ."

"And have them published, and you would be famous—a superb young talent, tragically cut down in his prime. Like Rupert Brooke, and just as good-looking."

My uncle's appreciative grin quickly faded to be replaced by the brooding expression I had often seen before. I knew why now; it was my resemblance to Kitty. I wondered whether it was torture for him to see me or a reminder he cherished, but I dared not ask him and risk this incredible moment of sharing. Too frequently I had seen him withdraw as a result of my prodding.

With his eyes still fixed on my face he grasped the arms of

his wicker chair and pushed himself to his feet. He said, "I wonder if you can imagine what it is like to be telling you all this."

I smiled up at him timorously, afraid to speak, afraid he was announcing the end of his memoir, but instead he reached out and lightly caressed my cheek. He said, "As long as we've gone this far I'd like to tell you the rest of it. I want you to see how it was for Kitty and me. But I need a drink to do it. What do you say?"

I nodded, still speechless, then stayed in my chair sifting my own sensations while he went to the kitchen. For him it must have been a much-needed catharsis to share the secret he had guarded for so long. For me it was a feeling of reaching bedrock at last, of feet firmly settling on long-sought ground. The relief was so enormous it was certain to outweigh any pain I might have to endure.

So I was ready when my uncle returned to the porch and relived for me the summer when Kitty Ryder became his at last.

"We didn't plan it, you understand. I had no idea of meeting her when I went to the city on leave." Uncle John had settled himself in the wicker chair once more. With his long legs stretched before him, his head resting against the seatback, he gazed past me with half-closed eyes. "I was going along East Fifty-eighth Street when one of those summer showers hit; it was July, around the tenth, I think. I made for the first recessed doorway and stood there feeling amused because it was the entrance to Schrafft's." He sat up straighter, smiling at the memory, "Do you remember them?"

I shook my head, and he said, "Well, they were a chain of tearooms that had grown into restaurants without losing their original gentility." He narrowed his eyes, still grinning. "Small round tables occupied by women wearing hats; tall, dignified hostesses in black dresses with white collars; a hum of ladylike voices. They were always crowded, but not with our sort of people. Nothing would have induced me to go inside—or so I thought.

"Anyway, I was standing there, feeling superior to all the polite, boring ladies I could see through the glass doors, when a woman scurried in to stand beside me. She was bent over, holding a soggy newspaper over her head, laughing and gasping because she was so wet, and then she looked up at me and it was Kitty." His eyes sparkled now at the surprise of it. "You can imagine the shock, for both of us. We stood there, chattering away, until I saw that she was shivering. She had gotten quite soaked, and the rain was still hammering down, so I suggested we go into Schrafft's and get some hot tea. I never felt the same about those places after that day."

He paused and slowly reached for the highball on the table beside him. "We had tea and cookies or something, and finally the rain stopped and we went outside again. We had never stopped talking, and we stood on the sidewalk, still going on a mile a minute until Kitty looked at her watch and said she had to catch her train. I flagged a taxi and rode to Grand Central with her. I remember the afternoon sun breaking through the black rain clouds and making the streets and buildings shine like patent leather, and the puddles that sent sheets of water spraying up beside our cab."

I could see it as he talked, and smell the unique, fresh scent of the city after a summer storm.

"We didn't say much on the way to the station. I think we both felt shy suddenly, sitting together in the steamy cab. Kitty's hair was soft and loose and the dampness had made it curl up at the ends the way it used to when she was a child. I remember I leaned across her to roll down her window, and a strand of her hair blew against my face. I caught a whiff of her Mimosa perfume. I felt dazed. It was like a dream."

He fell silent, and there was such tenderness in his eyes that I had to look away. I cleared my throat, and he resumed his narrative, lingering over the words as if to prolong the memory.

"The taxi entrance was full when we pulled up, so Kitty jumped out at the sidewalk there on Vanderbilt Avenue. I stayed in the taxi, saying good-bye with the door open, and then when she turned away and started into the station something made me call after her. I called her name and she turned around, starting to smile as if she'd been expecting it. I said, 'I've got to be back at Schrafft's two weeks from today. How about you?' She laughed, the happiest laugh, nodding and waving at the same time, then she called back, 'What a coincidence, so do I!' "

I sighed, curling up my toes with pleasure. I could see them so clearly. I could feel the excitement of the dare they were tossing out to one another.

My uncle sighed too. "It's hard to describe the way we felt about it. All I know is that it wasn't real life; it was time out, with no connection to past or future. We were alone in a bubble, cut off from family, friends, duties, the war; we had no responsibilities, no tensions. I don't think we had ever been in New York together, even with a group, and that removed it all the more from reality. Have you ever spent a summer in New York, Sal?"

"Never; no. The heat must be excruciating."

"The heat increased the unreality of it—as if we were in a story by Maugham. I never think of that time without a background of electric fans going; in the small restaurants we went to, and in the apartment on Fifty-fourth Street I'd borrowed from a friend. We couldn't use Mother's apartment, of course, partly because the doormen and elevator boys knew us, and partly because it was involved with all that we were pretending did not exist."

"Where did Granny think Kitty was going? How did she explain all those trips to New York?"

Uncle John smiled, and again his eyes held a tenderness I had never seen until that day. "Mother really loved Kitty; she was like a real daughter to her, and she worried about her getting restless and bored with Bill away. So she encouraged her to get into the city, to the museums, the theater, and to see her college friends who were in the same boat." He grinned over at me. "The funny thing was that Kitty was never particularly interested in the arts and she had never cared much about going in to New York. Then all of a sudden it's the Impressionists at the Museum of Modern Art, Menuhin playing at Carnegie Hall, a matinee of *Guys and Dolls*. Mother must have thought she had finally succeeded in getting Kitty to enjoy the things she should."

I must have looked disapproving, for he said quickly, "We didn't make fun of her, Sally, don't think that. But building a cultural framework to cover our meetings brought out our own creativity. We would pick up bulletins from the museums and concert halls, then read the reviews of the exhibits and recitals Kitty was supposed to have seen. She said she'd never thought having an affair would be like taking a course in art appreciation."

I laughed. It was startling not only to hear my mother quoted, but to find myself enjoying her sardonic viewpoint.

"We invented a whole cast of characters too, old friends of Kitty's from Wellesley who supposedly came to New York. They had to be from out of town, or Mother would have wondered why Kitty didn't see them more often. We had a wonderful time making up names: Bunny d'Alessandrio, for instance, whose parents had disowned her for marrying a San Francisco fishing boat captain; or Elaine Hogenwelter Tremaine, who admitted that she had married her husband for his name alone. We would lie in bed, laughing . . ."

I supposed it was the mention of bed that made him stop abruptly; but I said in the most casual, relaxed tone I could muster, "Wasn't it a problem to spend the night? Where did she tell Granny she was then?"

Uncle John picked up his glass and studied it closely while he rattled the melting ice. "There weren't many nights. She would have had to leave a phone number where she could be reached, because of you and Phil, and that meant working out such an elaborate lie she was afraid she'd never keep it straight. Oh, a couple of times a real friend came to town, her roommate, as a matter of fact, from Michigan."

I sat up straight. "The girl who told her about Dr. Josefson, I'll bet."

My uncle nodded. "Probably. She was the kind who would have known of an abortionist."

"He isn't. I mean, I know Mother went to him thinking he was, but he explained to me why some people had that impression. He's a liberal, you see . . ."

"It doesn't matter now, does it?" Uncle John was frowning; he'd been jolted out of his dream world, and although I wanted to protest that Dr. Josefson did matter a great deal, I also wanted the story to continue, so I subsided.

"This girl was named Jane Thompson then, but she's been married several times since. She stayed at the Waldorf in the rooms the Junior League had there. That worked out because if Mother should call, Jane could take a message. She didn't come to town very often that summer, though; only twice, I think. So we usually had just a day together at a time, which we stretched into the evening as often as we dared. There were a lot of delayed trains that summer; the service on the New Haven was disgraceful."

He grinned at me, and again I was caught in the enchantment, the adventure of it. What should have been a sordid story wasn't that at all. Because of what they were like, I decided, so young and beautiful and lighthearted.

And adulterous.

I twisted uncomfortably in my chair. I had to ask it. "What about Bill? Did you talk about him?" Again my uncle's face sobered, but I went on. "I'm sorry, Uncle John, but if you really want me to understand I have to ask how you felt about being disloyal to him. Especially since I get the impression that you both loved him."

"Well, that was a problem, of course. And I have to say that most of the time we didn't face it." The wicker chair creaked as he pulled himself out of it, picked up his glass from the table, and strode over to peer through the screen. It had gotten late; the afternoon sun gave his face a warm coppery glow as he stood frowning out toward his garden.

"I guess we knew that if we talked about it, if we faced it squarely, we'd have to end it." He turned, still frowning as he tried to work it out. "I don't mean to make excuses for us; we knew what we were doing, but we also knew, without actually saying it, that it was just for then. It couldn't last; we never even said we wished it could. We both looked at it as time out. Soon I would be back in Korea and Kitty would be lonely again; then the war would be over and Bill would come home. They would lead their lives; I would get married and lead mine." He ran his fingers through his hair in a distracted gesture that reminded me of Terry McGinnis. "Hell, Sally, it's impossible to justify. I'm sure that's why I never wanted you to know. My only excuse was, is, that I had loved her so long, and so fruitlessly, and to have her suddenly love me was too much; I couldn't resist. It was like a special treat—not meant for every day—just a lovely, magical . . . and then, my God, the way it all turned out."

He stopped. His face was rigid as he stared down at the glass in his hand, fighting for composure.

I felt an ache in my breast as if my heart had swollen out of shape. I could not speak, but I got up and went over to him and just brushed his forehead with my lips, then took the glass from his hand. I said, "I'll get us a drink," and left him alone while I went to the kitchen.

"It lasted a remarkably short time when you consider the impact; only a few weeks, really. Because Bill was killed in early September, and of course that was the end."

I had returned to the porch to find Uncle John once more seated in the wicker chair. I handed him his already sweating glass, then placed mine on the round table beside him. The light had grown so dim that from across the porch I could not clearly see his face, and the rhythmic chirping of the tree frogs had begun. I sensed the tenuous quality of my uncle's confiding mood; having to raise his voice to be heard might easily destroy it, so I hitched my chair closer to his.

"I can imagine how guilty you must have felt when he was killed."

"Oh God, yes. Both of us, but Kitty in the most disastrous way. She saw Bill's death as punishment for her unfaithfulness. It was absolutely shattering to her, and to the feeling she had had for me. She changed overnight. She wouldn't talk to me; she was barely civil. But I was still fool enough to hope that when she got over the shock she would come back. I thought eventually we might be married."

"Hadn't you ever considered the possibility that he might be killed and wondered how it would affect you?"

"No. At least I never had, and Kitty never mentioned it. That was part of the charade, I saw later, part of the make-believe world we had unconsciously created." He shook his head slowly. "Boy, when our bubble burst it was with a vengeance."

"Well, Uncle John, I know this sounds heartless, but since she was pregnant wouldn't it have made sense if you had gotten married? I mean after she had recovered from the initial shock?"

"That's what I would have thought. It's what I would have urged her to do—if I had known; but, you see, I didn't."

"You didn't know? Well, I don't understand. Why wouldn't she have told you? And where did you think she was all that time after she went away?"

I was suddenly too agitated to sit still, and I jumped up from my chair and began groping on the table top for a book of matches. It was quite dark by now and I could dimly see a half-burned candle standing there in a small glass holder.

"Oh, I can see why she didn't tell me. It was part of what I can only think of as her temporary insanity." He too groped on the table, coming up with a folder of matches that he handed to me. "She was obsessed by the notion of punishment, the idea that any suffering of hers was just retribution for the terrible thing she had done. Going off by herself to have a baby, or an abortion, was no worse than she deserved." He fell silent, watching as I lit the candle.

I sat down again and, looking across in the small circle of light, saw that he wore an expression of faint perplexity.

He said slowly, "What do you think, Sal? Was Kitty over-reacting or am I totally amoral? Because I didn't see it quite that way."

"No, a man wouldn't, I guess. But there's nothing like carrying the evidence around in your own body, seeing it grow, feeling the physical result of your behavior more intensely with each passing day, not less." I paused. I had never thought of it like this before. "Didn't you understand her reaction when you found out about the baby?"

My uncle slowly shook his head. "I can't say that I did, no. Mostly I recall being appalled because she had gone through the whole thing without a word to me. That hurt a lot, Sally. That made it clear that whatever might have happened it was Bill she loved, not me. She was ready to sacrifice her future and mine and even her baby's to protect his memory."

"You mean, to keep anyone from knowing that she had been unfaithful to him? Oh yes, of course. Otherwise she'd have had to face Granny; even Philip and I might have found out eventually. She had to do what she did. It was her last proof of loyalty." I felt overwhelmed, suddenly, by the scope of it. Again I had the sense of having reached the core of my mother's being. I could feel in myself the sureness, the stubborn conviction that had kept her on her difficult, lonely path. Her affair with Uncle John had been an aberration. In her loneliness she had been swept away by his formidable charm, but my father's death had shocked her back to reality.

I sat gazing abstractedly at my uncle's face, noting in a corner of my mind how dramatically the flickering candlelight highlighted his fine bone structure. Had my mother seen him thus one evening in an eastside bistro and sensed, as I did now, his awareness of the picture he presented? Had she recognized, if only for an instant, the vanity that possessed him, but pushed the insight to the back of her bedazzled mind? I could imagine with what a sharp, wry pang she later recalled the scene, and how she might have vowed never to give such a man the satisfaction of displaying to the world that he had seduced his brother's wife.

And did her vow and her terrible penance compensate

for her betrayal? I doubted that she ever thought so, but then she had not known the full extent of it. She could not have predicted that fatal encounter on the Hutchinson River Parkway.

I cleared my throat, but my voice was husky when I asked, "How did you discover what was going on? Did you track her down in Michigan?"

"Well, no. I was sent back to Korea a few days after Bill's funeral. I was pretty well occupied there, as you might imagine, but of course I thought about her a lot. I wrote one or two letters, but I couldn't put on paper the questions I really wanted to ask. I figured it was just as well, after the way she had treated me." He looked over at me almost anxiously. "I thought that as her grief wore off she would gradually feel less guilty about us, so in a way it was good that we were separated for a while. She was the woman I wanted to marry; I knew that. I was willing to wait as long as I had to."

"So then I suppose you came home to find she'd gone. That must have been a blow."

"It was the following June before I got home again. The war was winding down, and I expected to be out of the army in a few months." He paused, then he said slowly, "I hadn't heard one word from Kitty, but I was confident that by now she would have recovered from Bill's death and be ready to start a new life. With me, of course. She'd have grieved enough by then to wipe out her guilt, and when she saw me all her old feeling would rush back. I thought we would get an apartment in that same eastside neighborhood where we had been so happy. There'd be room for you and Phil, of course. God, how smug I was!" He pushed himself to his feet and stood looking down at me from beyond the rim of candlelight. Perhaps it was only with his face in shadow that he could say, "I was a conceited ass, Sally. And worse. But I really loved your mother, and I never really wanted anyone else."

I slowly stood up and we faced each other in the dimness. My uncle said, "There was only one way I could ever prove it, and you may think it's a strange one. When she was dead, and Michael Harris told me about Tommy, I swore I would keep her secret for her if I could. Oh, not that I wanted to raise him as my son." His hand flashed through the darkness in an impatient gesture. "It was no sacrifice for me. I could hardly stand the sight of him, knowing that if he hadn't been born Kitty might one day have married me. But all these years, while Michael has been bleeding me for every cent he could get, I've kept quiet. Because that's what Kitty would have wanted."

Again the whiteness of his hand cut through the dark, as he raised it to stroke my cheek gently. "I think she would have wanted you to know though, Sally. You're so like her; if she could see you now she would expect you to understand . . . all of it."

"All of it. Yes, I think I do." All of her part, I thought, then immediately felt ashamed, for my uncle had gathered me to him and stood holding me with a tenderness I doubt he had bestowed on any other woman except Kitty Ryder.

CHAPTER 21

Granny's funeral service was held in a tall, gothic Episcopal church which she had attended sporadically, but supported with generous annual donations. The building, with its lofty spires and intricate stonework, had been modeled on one of the great cathedrals of Europe. The parishioners, however, were very different from the black-garbed peasants with seamed, patient faces, who saved their pennies to buy votive candles. From this elevated pulpit the preacher looked down upon a gathering of prosperous, self-assured suburban couples, whose thoughts during the Sunday sermons had to be distracted from their golf swings and dinner party menus.

Stepping out of the black limousine that had been hired to convey family members to the church and cemetery, I felt awed by the numbers of dignified, well-dressed people filing slowly up to the arched doorway. It was as if they had come to claim Granny; on this day at least, she belonged to them. I nodded nervously in the direction of one or two I thought I recognized, then wondered whether I was meant to ignore them, in my grief, until after the service, when the family members would receive them in the church parlor. Altogether I was finding it a very self-conscious occasion. I wasn't at all sure what I was supposed to do in order to be a credit to Granny, and I had certainly started on the wrong foot by wearing my ill-fitting, dark crepe dress. I could imagine her lips tightening as she cast a critical eye over me; could almost hear her saying tactfully, "Surely you can find something just as appropriate that is a little more becoming, dear."

Uncle John took my arm, and a somber man from the funeral home led us into the church through a side door, then along a hallway until we reached the parlor, where the minister waited to greet us. He shook hands with each of us, Barbara, Phil, Uncle John, and me, giving my shoulder a reassuring squeeze as well, either because he sensed my nervousness or because I was last in line, I wasn't sure which. Barbara also seemed to feel protective that morning. She came toward me wearing a reassuring smile and carrying two styrofoam cups of coffee.

"We'll need a lot of this to get through the day," she said, handing one to me. Then she went on, "Chip takes that adorable bunny to bed with him every night."

"Oh, I'm glad. I wasn't sure he'd like it." The thought of the winsome little boy was a welcome distraction. "I've got to see more of that child, Barbara; and I hope you have a snapshot I can take with me to Chicago. I want to show him off."

We talked then about my new job, my prospects of finding an attractive apartment, her eagerness to visit when I was settled out there; and although it was all very superficial, I saw the warmth in her eyes and felt again that the bond formed between us that evening at her house was a firm and lasting one.

I wanted to say something about it, but of course this wasn't the moment, any more than it would have been the time to tell Philip that he had finally become a real brother to me. I looked about the room for him. He was standing beside the coffee urn with Uncle John and the black-robed minister. In a moment the latter consulted his wristwatch, murmured a few words to the other two men, then came over to tell Barbara and me that it would soon be time to begin the service.

We thanked him, then automatically moved together in the direction of a gold-framed mirror that hung on the wall beside the door. There we exchanged the usual remarks about one another's hair and dress, regrets countered by compliments in a routine we could have recited in our sleep, and perhaps did. The idea amused me, and I started to make some flip comment to Barbara when I was stopped by the expression on my brother's face as I saw it reflected in the mirror. I had become accustomed to his pallor, and certainly it was justified by the events of recent months, as was his tense demeanor. But never had I seen his eyes blazing with such intense emotion; they were fixed on my uncle's face with what appeared to be a mixture of anger and shock, and I wondered what in the world Uncle John had said to him.

Could he possibly have chosen this moment to unburden himself to Phil? Might he have reasoned that since I had discovered the strange, sad truth about our mother, Philip was also entitled to know?

Hurriedly stuffing my hairbrush into my pocketbook, I darted over and seized my brother's arm. "What is it, Phil? You look positively murderous." I kept a firm grasp on his arm, trying to draw him away from my uncle. The first shock of disclosure might well trigger an ungovernable anger; certainly Phil appeared to be on the verge of striking Uncle John.

He turned his coal-like eyes to mine, but I saw no comprehension in them. He was talking to himself as he said, "An autopsy. That's disgusting. Disgusting and unwarranted." He went on saying the words tonelessly, like some robot that could not be switched off, until I could bear it no longer.

I shook his arm furiously. I wanted to slap his fixed, tense face, but instead I breathed soothingly, "I know, Phil. It hit me like that too. But it's over now. I'm sure it is often done." He blinked and his expression softened as I went on. "It's just routine, Phil. You mustn't let it upset you so."

Barbara had joined me and she took up the refrain, speaking softly just as I had done, while my uncle watched in amazement.

"Excuse me." I turned to see that the solemn-faced man from the funeral home stood waiting respectfully at the edge of our little circle. "It is time for the family to go in now," he said, and indeed I could hear through the partly open door the closing bars of Bach's "Sheep May Safely Graze" and felt an instant's gratitude to whoever had selected that well-loved melody.

Phil seemed to have regained his composure; still I saw that Barbara kept his arm in a firm grip as they walked out of the room. Uncle John grasped my elbow and we proceeded into the nave of the church, where the assembled mourners stood waiting for us to take our seats in the front pew. I felt awkward and conspicuous as I confronted the ranks of sympathetic faces. The majority were strange to me; only here and there could I pick out a remembered acquaintance of Granny's or a local tradesman. Then, with a surge of relief, I saw that the pew behind our empty one was occupied by the members of Granny's household: Mrs. Berger, the maid Jenny, the cook, the night nurse Miss Nelson. Beside her sat Jane Kelly, her eyes red-rimmed, her lips trembling as she attempted to give me a reassuring smile. I saw that Nancy and Michael Harris sat next to her, then Tommy. Tommy Harris, nee Ryder, I thought.

I could hardly tear my eyes from Tommy's face. This was

our first encounter since I had known that he was my brother. My brother. Were those blue eyes like my uncle's or my mother's? My knee bumped painfully against the edge of the wooden pew, and I felt Uncle John tighten his grasp on my elbow. Good God, I was stumbling toward my seat like a drunk. Dizzily, I wrenched my gaze from Tommy's face, only to see Nancy Harris staring at me with what I fancied to be total comprehension. Of course she would understand the reason for my agitation; she probably thought me a fool for not having figured it all out years ago.

I sat down on the smooth wooden seat and heard the bumps and rustles and coughs of the congregation settling back into theirs. All those years Nancy, my friend Nancy, had pretended Tommy was her son. She must have loved my mother dearly to go to such lengths to protect her secret. Or had her husband kept her quiet in order to assure the continuing flow of money from Uncle John's pocket to his? She must have been deeply ashamed of that blackmail; she wouldn't have wanted me to know of it, ever. That shame would have been reason enough for her silence—that and the fact that she had come to feel a mother's love for Tommy. I thought of what an adorable little boy he had been; many a barren woman would condone the crime of blackmail to have such a child for her own.

I forced my attention to the minister's words, which flowed forth in a soothing stream. I felt baffled, as always, by the obscure, tortured phrases: Like as a father pitieth his children, so the Lord pitieth them that fear him. What was the psalmist implying there? Was it natural for parents to 'pity' their children? I had never thought of including pity in the complex of emotions called forth by parenthood.

Uncle John was a parent; but he seemed to have none of the feelings that normally accompany the role, certainly not pity. Yet his son, Tommy, was the product of the great love of his life. What if Tommy knew that? What would he think of having a father who not only felt no 'pity' for him, but refused even to acknowledge him?

And now I faced the hard question, the one that had formed in my mind as I stood in my uncle's embrace on the previous evening. Was it truly to honor my mother's wishes that Uncle John had kept silent, or was it to keep Granny from giving Tommy a share of her estate?

As indeed she would have done if she had known. And after all those years she might have found out if instead of waiting until I was in Chicago I had gone to see Dr. Josefson at once, then immediately confronted Uncle John. After that I would have had to get to Granny with the interesting facts of Tommy's birth before her mind was once more dimmed—possibly by unauthorized doses of Haldol administered by Gillian.

If all those conditions had been met there would have been no reason for anyone to want to hasten her death. No advantage would have been gained by it. She might still be alive.

Or was it my coming so close to the truth that had caused my uncle, or more likely his resourceful lawyer, to take the desperate step of adding a lethal quantity of potassium to her intravenous solution?

My head began to throb, battered by a confusing mixture of anger, resentment, incredulity; and through it pierced the knowledge that the horror I imagined was not only possible, but probable. A man who seduced his brother's wife, then schemed to keep his son from his share of the family fortune, was probably quite capable of giving his comatose mother a nudge toward the grave. Especially if the act could be performed by his able and willing deputy, thus allowing him to remain in the state of self-delusion he had occupied all his life.

The pulsing in my head had become a sharp, stabbing pain.

I wrenched my attention back to the sermon. It was too bizarre to sit at my grandmother's funeral service and imagine her only son plotting her murder.

The minister had gotten to the Twenty-third Psalm. "He maketh me to lie down in green pastures; He leadeth me beside the still waters." I remembered crossing Granny's green lawn to reach the sparkling trout stream. Where I met my brother, though I did not know it. A brother who was a penniless drug addict. And a medical student. If an addict will rob and kill to get funds to support his habit, would he balk at adding a toxic substance to the IV of an already dying woman? A woman he had perhaps always resented because of her hold on his parents and whose death would solve his financial problems and theirs? It seemed likely that Nancy and Michael would have been informed of the bequest that awaited them, and might very well have told Tommy in order to provide added incentive for curing himself. The information might have had a very different effect from the one they intended, however.

I swallowed hard, imagining Tommy's eyes fixed on the back of my head. I wondered if they were shining with the strange, wild light I had seen on that morning when he'd kissed me. The shock of the memory cleared my head. Perhaps that was the reason his kiss had struck me as so very unseemly: not because as a toddler he had been my charge, but because he was my brother. My reaction had been a protest of the blood.

Thank God for Philip, the brother I knew—or was finally coming to know. I bent forward slightly to look beyond Barbara and possibly catch his eye. Before the service I had felt the closeness he could only seem to allow when he was troubled. Perhaps the anguish of the last few weeks could be justified if it had broken down the barrier between us.

I saw that Phil's face was still drawn and white as he sat stiffly in the uncomfortable wooden seat. His head was bowed, but his open eyes were fixed on the hands he held tightly clenched in a manner that appeared more pugnacious than prayerful. Barbara seemed aware of his tension; as I watched she unobtrusively placed a steadying hand on his arm, neither lifting her head nor turning to look at him as she did so.

"Be ye steadfast, unmovable, always abounding in the work of the Lord." It was the Lord's work to decide when people were born and when they died, not yours, Uncle John; not yours, Tommy Harris; not Gillian Clark's, or mine, or Phil's.

It was nearly over. The minister was pronouncing a blessing over the gleaming mahogany coffin, and at the sound of the simple, compassionate phrases my eyes filled with tears. "The Lord make his face to shine upon you and be gracious unto you." Unto *you*, Granny. "The Lord lift up his countenance upon you and give you peace both now and evermore."

Evermore, Granny, evermore. Blinded by my tears, I followed Philip and Barbara from the pew toward the parlor where we would gather once again. As I reached the door something made me turn and look back at the rows of somber faces watching respectfully as we moved to our private retreat. There in the third row Terry was standing next to Betsy. His warm brown eyes met mine and I thought I saw him start forward as if to leave the pew, then restrain himself. He was not one to stand and watch while others suffered, and I felt a sudden longing to have him at my side. What strength would come to me if he were to take my hand in his! But that strength was for Betsy, and for all I knew her need of it might be as great as mine. I seemed to move in a lonely vacuum as I turned away and entered the room to join the others.

Of the two hours that ensued I remember very little, except that the emotions that had clamored within me, all the grief and fear and suspicion, had been subjugated to an overwhelming need to escape. The desire to get away increased with every second that I stood accepting the condolences of our friends. Even when Terry kissed my cheek and spoke to me I heard only the humming urgency in my head. Then Betsy's face swam into my ken, and something sparked in my mind: the idea that she could help me.

I did not grasp it, however, until I stood in the cemetery at the graveside. Glancing along the row of bowed heads, I did not even attempt to comprehend the ritual words intoned by the minister, but thought only that his black-robed figure suddenly resembled a hovering bird of evil. I needed to run from it and from these people who stood so close beside me. There was a falseness in one of them; I could not bear to speculate any more as to which it was. And I could not be with them any longer. I was suffocating.

I kept going somehow. I did not disgrace myself and discredit Granny by running away from her grave. But when the limousine arrived back at the house I pushed the door open immediately. Before the chauffeur could reach it I was halfway up the front steps, and I brushed past Mrs. Berger and the servants who waited in the hall and flew up the stairs to my room. My thoughts were clearly organized as I telephoned Betsy and tersely asked to borrow her parents' Vermont house for a day or two. She responded as I had known she would, and I said I would pick up the keys in twenty minutes. Betsy offered to come along, but I explained that I needed to be alone, then cut her off rather abruptly. I had one more call to make, to Mike Alwyn in Chicago; then I would pack a few clothes and be gone before anyone could have an opportunity to persuade me otherwise.

I pulled off the crepe dress and hurled it into a corner of the closet. Nothing would ever induce me to put it on again.

I tore off my stockings and reached for a pair of blue jeans. I was being unforgivably rude; I knew that, but it couldn't be helped.

I'm getting somewhere, Dr. Zeigler, I thought as I tossed sweaters and underwear into my duffle bag. I'm listening to myself at last, and the orders are to get out of here fast—before I explode.

I was on the point of chuckling fiendishly as I ran down the back stairs and out to my little red car. I had parked it that morning in the service road at the rear of the house in order to make room for the numbers of people who were expected to call. I could not have done a better job if I had been planning an elopement. I tossed my bag into the back seat, climbed in, and switched on the ignition, praying it would not be heard. No one called after me, no one tried to stop me as I drove down the winding lane and, with a grateful sigh, turned onto the road that led to Betsy's house.

CHAPTER 22

The drive to Vermont was blessedly numbing. I did not have to think very much about the route, as ski weekends at the Marshes' had been an important feature of my prep school and college years. I made my way north, observing how the villages changed, becoming less suburban, with older and more sizable houses set far back on broad green lawns. It was soothing to pass through these old, established towns, comforting to think of the generations of families that had grown up there. They too must have been a mix of weak and strong, though the substantial white houses implied otherwise. Those families too had known illness and death, failure and disillusion. Although life in the early years of our country was more precarious, the pain of bereavement could not have been less than it was today. The mothers who buried one baby after another must have felt indescribable agony. I thought of what my mother had gone through, first to give birth to her baby in secret, then to make it possible for him to grow up. Her efforts might seem disproportionately heroic in view of the way that child had turned out, but that would have made no difference to her, nor would it have to the women of these villages I passed through.

The countryside became more rolling, the towns smaller and more rural. Soon I observed that the fast-food shops were giving way to vegetable stands, and I became aware that my emotional tumult had been replaced by a gnawing hunger. I slowed the car at every roadside cluster until at last I was rewarded by finding a gas station that was annexed to a lunch counter. While my car was being serviced I ate at the counter, surrounded by the seductive aroma of onions, pickles, and sizzling beef. Thinking ahead to evening, I ordered a second hamburger to take with me, along with a supply of Coca-Cola and potato chips. The grocery stores would probably have closed by the time I reached Manchester.

Indeed it was dusk when I arrived in the outskirts, and I could spare no time for shopping. I needed the last minutes of twilight for finding the road to Betsy's house. The town had changed considerably since my last visit. I recognized only one or two landmarks, one of them, luckily, a barn-red antique shop that marked the turn onto Betsy's road.

The house stood several miles northeast of the town, and I drove carefully along the winding, hilly road, straining my eyes through the dimness to pick out the names on the mail-boxes I passed. At last I saw Marsh lettered on a white box mounted on a tilted fencepost, and gratefully pulled into the driveway.

I turned off the lights and the ignition and sat in the car for a moment, feeling the spacious silence of the evening around me. Then I climbed out and walked slowly around the house, breathing the cool, crisp air and observing that everything appeared unchanged from the way I remembered it. The small, square farmhouse had a wide porch across the front, where we had stacked our ski equipment. Though the clapboard exterior looked freshly painted, nothing had been done to make the place chic. No picture windows had been added and, peering through a small-paned one into the kitchen, I saw that that room remained comfortably outdated. The bulky white refrigerator was a twin of the one Granny had given away the year I graduated from college.

One of her tenets had been that mink coats and good refrigerators never wear out, but must be sternly disposed of when their time is up. I smiled to myself, wondering if she had acquired those firm opinions from her own mother, then felt a shock as I realized that question would remain forever unanswered. And there will be others, I thought, so many other questions only Granny could answer that I never thought to ask.

I walked back to the car to get my bag, marveling at the silence of the place. The only sound I heard was the soft sigh of the breeze passing through the tall firs at the edge of the lawn. I shivered, suddenly eager for the cosy warmth of the house. Perhaps I would light a fire and settle down with an old novel from the Marshes' overloaded bookshelves.

But after I had pushed open the swollen kitchen door and stepped in onto the linoleum floor I could not even summon the energy to eat my second hamburger. I stowed it in the refrigerator, and after raising a window in the kitchen and one in the living room, climbed slowly up the creaky stairs to the floor above. There I went around the simply furnished bedrooms, opening windows here and there, until I had settled on one, the smallest, for myself.

I did not turn on a light, but washed my face by the pale glow of the night sky in the bathroom window. I rummaged in my duffle bag until I found my nightgown, changed into it and, after taking a spare blanket from the foot of one of the other beds, climbed into mine. I lay staring at the light that came through the thinly curtained window, thinking of nothing, not even the relief of being free at last of the clamor in my head. I listened to the soughing pines until I fell asleep like an exhausted child.

I was awakened by the morning sun shining on my face, and after opening my eyes to confirm my surroundings I closed them again, smiling to myself. Mornings at camp had started like this, with the warm sun on my cheek, only then the other girls in my cabin and I had been briskly routed out by our counselor; there was none of this heavenly peace and privacy.

I took my time getting dressed, then went down to the kitchen and found a jar of instant coffee. While the water heated in the kettle I looked around for fishing gear. It was a perfect morning to wander along a stream and possibly catch a couple of trout for my lunch. In a small room that had probably been the original pantry I found several fly rods packed in their olive drab cotton cases, and a selection of reels, flies, and all the other equipment I would need. All these things were neatly arranged on shelves, and several wicker creels hung from hooks on the wall, along with green rubber waders in various sizes.

I outfitted myself while I drank my coffee, then set forth to find a stream, locking the house behind me. It was a morning designed to banish dark thoughts and tremors, and as I walked to the back of the property where the sloping land suggested the possibility of water, I congratulated myself on my decision to come to Vermont. The sky overhead was clear and blue, with a scattering of white cirrus clouds that looked like feathers carelessly tossed. The budding leaves of the bushes and trees trembled as if rejoicing in the long awaited sunlight, and I too stood for a moment with my face tilted up to its warmth before I began pushing my way through the foliage.

I soon came upon a shallow, rock-strewn brook, its water too low for fishing at that point, but worth following to where it might become broader and deeper. I made my way along the bank, climbing over roots and stones, pushing aside low-hanging branches, occasionally making a detour around a fallen tangle of trees. Soon the chuckling, fast-flowing water grew deeper and I began casting my line into the small pools formed by rocks and old tree stumps. I made short, careful casts to avoid getting caught in the branches, and quickly retrieved the fly before it could snag on the jumble of rocks just beneath the surface.

For the first hour my attempts were fruitless, but it didn't matter; I was caught up in the sport of it. Wherever I looked I saw spots that would invite a fish to hover, barely moving in the water, until a tempting fly touched the surface above: beside a fallen branch, in the shadow of an overhanging fern or in the rushing eddy formed by a beaver dam. My casting became more accurate as I tossed the fly again and again, enjoying the rhythm of it, lulled by the repetitious activity that might reward me at any moment.

After tying on several different varieties, I finally selected the fly of the day and the real fun began. I cast into a still, dark patch of water at the grass-rimmed edge of the stream and immediately felt a sharp, wriggling tug. Keeping the fish in the water, I quickly twisted the tiny hook from its lip to set it free. There would be others, I felt confident of it, and I wanted the adventure to last.

I could tell when it was noon by the empty feeling in my stomach and by the changed direction of the sun's rays that shone through the trees onto the rippling, brown surface of the water. By that time I had caught and released eight small trout and two more were nestled damply in my creel. It was time to start back to the house. I knelt on the bank near a

spot where the current was fast to slice open the fish and clean
them against the flat surface of a rock. Replacing them in the
creel, I trudged back along the bank for a mile, then pushed
through the bushes and emerged on the lower slope of a wide,
grassy field. From where I stood it rose to a crest that concealed, I presumed, my view of the road beyond.

I trudged over the gently rising ground, enjoying the sun
on my back after the coolness of the shaded stream. When I
reached the top of the rise I saw the road just a hundred yards
away, and I picked up my pace. The Marshes' house lay about
half a mile to my left, I figured, and I allowed myself to start
thinking about lunch. I hoped I would find some flour in the
kitchen, and a bit of oil for frying the fish. In my mind's eye
I could see them sizzling side by side in a black iron skillet,
two perfect, plump trout turning crisp and brown on the
surface, while the pale pink flesh within remained sweet and
juicy. Might the Marshes have left a can of beer in the back
of the fridge? Surely they had; everyone did.

While I was trying to remember whether I had noticed one
I rounded a curve in the road and saw the house standing
several hundred yards to my left. I climbed up the grassy
bank that edged the road and made my way toward the back
lawn in order to enter through the kitchen door, the only one
for which I had a key. I stepped in among the fir trees that
bordered the property and paused to savor the scent of their
dark, fragrant branches; then I proceeded across the lawn to
where it met the rough driveway.

I turned the corner of the house and stopped abruptly.
There in the driveway stood my small red car, where I had
left it; but there was now another vehicle parked just beyond
it. I hesitated, then slowly started forward to examine the
strange car. As I did the kitchen door swung open and Terry
McGinnis stepped out.

I gasped in astonishment, but my first reaction was to wonder how he had gotten into the house, not why he had come, and as if he had read my mind he said, "They keep a key hidden under the stairs right here. Look, I'll show you."

He descended the four wooden steps as I approached, then reached under the top one to feel the hook that held the key. He reached for my hand and guided it to the spot, and I smiled up at him. "That's a useful thing to know about." I moved away then and said, indicating my creel, "It's lucky for you I kept two trout. Come on in and we'll have some lunch."

I was about to mount the stair, but Terry grasped my arm to stop me. I looked up questioningly and when I saw the gravity in his face I felt a stillness grip me. My mouth was dry as I whispered, "What is it, Terry? Why are you here?"

Still holding my arm, he took the fly rod from my other hand and propped it against the clapboard wall of the house. He said, "You'd better sit down, Sally. A terrible thing has happened."

My eyes were riveted to his as I slowly sank down onto the bottom step. He knelt beside me and said very gently, "It's Phil. He has taken his life, Sally. He shot himself last night."

I felt my whole body begin to tremble, and Terry must have felt it too, for he released my arm and pulled me over to rest against him. I pushed away, however, and sat upright to look into his eyes. Though my body was reacting to his words, my mind was unwilling to grasp their meaning.

Terry went on. "He seemed all right when I saw him after the service. But that night after Barbara and the baby had gone to sleep he left the house. He went to a motel, Sally, so Barbara wouldn't be the one to find him."

"Did he leave a note, or what? How did she discover . . . ?"

"Apparently he left a note in the kitchen, where she'd find

it when she went downstairs in the morning, but not before. If Chip got her up in the night, or something." Terry was watching me closely as he talked, and now he gently pushed my hair back from my forehead. "He had thought it out very carefully. He didn't want to be stopped."

"But did the note say why? Why would he do it now? His troubles were over . . ."

"I haven't seen it, but Barbara said he merely told her where to find him and gave some instructions about his insurance policies." He had taken my hand in his and was holding it tightly. "Barbara was in shock, of course. I gave her some sedation and called Jane Kelly to stay with her. She's there now, and so is Betsy. Barbara wants you, though, and I offered to come and get you."

"Yes," I said. I was nodding my head as if at the logic of it all, when actually it seemed that the world had gone completely senseless. I was still trembling, and although the noon sun beat down from directly over my head, I felt icy cold. I peered toward the fir trees whose cool fragrance I had enjoyed so recently. They seemed to be trembling with me; I could not distinguish their branches, they had become a soft, dark blur at the edge of the bright lawn.

I sighed; then, to my surprise, I yawned deeply. I turned to Terry and my voice seemed to echo from some distant point as I said, "We'd better get started, hadn't we? I'll go in and get my things. Or shall I just leave them . . . ?"

I was sagging against him then, incapable of thought or words, conscious only of the fact that his voice too seemed to come from far away as he soothed me. "You'd better have something to eat first. I'll go in and fix some coffee and see what I can find." It sounded as though he spoke through a thick layer of cotton. "You stay right here, Sally. Don't try to do anything."

He propped me against the steps like a rag doll, then he

took the creel from my shoulder. "I'll put the fish on ice," he said as he disappeared through the kitchen door. "Just sit still now."

I did as he ordered. The door banged behind him and I sat there in the sunshine, feeling the light, cool touch of the Vermont air against my cheek, and tried to force a place in the peaceful scene about me for the pale, tense features of my brother. Oh, but they wouldn't be merely pale and tense any longer, I reminded myself. Now his face would wear an embellishment: a small, red hole, the skin at the edges turned inward by the passage of the bullet that had made it. In his forehead, I wondered? I tried to think how it would look. Or had a piece of skull blown off, allowing blood and brains to cover the pillow? How horrible for the innocent people who ran the motel. Which motel? I got to my feet. I had many questions to ask Terry all at once. I hoped he would tell me the truth.

As I pulled open the screen door I started to speak; but all the questions I wanted to ask began tumbling through my mind in disarray, and I merely stood gaping silently while Terry placed the coffee pot on the counter and came to put his arms around me. And then the tears began.

CHAPTER 23

The mundane preparations for departure proved therapeutic. I had to set aside my grief while I packed my duffle bag and closed up the house, then followed Terry into Manchester to leave my car at a leasing office. Although I felt perfectly capable of driving myself back to Connecticut, Terry would not have it, and when I climbed in beside him I was glad he had insisted. It was an unaccustomed luxury to lie back and relax while he bought the gas, selected the route, and took the wheel with apparently every intention of driving the entire way, even though he had already done the trip once that day.

If I were married I'd have it this way all the time, I thought. No wonder some wives become so dependent; it's nice. Then I tried to remember whether I had enjoyed having Joe make all the decisions during our marriage and, as far as I could recall, it had felt more like condescension than pampering. I must remember that, I thought drowsily; mustn't let that happen again.

I slept, waking occasionally when we slowed down to pass through a town or stopped at a traffic light. We had reached the outskirts of Great Barrington, Massachusetts when Terry stopped for a cup of coffee. He brought one to me, and when I saw the weariness in his face I begged him to let me drive.

"Just for an hour, Terry. You need to rest, and I'm slept out." He relented without much argument, and climbed into the passenger seat, pushing it back as far as possible so he could stretch out.

For the first few miles, while I felt certain Terry was still awake, I concentrated on my driving. Then I saw that his legs had relaxed in an easy sprawl and his mouth had fallen open, and I turned my thoughts back to my brother's suicide.

There was something I had to face, something I had buried in my consciousness during my anguished speculation regarding Granny's death. I recalled the dreadful thoughts that had occupied me during her funeral service, and remembered that I had imagined compelling reasons for Uncle John, Gillian Clark, and Tommy Harris to want to hasten her death, but not Philip. Not Philip because surely Bill Watkins would have been willing to wait for his money the few more days or weeks it would take for Granny to die. He had waited six months already, so he clearly possessed some compassion, some fellow feeling for his old friend and colleague.

But then I remembered overhearing Phil with Gillian Clark; I recalled the angry desperation with which he had demanded to know when he would receive his share of Granny's estate. He had not behaved on that occasion like a man who had just been saved from disgrace; quite the contrary. And what about his agitation when before the funeral Uncle John had told him an autopsy had been performed on Granny? I had assumed that, like me, he was horrified at the idea of it; he had always been fastidious, easily repelled by the gross physical aspects of life.

But supposing his shock had been due to fear of what the

autopsy might disclose? At the thought a pulse began hammering in my throat and my palms turned damp on the steering wheel. I glanced at Terry in annoyance. Where a few minutes earlier I had enjoyed watching him sleep, and thought that he resembled a vulnerable little boy, I was now impatient for him to wake up. I needed to ask him about the autopsy now, right now, and I began driving with less care for the bumps and sudden pauses that might jolt him back to consciousness.

And the note. I must get Barbara to show me the note Phil had left for her. Perhaps he had disclosed his motive; he would seem to owe her, at least, an explanation.

But would she ever get over the hurt of it, whatever his reason had been? I had read somewhere that suicide is an act of anger, of aggression; and now that it had touched my life I understood. I will take myself from you, Phil had said to us. It was like a slap; I felt the pain as well as an answering anger in myself. How could he do such a thing to Chip?

I pressed harder on the accelerator. I prayed that Barbara would never tell Chip his father had taken his own life. Such knowledge haunts the survivors; I knew it from one of my friends. All their lives they fear they will do the same thing; they sense that the capability exists within them like a seed that might one day germinate. We couldn't have that for Chip.

Terry stirred. He rearranged his legs, but in the small space he could not find a really comfortable sleeping position, and after a moment of twisting about in the seat he gave up. He sat up, readjusted the seat back, and turned to smile at me.

"Want me to take over?"

I returned his smile, then gave my attention to the winding country road we had entered. "Not unless you're dying to. We're just outside Ridgefield; we'll be home in half an hour."

Terry yawned and leaned back again, his eyes half closed.

"You'll be interested to hear that the results of the autopsy were inconclusive," he said.

I swerved the car to avoid an indecisive squirrel, and Terry grabbed for the dashboard. I said, "Sorry. That wasn't because of what you said, but it could have been. I've been longing for you to wake up so I could ask about the autopsy. You mean they found nothing, no extra amounts of anything in her system?"

"Not measurable, no."

I drew a deep breath. Relief flooded through me, and I felt suddenly buoyant. "Oh, thank God. I was so afraid."

Terry said, "Why don't you pull over, Sally? I want to explain something to you, and you may find it upsetting."

Obediently I drew the car to the side of the road and stopped. He was right; I shouldn't be driving. I was on an emotional trampoline that day.

"Jane was afraid someone had added potassium to your grandmother's IV solution; I know that. And I have to tell you that the coroner's findings do not rule out that possibility."

He had unbuckled his seat belt, but he stayed quietly watching my reaction to his words.

"I don't understand what you mean."

"It will take some explaining. Do you have any idea of the function of potassium and sodium in controlling the body's electrical system?"

I had begun nodding eagerly before he finished. "Jane described it to me, yes; the balance that has to be maintained in order to keep the electrical impulses going—the ones that keep our hearts beating."

"And our brains working." Terry reached into the back seat and after a moment's fumbling, pulled a pencil and notepad from the pocket of his jacket. He hunched forward, opened to an empty page, and drew a line across it. Along the line he added arrows going in and out, each identified with the chemical symbols for potassium and sodium, K and Na. He said, "You apparently understand that an interchange of these elements is essential to providing the electrical voltage that stimulates the heart muscle."

"Yes, I think I get it. And if there is too much of one of them the rhythm of the process is destroyed and there is no stimulus to keep the heart muscle going."

"That's the idea." Terry added some arrows along the line he had drawn. "The thing that happens then, at death, is that the tension in the cells breaks down. There is no longer a dividing force to keep the sodium separated from the potassium. One rushes out through the membrane and the other pours in, because the system of regulation has stopped functioning." He paused. "So of course in the resulting chemical confusion there is no way to measure the amounts of either sodium or potassium that would have been present at death."

I stared at him wide-eyed, trying to understand the implications. "Then there's no way of proving anything; either that someone added potassium or is innocent of it."

Terry nodded. "The additional potassium in the IV bottle was reason enough to be suspicious. But all we could hope to find in an autopsy would be evidence of drugs or some other cause of death, such as asphyxia. We had to do the autopsy though, Sally; you can see that, can't you?"

"Yes, I've understood that ever since Jane explained to me about the potassium-sodium balance." I paused. My thoughts were tumbling confusedly. "But Jane didn't tell me that an overdose of potassium wouldn't show up in an autopsy. I wonder if she knows . . ."

"Anyone with her medical training would know, or should." Terry spoke in an even, neutral tone. He did not look at me, but reached over to give my shoulder a friendly squeeze, then pushed open the car door on his side.

Anyone with medical training. That included Tommy Harris, certainly, and probably Gillian, who if she didn't know the facts would know where to find them. And through her it probably included Uncle John. I could not imagine him going into the scientific aspects himself, but Gillian would be certain to give him the necessary guidelines.

So any one of them could have done it and felt perfectly confident of never being found out unless they were actually seen adding the substance to Granny's IV, or made some slip that would point suspicion in their direction.

Some slip like committing suicide.

I did one thing for Barbara. I never told her.

She showed me Phil's note, all of it, not just the fourth page, which was all the police ever saw. The message was rambling, nearly incoherent, and when I saw the shaky handwriting, large and sprawling like that of a very old man, my eyes filled with tears.

In broken, erratically punctuated sentences he expressed his love for Barbara and Chip and his desolation at having to leave them. By his misappropriation of funds he had tested her loyalty, her love, as no husband ever should; he had risked her future, jeopardized the family's good name. He could not bear to heap more disgrace on her. He couldn't stand the thought of being there when she learned how he had panicked, when she discovered the incredible extent of his cowardice. He loathed himself for what he had done; he couldn't bear it if she hated him as much as she surely would. The thought of her judgment or mine, and later Chip's, was unendurable. She must see that it was panic, pure panic, that had seized him because Bill Watkins would not wait for his money beyond the deadline he had established; said he couldn't. Phil could not understand it; Bill had been so fair, so understanding till then. But the strain was too much; it had weakened him, demoralized him, mixed up his mind. All he prayed for was her forgiveness. She should start a new life, change her name if she must, do anything necessary to protect Chip. . . .

There were three pages of it; then he must have stopped, either because he was exhausted or running out of time. I pictured him seated at the kitchen table in his shirt-sleeves; imagined his distraught, white face as he glanced up at the clock on the wall. He would have taken a deep breath, it seemed to me, seeing that the hour was nearly at hand; then he would have looked down at the untidy pages before him and realized he must turn to practical matters.

On the fourth page the handwriting was more recognizable. He must have felt almost like his normal, businesslike self while he listed his insurance policies, suggested a lawyer to handle his estate, and told Barbara the number of the room he had reserved at the Holiday Inn.

I read the entire message twice, while Barbara watched me, then I placed the fourth sheet on the table and turned to face her. She said nothing, just reached out her hand and I gave her the first three pages. With her eyes locked on mine she slowly tore the sheets of paper into bits. Careful not to drop a single scrap on the floor, she walked to the kitchen sink, where I saw she had placed a small pan made of aluminum foil. She piled the scraps of paper in the pan, reached for a book of matches that lay on the counter nearby, and set fire to the remnants of Phil's note.

I said nothing. I went to the stove and turned on the exhaust fan, then I opened the back door. I went to stand beside Barbara, and together we watched while the flames quickly consumed my brother's disjointed final message. As I watched the bits of paper blacken and curl into ash, I wondered what instinct had guided Phil's hand so that there was no mention of Granny or of his dread of the results of the autopsy, not one concrete indication of the real reason for his terrible guilt. Though much more was implied, it would be quite possible for Barbara to believe that it was the unexpected pressure from Bill Watkins that had driven her husband to suicide.

When she had shaken the ashes into the garbage disposal and run it, she crumpled the foil pan and placed it in the wastebasket. She turned to face me and I met her glance squarely. I took her hand and said, "Let's go and see if Chip is up from his nap."

CHAPTER 24

Two years have gone by, and I am able now to think of the events of that beautiful Connecticut spring with some detachment. It was a long time coming, this philosophical viewpoint I've managed to achieve. My first reaction to Philip's implicit confession was outraged anger. I could not imagine what our relationship would have been if he were still alive. Suspecting what I did, I could not have treated him as a brother, any more than I could have resumed the old, comfortable rapport with Uncle John or Tommy, or treated Gillian Clark with even the barest civility.

I would have lived out my life never knowing which of them had murdered my grandmother, or—most macabre thought of all—whether perhaps every one of the four had poured additional potassium into that IV bottle.

Murder by committee, but with the committee members unaware of one another's participation. I felt grateful to Phil for sparing me the bizarre image of those four figures slipping in and out of Granny's bedroom like characters in a French farce.

He had also spared me the necessity of forgiving him—or the anguish of being unable to. The latter would surely have been the case if Phil were alive and if Granny's death had occurred even a few weeks earlier than it did. But those weeks spent at her house had changed me. In a short space of time I had come to love my brother's child; I had developed a warm and protective feeling for his wife; and I had begun to see the possibility of a newly loving relationship with Philip himself.

But it was the revelations about my mother that had the most stunning impact. After my lifelong questioning, what an unexpected boon it was to be led, in an almost mystic manner, to a true and intimate knowledge of her. And then how ironic was the discovery that the woman with whom I could so joyously identify had committed adultery with her own brother-in-law. My beloved uncle had played out his paternal role in my life more fully than I had realized.

As for his own son, I gather that Uncle John's feelings toward Tommy remain the same. Whenever I see Uncle John now, I call attention to Tommy's strength of character in curing himself of his addiction and to the fine record he is establishing as a resident in one of the country's most respected children's hospitals.

But my uncle cannot or will not admit that he is pleased with Tommy. The subject seems to embarrass him. It is as if he cannot break the habit of silence established over the years when he controlled the secret of Tommy's parentage.

He is equally reluctant to talk about Phil, and I wonder whether something in my manner might have hinted at a dark reality he wishes to avoid facing. His talent for evading unpleasant truths still serves him well, it seems, as it must have done all the while he tacitly condoned Gillian's treatment of his mother.

I am able now to see their transgression more as weakness

than depravity, and I am grateful for the way my knowledge of their wrongdoing has softened any judgment I might pronounce upon my brother. It is as if a curtain was twitched aside to show me a glimpse of the evil that lurks in us all, in me as well as everyone else, like a beast that should not be denied, but faced and controlled.

When I think of it I sometimes fancy I can hear Granny saying, "You see, dear, life is not simple. You must not be quick to condemn, but cultivate forgiveness, never knowing when you may be in need of it yourself."

I'm sure it is thinking of her, imagining what she would advise, that has made it possible for me to forgive Gillian Clark, as well as my brother. Gillian must have seen quite early in their relationship that John Ryder did not share her all-consuming passion, and that without her ability to manipulate Granny's funds for his benefit he would quickly drop her. As indeed he did the moment he inherited his own fortune. Her desperate craving for his love must have made it seem quite reasonable to drug an old woman in order to keep her from tightening her purse strings.

To Gillian that was simply an ingenious way of insuring the necessary flow of payments to Michael Harris. I could imagine how she might have congratulated herself on possessing the medical knowledge she needed, where a less-informed person might have used the wrong drug, perhaps a drug that could kill. When the whole point was to keep Granny alive, alive but helpless, until the longed-for time when my uncle might come to love Gillian for herself alone.

It seems incredible and somehow pathetic that a woman of such strengths could lose all moral perspective because of love for a man. And if anyone had suggested that my uncle was not worthy, I can imagine Gillian's response; I can picture the scornful flash of those proud, dark eyes.

I think of her extraordinary poise and beauty when I see

her name mentioned in the *Times*. I gather she has gotten the upper hand over her passions at last, for she has married a financial savant, a man whose picture appears frequently in the business pages of the New York papers, and whose spectacled face and rotund body would be unlikely to awaken memories of my Uncle John.

Occasionally Bill Watkins's name jumps out at me from those same sections of the paper, usually in connection with the lawsuit brought against him by his Wall Street firm. When that happens I wonder if he ever feels remorse for what, in his own desperation, he provoked my brother to do. It seems doubtful, caught up as he must be in his own ongoing predicament; but I am swept with undiminished bitterness each time I see a mention of the scandal that erupted shortly after Phil's death.

Poor Phil, with his six-month deadline for replacing the two hundred thousand he had misappropriated. It was his suicide that caused federal officials to look into the firm's transactions. If Watkins had not hounded Phil so relentlessly his own criminal mismanagement might never have been discovered. As it is, even with his guilt clearly established, there remains the complicated task of sorting out the tangle before he can be sentenced. It has already taken two years and may easily go on for two more. Phil would have had plenty of time.

Fortunately for my peace of mind, I see the New York papers only occasionally. It is invariably after picking up a copy of the *Times* at Walt Mitchell's store that the questioning starts up in my mind again; and there goes Terry's evening. Still, no matter how long and busy his day has been he listens and comforts me. I can tell that he respects my need to understand, even though it seems to me that he was born knowing what I so recently discovered. We sit together before the fire, and when I sink back against him, spent from the effort of putting it all into words, I feel his solidity. I look up and see the love and kindness in his quiet face, and I think that in him the beast of evil must be a very small one, probably existing only to make him aware of its presence in others.

In June we will have been married for a year, and I am expecting a baby in September. We live in a small red farmhouse a few miles from the Vermont village where Terry has bought a practice. Sometimes I go along when he makes house calls; I find it an excellent means of getting acquainted with our neighbors. I also enjoy seeing how his patients respond to Terry. Often I read in their faces the same wonder with which I watched his compassionate treatment of my grandmother, and I am shaken by the intensity of my love for him.

More often I spend my days painting woodwork or stitching up curtains, for I am determined to have the house in shape by September. The baby's room is ready, and I love to sit there when I am tired, and imagine how different everything will be in a few months. Sometimes I sink into the big wooden rocker in which I plan to nurse the child, and start it slowly rocking. I am usually wearing paint-spattered blue jeans, cut out over the tummy to accommodate my interesting shape, an old blue cotton shirt of Terry's and, if I have been painting, a red and white bandanna tied over my hair. The motion of the chair soothes me and I lean back with my eyes half closed and feel a foolish smile of contentment come to my face.

Often at such moments I think of Betsy, of how it would amuse her to see me like this. And Mike Alwyn. I can hear him saying he could have predicted the outcome when I made that timid selection of a female secretary. I keep meaning to have Terry take a picture of me in my rocker, so that I can send each of them a copy. They both deserve a treat for the way they behaved when Terry and I told them what had happened to us. Although he and Betsy had agreed during their final weekend trip to Vermont that, regrettably, they could never make a life together, they still felt a lingering fondness for one another. I sensed the tug of it when I saw the look they exchanged after we had told her and felt the wetness of her cheek when she gave me a congratulatory kiss.

She writes me wonderful letters. I tell her we are among the few practitioners of a dying art, for most people nowadays communicate only by telephone. Betsy's carelessly typed pages crackle with life as she describes her clients and the imaginative things she does to keep them before the public. She always includes news of the marketplace and often mentions a free-lance writing assignment she's heard about, as she is terribly afraid I will rusticate here in the country.

What I haven't told Betsy—because it's so new, so fragile —is that I have spent several recent mornings writing, just fragments so far, but totally out of my own imagination. This is my first attempt at writing with no commercial framework, no deadline to meet, and I am finding it both frightening and exhilarating. It seems a new kind of freedom, one I might never have known if I had accepted that job with its admittedly tempting rewards.

Here my rewards are different: a clear and certain sense of purpose, for one; for another, a connection to nature I've never felt before. The fresh, clear air, the snow-covered mountains sparkling in the winter sun, the dark days of buffeting wind and rain, all form a harmonious accompaniment to the momentous changes taking place in my own mind and body. Sometimes I feel like a force of nature myself.

From what I've learned about her, I think my mother must have felt this way too, and of course that sense of a shared experience is the greatest reward of all. We were allowed to share so little, my mother and I, but I hope with my children to make up for that. I will try to pick up the threads my mother was forced to drop, and weave a connection reaching back into the past and forward into the unfathomable future; those long years of wondering taught me the value of that. For not until I grasped the essence of my mother's spirit did I begin to recognize the shape and substance of my own.

With luck, my children will be spared any wondering. Like it or not, like me or not, they won't have to go looking for me. I'll be right here.

DISCARD